The Stories of the Surge

an anthology of new fiction written in a new style

The Stories of the Surge

an anthology of new fiction written in a new style

by

James Lofton

Mary Rhinehart

Betty Hargrove

Ted McConkey

John Hardrick

Debra Killian

Robert Crossland

and

Christopher Hight

edited by THESURGE.NET

iUniverse, Inc.
New York Bloomington

The Stories of the Surge
an anthology of new fiction written in a new style

iUniverse books may be ordered through booksellers or by contacting:

iUniverse
1663 Liberty Drive
Bloomington, IN 47403
www.iuniverse.com
1-800-Authors (1-800-288-4677)

Because of the dynamic nature of the Internet, any Web addresses or links contained in this book may have changed since publication and may no longer be valid. The views expressed in this work are solely those of the author and do not necessarily reflect the views of the publisher, and the publisher hereby disclaims any responsibility for them.

ISBN: 978-1-4401-4500-1 (sc)
ISBN: 978-1-4401-4502-5 (ebook)

Printed in the United States of America

iUniverse rev. date: 5/15/2009

Cover photo copyright 2009 G. Cima, M. Slaby

For A.J.

Contents

Patsy

by James Lofton

Patsy Peplowski was no ordinary cop. He didn't work vice; he wasn't on homicide; he wasn't on the special victims unit or the gang squad. He worked for the United States Park Police. "The oldest uniformed police force in the country," as he liked to remind his mother. As such, he worked on the beach—for the most part.

From his headquarters on the Rockaway Peninsula in the borough of Queens, his duties involved shaking down the owner of the mini-golf course, chasing teenagers off the dunes, and teaching the lady lifeguards how best to assert their authority. "The great thing about the double leg takedown," he would say, "is that it keeps your chest close to the opponent. Who wants to try it on me?"

Through his diligent efforts, Patsy (short for Patrick) was promoted to the Jamaica Bay Station, located on the other side of the bridge. From here, when he wasn't shaking down the owner of the driving range, he was visiting the girls at the tack shop. "My horse has a humongous barrel," he would tell them. "Thanks to you girls, I've never really needed a girth extender."

Patsy knew something big was coming his way. He could feel it every time he saw the same man with the hunched shoulders visit the Dead Horse Marina. Something about it smelled fishy.

His commanding officer, Captain Winthrop, was skeptical. "Captain," Lieutenant Peplowski said, "I know this guy. I checked his rap sheet. He did time for distribution. I'm telling you he's back in business. Why else would a guy like that have a twenty-foot pleasure craft?"

"For pleasure?" was the Captain's response.

"Please. Let me check it out. Give me a day just to follow him around in your boat."

"You want to borrow my boat."

"I'm going under cover," explained Patsy.

The Captain wouldn't hear of it. Patsy went to the Captain's wife, telling her, among other things, that he was hot on the trail of a drug trafficker and was planning to rent a boat and take a day off from work to follow him. "Wait a minute," said the Captain's wife. "Why rent a boat? Why take a day off from work?" Eventually, the Captain gave in.

Patsy chose to follow his suspect on a bright summer day. He took his fishing poles with him to blend in. "New York Bay is full of fishermen," he explained. He followed his suspect right past the fishermen, all the way to the brackish waters of the Raritan, turning at the Navy Pier straight into the grimy serenity of Sandy Hook and Horseshoe Cove.

"I spooked him," thought the young lieutenant. Observing his suspect drop anchor and swim ashore, Patsy got nervous. "I better call this one in," he said to himself. Raising the Park Ranger Station on his radio, he asked for Ranger Rosales. "Hey, baby," he said. "Are you at area L?"

"Yes," said Rosales. "Don't call me baby."

"That's just squawk talk, honeypie. Listen: I've got a guy coming towards you with bright red swim trunks. Keep an eye on him for me, will ya?"

"Affirmative. Over."

"And have Ingleberry get me a towel."

"That's Inglebert," said Ingleberry, snatching the radio from Rosales. "Why do you need a towel?" he asked.

"'Cause I'm about to get my pants wet," said Patsy. "Don't worry, Ingleberry. This time, it's got nothin' to do with your mother."

The rangers followed the man in the red shorts to a parking lot where he met a man with a beard next to a car with a tandem kayak. "Don't tell me he came here to go kayaking," said Patsy.

Inglebert said, "Maybe it's gay sex."

"He always thinks it's gay sex," said Rosales.

"Maybe a single man with a beard and a tandem kayak is code for gay sex."

"Maybe," said Patsy.

They watched as the two men unloaded their kayak.

"If it's gay sex, why don't they just meet at the gay beach under the rainbow flag?" asked Rosales.

"They don't want to be seen—obviously," said Inglebert. "The closest gay beach is clothing optional. Not everybody is comfortable with that, my dear."

They watched the two men put their paddles together.

"Gay sex notwithstanding, I still think there are drugs involved," said Patsy.

They watched the two men put their life jackets into the kayak.

"At least they play it safe," said Inglebert.

They watched the two men put more life jackets into the kayak.

"Wait a minute," said Patsy. "That's a whole lot of life jackets."

"When it comes to gay sex," said Inglebert, "you can never be too safe."

"Don't you get it," said Rosales. "They're smuggling the drugs in the life jackets."

Probable cause, for the Park Policeman, comes in many forms. For Patsy Peplowski, an excessive number of life jackets in combination with bright red shorts was cause enough. "I'm going in," he said. Turning to Rosales, he asked, "Can I borrow your gun?"

Crawling out of the bushes where they were crouched, Patsy did not appear like an ordinary cop. Having stripped down to his underpants to swim ashore, he was still dripping wet. Armed and half-naked, with a gun belt around his shorts, it probably didn't matter that he identified himself as a park policeman. The suspect ran.

Perhaps flashing a badge in the midday sun blinded him, as Rosales later testified; perhaps he was frightened by Patsy's bare chest, as Patsy himself claimed. Regardless, he ran over the dunes, through the bush, across the main road, and right past the sign that said, "From this point on, you may encounter nude sunbathers."

Patsy, who had led the chase, stopped to catch his breath. Rosales was close behind. "God," he gasped, turning around, "I love it when you run."

Rosales was all business. "Where did he go?"

"Don't worry," said Patsy, "we've got him blocked off. Put a detail on the road. Get somebody on either end of the beach. I'm going in."

"Dressed like that?"

"You're right," said Patsy. "I'm a little conspicuous."

"Give me back my gun."

"Where's Ingleberry?" asked Patsy, returning the gun.

"Detaining the other one."

"He made you run?" asked Patsy, incredulously. "Remind me to thank him. Now keep your eyes open to either side. He may have thrown something into the bushes." Sure enough, several yards down the boardwalk, Rosales found something.

"What is it?" asked Patsy.

"It's a pair of red shorts."

"My God," said Patsy. "How are we going to recognize him?"

"What are we going to do?" asked Rosales.

"I'm going to blend in," said Patsy, taking off his shorts.

"Dios mío," said Rosales.

"What's wrong?" asked Patsy. "This is what they call the long arm of the law. Stay here."

Down the boardwalk, Patsy encountered a naked old man sitting on a bench with his dog. "Excuse me, sir," said Patsy. "Park Police. Did you see a naked man run through here?"

"What's that?"

"A naked man."

"So it is."

"Have you seen one?"

"What's that?"

"Have you seen a naked man?"

"More than once—although I used to see a lot more before my eyes went bad." Patsy noticed the sign on the dog. It said, "I am working."

"Is that a service dog?" asked Patsy.

"Yes, sir," said the man, stroking his dog. "This here is Inspector Paw. We used to be on the force together. Caught a lot of bad guys, didn't we, Paw? Now he just helps me to get up. I'm Sergeant Majors, by the way," said the man, offering his hand. "Retired law enforcement. How can I help you, son?"

Though Inspector Paw was an old dog, Patsy was convinced that, given half a chance, and some quality time with the red shorts, he would sniff out his suspect from among the throngs of happy-go-lucky nude sunbathers on the beach. Little did he expect that this old dog, from his relatively low position, would take such immense pleasure in the sights and smells afforded him.

Nor did he expect how ridiculous he would feel, smiling down at the naked ladies, each with their beautiful round shoulders and lovely ankles exposed, as he tried to get the dog out from between each of their legs flashing each of them his badge and saying to each of them, "Excuse me, ma'am. Police business." The mortification was short-lived.

Somewhere between the ladies' beauty contest, which Patsy took a few moments to enjoy, and the dancing, which he also enjoyed, and the volleyball game, which was also pleasant, Inspector Paw found his mark. Unfortunately, so had Patsy.

To the canine, the scent came undoubtedly from the shore, the sea breeze bringing not just the fragrance of flounder and bluefish with a touch of green crab mixed with striped bass, but, above and beyond this briny bouquet, the distinct nutty flavor of bright red shorts.

Patsy, on the other hand, was drawn by a different feast: the confident stride of youth, emerging from the sea, hands pushing back wet strands, an elbow pointing up, pulling with it a tortuous line of shade across flesh, a motion of such immense gracefulness that, once reaching its climax, it just as soon hid the soft, pale underbelly of the arm that led down to a freshly matted pit of delicately trimmed hair, still peaking from beneath those drawn shoulders, pointing to a pair of bubbly breasts, which, ever so mournfully, turned away, presenting the elegant boxwood bouts of the back, dimpled above the ass, bending now at those generous hips before pushing off with the springiness of freshly leavened dough, and disappearing like satin gauze upon the waves. Now that, thought Patsy, was a girl in desperate need of police investigation.

Inspector Paw wouldn't have it. The desire to find red shorts being so strong, and the insensitivity coming from the opposite end of his leash so great, the beast broke his collar. Dashing towards the shore, leaping over bare bottoms, kicking up countless amounts of sand into innumerable private places, the dog finally jumped onto his prey.

The poor devil, crouching at the water's edge, his back to the beach and the waves lapping at his balls, had no idea what hit him. The dog, doubtlessly overjoyed to be out of retirement for the day, hit the man with such force that a slender plastic bag full of green little herbs dislodged itself from underneath the sign on its back.

"Cannabis!" yelled Patsy, running to the scene of the crime. "Cannabis!" he yelled, flailing all five limbs.

"It was cannabis," said the Captain, pushing back his chair and getting up. "This must be the worst example of police work I have ever seen. You allowed an attack dog to run wild on a nude beach?"

"There is a good explanation for that, sir," said Patsy, who, for the first time, sat upright in his chair. "He was wearing a break-away collar. They were invented to prevent strangulation. When the pressure on the safety buckle gets too—"

"Shut up," said the Captain, digging his knuckles into his desk. "You're lucky the Governor had his own naked business to attend to."

"How was I supposed to know the boat was owned by a parole officer?"

"By checking it out."

"And the bearded man?"

"That was the parole officer," said the Captain.

"The life jackets?"

"They were for his boat."

"What was he doing in Jersey?"

"That is none of your business, lieutenant."

"The drugs?"

"Sergeant Majors confessed to that."

"Did we book him?"

"No, we didn't book him." The captain breathed out a heavy sigh.

Patsy's puppy dog eyes turned into a vacant gaze. "I guess that's for the best," he whispered, catatonically.

When he was placed on administrative leave, he said it again. When he was transferred away from New York, he said it once more. He told his mother it was a promotion. In reality, they were keeping Patsy as far away from the field as possible. The Park Service wanted nothing to do with him.

He was sent to a congressional office—not even to the chairman of the committee with oversight over something, but to the junior member. This, they claimed, was simply a matter of available space. Consequently, when a girl was killed falling off the Statue of Liberty that summer, Patsy Peplowski was miles away.

He didn't even follow the investigation. He didn't know it was ruled a suicide. He didn't know that the mother, who was all over the papers, was unconvinced. When a staffer came into his office one day, interrupting a very important game of solitaire by shouting, "Hey, Patsy, Liberty Girl's mother is here: take care of it," Patsy said, "Who?"

Liberty Girl's mother was a middle-aged, bereaved and not unattractive woman in black. Patsy, feeling a surge of interest in his work, paid as much attention as he could. When shown a picture of her daughter, he was shocked.

"I'm telling you, Lieutenant, my Denise would never have jumped—the Statue of Liberty of all places. She was a good girl, that's the God's honest truth. She was ambitious—true. She wanted to achieve great things. Not that she couldn't, but—you know. She was a very good student. Not great, but good."

All Patsy could think about was the young and beautiful woman who, before his very eyes, resembled the one who had dove into the water those many weeks ago. "Excuse me, Ms. Cartwright," said Patsy. "Do you happen to have a picture of your daughter naked?"

The woman was, naturally, flabbergasted. "I'm sorry," said Patsy. "Your daughter looks very familiar."

By the time Patsy explained himself, he was convinced that it was the same girl. "Ms. Cartwright, I can assure you I will do everything in my power to further this investigation. You have my word."

The chairman of the committee was of a different mind. Patsy went to the chairman's wife, saying, among other things, that, though he proposed to pursue full time his own investigation into the suspicious death of Denise Cartwright, he was told that dead young women don't vote. "Excuse me?" said the chairman's wife. Eventually, the chairman gave in.

Patsy's colleagues in New York were less than excited. "Denise Cartwright committed suicide," said the Captain.

"She was murdered," said Patsy, wagging a finger.

"You have no evidence of that."

"I have a theory," said Patsy.

"What's that?"

"She was murdered."

"How?"

That was not an easy question to answer. Going through the investigation step-by-step, Patsy felt sure he was getting close. He interviewed the rangers who had witnessed the tragedy. "She was definitely alive when she fell," said one of them. "I saw her from the back of the pedestal. She was screaming and waving her arms."

"Why would she scream if she wanted to jump?" asked Patsy.

The ranger shrugged. "They say everybody regrets it half-way down."

Another ranger said, "I saw her falling from below the shoulders. It looked to me like she had slid off. I don't know if she had meant to do that, but, to me, it looked like she was panicking."

"For how long did she scream?" asked Patsy.

"Not long," said another one. "She hit part of the robe and that must have knocked her out."

The maintenance workers were baffled and defensive. "That door was locked when I went to open it. There was nobody up there. The only thing I found out of place was a rope tied to a grab bar. That lady must have used it to help her climb through the access hatch."

"Why would she use a rope," asked Patsy, "if she were trying to kill herself?"

The man raised the ends of his eyebrows. "Is that a rhetorical question?"

"These maintenance checks are routine," said the foreman. "A guy goes in the morning. A guy goes in the afternoon. They're supposed to lock the door. It doesn't always happen. Sometimes they jam it. I've done it myself."

"With what?"

"Anything: a piece of rubber or a cotton ball: whatever's handy."

"The door was locked in the afternoon."

"That's right. The girl must have snuck in there in the morning. If she didn't fall until later, she must have been up there for a while."

"What was she waiting for?"

The man shrugged. "How am I supposed to know? Maybe she was thinking about it."

The technician who had the morning shift that fateful day couldn't remember if the door had been jammed. A close inspection of the mortise revealed dried bits of something. "This is evidence," said Patsy to the worker. "I'm going to need you to replace this doorjamb."

"It's bubble-gum," said Patsy, dropping the report onto the Captain's desk. "Denise Cartwright's bubble-gum. I don't know how you guys missed this. Why would a girl who's planning to kill herself jam the door?"

"I don't know," said the captain.

"The epithelium is haplogroup 03-M122. That's an Asian genetic marker, Captain. He's our guy."

"Maybe," said Winthrop.

"All of the victim's friends say that she was happy. She would never commit suicide. Some said she was political. Unlike the media speculation, none of them thought she was capable of something as stupid as throwing herself off the Statute of Liberty to make a point. Three of them knew she was seeing somebody. Two of them knew he was Asian. One heard him speak over the phone in a heavy accent. The other saw him briefly. She can't describe him."

"Don't get too excited," said the captain. "Remember, there was nobody there."

Patsy had a grim look on his face. "He wanted to watch," he whispered.

"Lieutenant, for all you know, they had a disagreement at the top of the Statue of Liberty over whether or not to get some fresh air."

"He did it," said Patsy, nodding his head. "I'm going to feed this through the FBI and Interpol. Anybody who would go to these lengths to get a sick thrill has to have started somewhere."

The FBI was not helpful. Patsy's concept of a serial killer who mysteriously left girls to be thrown from tall statues made them laugh. The memory of nudie narcotics was still fresh in their minds. Patsy paid no attention. Sifting through reams of newspaper articles and police reports, he perused every detail of every person in the United States who had fallen from more than thirty yards. He found nothing.

"I don't get it," said Patsy, digging his feet into the sand. "With only a rope and nobody around, how does a woman get dropped from the top of a tall statue?"

"What's that?" asked Sergeant Majors.

"I said: how does a woman get dropped?"

"She talks too much," replied the naked old man, stroking his dog.

"That's right," said Patsy. "She must have been drugged."

"What's that?"

"I say, he must have used some kind of drug."

"Go ahead. Help yourself."

"There are so many risks," continued Patsy. "So many things could go wrong. He must have tried it once before: someplace safe. A statue or a monument he was familiar with. If not in the United States, then where?"

"What's that?"

"I said, where?"

"You know where. I keep it underneath the sign on the dog." Patsy looked. The sign said, "I am working."

"That's right. He must have been working there. I'm looking for a man from Asia who has worked in some capacity on a giant statue. There are five statues in Asia taller than the Statue of Liberty, if you include the pedestal, and twelve excluding it—all of them representations of the Buddha."

"What's that?"

"Of the Buddha, I said."

"No," said Sergeant Majors. "I've got some cheddar—in the cooler."
Paw barked. "What's wrong, boy?"

"He wants cheese."

"He hates cheese," said Sergeant Majors. The dog barked again.

"That's strange. Service dogs aren't supposed to bark for no reason,
are they?"

"No," said the old man. "I wonder what's got into him."

Patsy surveyed the length of the beach. There were only a few
people around: two couples to the north and a pair of men to the
south. As Inspector Paw's growling and barking reached its peak, Patsy
noticed, directly ahead, a jogger—an otherwise ordinary, random,
not-to-be-mentioned-twice jogger—except for one, small, apparently
beachcombed pair of bright red shorts. "No," whispered Patsy. The
sentiment came too late.

Inspector Paw had already broken through his collar. Once more,
he was dashing madly across the sand, kicking up whirlwinds, caving
in countless ghost crabs, in pursuit of what he must have thought his
last great prey. The poor jogger never knew what hit him.

"A hundred pounds of angry cop," said the sergeant, as Patsy led
the beast back to its leash.

"How do you put this thing on?" he asked, fumbling around with
the collar.

"Allow me," said the old man. "This safety buckle is tricky."

"What are these for?" asked Patsy, referring somewhat disingenuously
to the small metal D rings on either side of the buckle.

The old man smiled. "I suppose we should use those. That way he
won't get free. Then again, I doubt any more joggers wearing bright red
shorts will come dropping by."

"Dropping by." Staring at the breakaway collar, the words resounded
within Patsy's head. Crouching next to that naked old dog, he looked
up to the naked old man and said, "That's it."

"What's what?"

"That's it."

"What?"

"You're a genius!"

Patsy asked Rosales if he could test out his theory on her. She agreed.
Dressed in a skirt for what seemed, at least to Patsy, to be the very first

time, and only to approximate the circumstances of the victim, Rosales placed around her neck a breakaway collar through which Patsy had looped a rope. Having her lie on a long conference table, Patsy attached the rope to the legs of the table on the side above her head. Similarly, he attached another rope to the D-rings on either side of the safety buckle. This uncomfortably pressed against the ranger's face.

"I apologize," said Patsy.

"It's alright," said Rosales, in a tone that Patsy could have sworn he had never heard her use before.

Lifting the table by its side, Patsy dragged it across the floor and lodged it high against a shelf. "You're so strong," said Rosales.

"How are you doing?" asked Patsy, removing the rope from the D-rings.

"Much better now, thank you."

Positioning himself at the bottom of the table, Patsy said, "Okay. It looks like it's holding. Let's pretend you're regaining consciousness."

All Rosales had to do was flex her neck. The collar gave way, sending her body down the slick surface of the table-top. Interestingly, through the aid of her hands, which at least seemed to be vainly trying to slow her progress, the ranger's bum ended up on the edge of the table, her legs to either side, and her skirt decidedly bunched around her waist.

When Patsy instinctively looked down at the protruding pelvis, he saw not panties nor pantyhose nor any other type of ladies' undergarment. He saw the lack of such things. Looking to the ranger's face, expecting shock or embarrassment, he saw only the blank stare of a child-provocateur who fears his parents' judgment.

"Alright," said Patsy, smiling sheepishly and nodding. "That went well."

Patsy wanted to show everybody how successful his test had been. Gathering all the rangers and the park policemen, he again prepared the long conference table and the ropes. This time, as he was about to put the collar on Rosales, he whispered into her ear, "Are you sure you're wearing panties?"

Inglebert interrupted. "It's not right for a lady to be put in that position. I should be the one to do it."

There was silence—not that anybody was particularly shocked by Inglebert's chivalry. He was always trying to impress his partner. She was a nice lady: very well-rounded. She had a great personality. Nobody was willing to mention that his weight, in all likelihood, more closely resembled the weight of the victim. "Alright, Ingleberry," said Patsy. "You're going to have to wear a skirt."

As the crowd laughed it up, Patsy was called away by an urgent phone call. It was a Detective Morimoto of the Tokyo Metropolitan Police. The detective explained that he was investigating a series of suspicious deaths from high-rise buildings in the Tokyo area. He had decided, upon being informed by Interpol of the investigation in the United States, to contact the lieutenant directly, since he was concerned that the deaths in Tokyo might have something to do with not only the Statue of Liberty death, but a girl who fell from a statue of Beipu in Taiwan.

"Wait a minute," interrupted Patsy. "A girl fell from a statue in Taiwan?"

"Yesu," said the detective. "A sutachu ofu Beipu."

"Who is Beipu?"

"He isu Buddha," said the detective, "witu bigu berry."

"A Buddha with a berry?"

"No," said the detective. "Witu a berry."

"A berry."

"No," said the detective. "He hafu berry—a raruju berry."

"I get it. What does the berry symbolize?"

"Hisu eatingu too machu."

"What does that mean?"

"Itsu shimboru ofu happinessu."

"Ah," said Patsy, "the berry is a symbol of happiness."

"No," said the detective. "Itsu hisu berry."

"What?"

Eventually, Patsy realized how much of an idiot he was. Because the letter P comes before R, and, in all fairness, because it was his first time with Interpol, instead of requesting information from both the Republic of China and the People's Republic, Patsy, embarrassingly, like some kind of lefty, had only expressed an interest in the People's Republic. Morimoto assured him his secret was safe. Their profile began to flesh out.

The suspect was probably Taiwanese, the Beipu incident having occurred first. Though he was present in the United States during the summer, he was now believed to be in Japan. He nursed a penchant for watching women fall from tall buildings, especially large statues. Presumably, he employed a type of breakaway collar on his victims. The FBI was paying attention. Help came from every angle. Rosales, of all people, came up with an idea.

"What if," she said, whispering into Patsy's ear, "the suspect witnessed the World Trade Center attack? That's how he realized he had a thing for watching people fall."

It was an admirable idea. Patsy explained that though it were possible, even if it were true, it meant he could have been anywhere except perhaps the desert. "Even there I think they have television. I'll look into it."

Meanwhile, the Tokyo Metropolitan Police, at Patsy's suggestion, searched rooftops near sites of questionable suicides for evidence of anything remotely resembling a breakaway collar. They found nothing. Detective Morimoto was discouraged. Sitting by the bay, he saw a white egret fly past him. Landing in a pile of refuse, it reminded him of the old saying, *hakidame ni tsuru*, meaning, a crane in the garbage dump.

The egret started fiddling around with something. It was a child's ribbon. It took the fabric in its mouth and flew away. Morimoto wondered. He ordered his men to search the rooftops once more. They found a piece of gabardine woven into a large nest. There was some kind of buckle on it. The laboratory found traces of a victim's skin.

Patsy was ecstatic. He asked the Secretary of the Interior if he could go officially to Japan and assist the Japanese in their investigation. "Absolutely not," she said. Patsy went to her husband, explaining, among other things, that if a U.S. Park Policeman were to make an arrest in the Liberty Island case, it would mean the Secretary of the Interior would be holding a big press conference. Television has a way of boosting a politician's prospects. Eventually, the Secretary gave in.

In Japan, Patsy worked hard to acclimatize to the culture. He learned words like *onna*, meaning "woman," and *utsukushii*, meaning "beautiful," which Patsy found himself using all the time. There were also more complex words like *kon'yoku*, meaning "mixed bathing," and *hadaka-mairi*, meaning "visiting a shrine naked." One never knew when those might come in handy.

Detective Morimoto's wife and daughter were lovely people. They asked him what he was doing in Japan. He tried to explain with his pocket dictionary that, "Over there," meaning America, "I was shown, by a mother, a beautiful woman whom I saw myself naked." They both giggled until they turned beet-red.

Patsy thought it was funny too. Morimoto explained that, due to his ignorance of grammar, it sounded as if he were saying, "Have your mother show me your genitals. You're a beautiful woman. It's time I saw you naked." Patsy denied he had any prior knowledge that "over there" was a euphemism for genitalia.

Customs had to be learned. Every time Patsy went to investigate a famous statue of Buddha, he would spend the night at a local hot springs. Japanese etiquette demands that, before entering a public bath, one first wash himself thoroughly with soap and water. To this end, a well-drained area is prepared with spigots, buckets and ladles.

At first, Patsy would squat down and humbly clean himself, paying particularly close attention to "over there." Seeing that this was the method favored by women and not by most men, by the time he visited the Dai-Kannon of Izu, and stayed in the shadow of Mount Fuji, Patsy's skill had increased so dramatically, he was able to stride into the bathing area, swoop down, grab a ladle without disturbing its bucket, splash his genitalia with what little water was there, the way a cook might add a bit of garlic to his Zampone, and, with a flick of the wrist, deposit the ladle in yet another bucket before crying "banzai" and cannonballing into the water. Though superficially disgusted by this when they were together, when alone, the ladies seemed to admire it.

One time, Patsy came close to capturing his suspect. The man had suddenly vanished from his post at the Dai-Kannon when Patsy and Morimoto had shown up to question him. Giving fruitless chase through the streets of Ito, Patsy returned to his Tokyo hotel to find none other than Ranger Rosales. She had taken leave from the Park Service to join him. "That's very kind of you," said the young lieutenant.

Somewhat less shockingly, two days later, Inglebert showed up. "I knew you were in love with her," said Patsy. "Go for it. Don't mind me. There's only one reason why she's interested."

"What's that?" asked Inglebert.

Patsy drew in his breath and leaned in. Batting his eyes and bobbing his head, he murmured, "She's seen me naked."

Patsy had his sights set on another woman: the beautiful Kubota Kumiko, whose name means, "Long-time lovely, little low-lying rice paddy," which is just what Patsy was looking for.

"I think I rubbed the little bastard the right way, if you know what I mean," he told her one night while "doing the *kon'yoku*." He was talking about his suspect. "That little chase in Ito means he'll lie low for a while. He won't stop. He likes it too much. He'll change his strategy: go back to buildings. What we ought to do is set a trap."

The best place for that was the tallest building in Japan, the Yokohama Landmark Tower. Rising more than three hundred yards above the ground, it dwarfed everything around it. More importantly, two-thirds of the way up, on the forty-ninth floor, a glass eave in the middle of each wall provided a perfect spot to leave a victim.

Morimoto arranged a hiring campaign looking for everything from window washers to security guards. Yokohama having a large Chinese population, Patsy felt it was a good place for his suspect to hide. Many applied. Unfortunately, the tenants did their own hiring.

To make matters worse, floors 49 to 80 were occupied by the Royal Park Hotel. Reception, security, and the maid staff received copies of the eyewitness drawing. Patsy wasn't sure it was enough. He convinced his superiors he would have to stake-out the building on his own. He received complimentary service.

One day, while waiting for Kumiko by the tea ceremony room on the sixty-fifth floor, Patsy looked out the window at the spokes of the Ferris Wheel on the quay. He caught sight of his man. He wasn't on the Ferris Wheel. He wasn't on the quay. He wasn't walking sixty-five floors below.

His face was being reflected in the window. That was the last thing Patsy remembered before waking up. It was freezing cold. It was dark. It was windy. There was something around his neck.

"This is embarrassing," thought Patsy. Knowing better than to look up, he guessed where he was: outside and somewhere above the forty-ninth floor. His hands were like chunks of dead meat. There was nothing he could do.

"I'll have to wait for the sun to come up. I only hope I'm facing east." He would regret those words. As soon as the sun rose, Patsy felt it on his skin. It was burning. "This glass gets really hot," he told the birds. He couldn't wait.

His first idea was to secure himself. Patsy could feel something cutting into his skull. He carefully reached back and found a steel cable. Though sturdy, it was impossible to climb. He assumed there was a ferrule. His collar had to be running through a loop. How large a loop was important. In this position, it was too risky to find out.

Patsy unfastened his pants. Ever so carefully, he wiggled them down. Next came his shorts. As much as they would burn, his cheeks had to provide traction. With the smell of burning flesh already seeming to fill his nostrils, Patsy clutched either side of his collar and gently inched back his fingers. Supporting more of his weight on the fabric was dangerous but unavoidable. He could only hope he reached the loop in time.

He wished he knew what time the sun rose. Above and to his left were the windows of the barbershop, which didn't open until ten o'clock. To the right was the aromatherapy salon, which opened at eleven. Somewhere below him were the windows of the Sky Pool, part of the fitness club. In the morning, it was open from seven to ten. It was too far to reach.

His fingers found the loop. His hands curled around it. He could afford to maneuver. Crawling like an inch worm with his buttcheeks, Patsy made it all the way to the barbershop window. He realized it was Monday. "Of course," he thought. "The barbershop is closed on Monday. How disappointing."

He considered dropping down his shoes along with the rest of his clothes. He realized the shoes would probably just fall on a lower roof. His clothes would drift away. "Besides," he thought, "it's bad enough my ass is burning." Moving it somewhat relieved the pain. He started inching towards the aromatherapy salon, one cheek in front of the other.

Somewhere along the route, whatever was keeping the steel cable from falling gave way. Patsy's heart leapt into his throat. Plunging down a few meters, he stopped. "Thank God," he thought. "I managed to hold my grip." On the bright side, he was now level with the pool windows. On the other hand, he might not last there very long.

Deciding to provide himself with more traction, he stripped the rest of his clothes. "I can't believe I'm getting naked," he thought. He was also crazy enough to squeeze his whole hand through the loop. He was convinced that this way, if he dropped over the side, it would only break his wrist and not his grip.

Positioning himself over a pool window, Patsy prayed. "Please, God, let somebody see me." Everybody was swimming breast stroke. "Are you kidding me?" cried Patsy. "After all the stroking I've done for you, this is how you repay me? Sidestroke! Why isn't that more popular?"

A woman who started swimming crawl must have noticed something in the corner of her eye. She stopped and stared at Patsy's naked body. He waved and smiled. The woman screamed. Instead of pointing, she began splashing hysterically. The lifeguard dove into the water. Everybody stared. "I'm over here," cried Patsy.

The window was too thick. He banged it with his fist. It hurt. He banged again. It was useless. He tried banging with both hands. The cable gave way. Patsy began screeching slowly towards the edge. It hurt a lot. Lifting his leg to assuage the burning, he dropped even faster. By the time he lifted his arm, his feet were dangling over. He made his peace with God.

Patsy thought he was finished. He was falling off the largest building in Japan. At some point, the cable held. Swinging wildly below the forty-ninth floor, he was no longer glad he was alive. The pain in his hand was unbearable. "Like a fish on a hook," he whispered. "I'll never go fishing again."

He thought surely somebody would see him now. The floors below the forty-ninth were all office space. Patsy realized how hard-working the Japanese were. With his last remaining ounce of strength, he whispered, "Take a break." For the first time in his life, perhaps rightfully so, he cursed the Capitalistic virtue of productivity, thinking, "Why couldn't I have gone to France?"

It wasn't until rumor of a hotel guest who claimed to have seen a naked man outside the Sky Pool circulated around the shopping plaza on the first floor that a woman on her lunch break returned to her office on the forty-seventh floor and told her co-workers about it. They didn't believe it. Though somebody glanced out the window, Patsy must have swung out of view.

Eventually, somebody complained of a water leak. A radiator was found crushed up against a window. Patsy was attached to the other end. Hoisted onto terra firma, he wasn't sure whether he was still alive. Opening his eyes, he giggled at the dumbfounded emergency workers. He whispered, "What beautiful angels."

By the time he came to his senses, he was being deified. People were associating him with the tiger-headed fish-mount of a god of law. The logogram was a picture of a fish next to a tiger. It could also mean "killer whale," which is what the newspapers and the less superstitious folk called him. All Patsy had to do was sit around and let his wrist heal. Kumiko took care of the rest.

In due course, Patsy learned his suspect had escaped to Hong Kong. He went after him. Hong Kong was an orgy of sloping skyscrapers: the Finance Center, Central Plaza, the Bank of China Tower, Nina Tower—all had perfect spots for his suspect's favorite pleasure. Despite the immense difficulties, Patsy tracked him down.

By now, he felt invincible. Chasing his suspect onto the roof of a skyscraper, he followed him onto a crane. His suspect, probably being more familiar with this sort of thing, reached the top of the mast with time to spare. He slipped into the operator's cab. He tried slewing the arm towards a nearby building. It wasn't going fast enough. Patsy was hot on his tail. The suspect started swinging across the jib.

If Patsy had stopped to think like a normal human being, he might have tried to move the arm back. Instead, he followed his suspect across the jib. He reached the trolley. He climbed down. There was a hook at the end. A long chain was attached to it. The suspect was holding on for dear life, trying to sway himself toward a pair of incredulous window washers on some nearby scaffolding.

Patsy fastened one end of his handcuffs around his arm. He started to shimmy down. The closer he got to the end, the more momentum his suspect had. The workmen were stretching out their arms. They almost had him. Patsy was running out of time. Only one swing separated the suspect from freedom. He was coming back. The workmen were getting ready. Patsy jumped.

The workmen grabbed a hold of the suspect. Patsy fell against the scaffolding. He handcuffed himself to the suspect. The window washers strained to hold on. Patsy lost his grip. He fell. Hanging over the edge, he thought to himself, "Not this again."

The Chinese authorities were not pleased. As soon as they had brought everybody back to the ground, they told Patsy he had to release the suspect. Patsy relented.

"Are you insane?" asked the American officials. "You risked your life for nothing. If we don't have any evidence, they're going to let him go."

Patsy smiled. He held up his hand. A pair of bloody handcuffs hung from his mangled wrist. He said, "This is all the proof we need."

The Chinese agreed to wait for the test results. The blood positively matched the epithelium from Denise Cartwright's bubble-gum. Patsy Peplowski had caught the Liberty Island Killer. Captain Winthrop was stupefied. Ms. Cartwright was grateful. Patsy's mother was proud. Kubota Kumiko was pregnant.

"All in a day's work," said Patsy. "For the U.S. Park Police."

The Song of Red Tower

by Mary Rhinehart

It's hard to say whether Panfilo loved his mother. She died of plague when he was young. Often he would try to remember what she was like by cuddling next to a pillow and pretending it was her. He grew out of that. Like many children who have lost parents, the energy that would have gone into pleasing his mother was devoted to a general resentment of other people, which he hid, and a feeling of entitlement, which manifested itself more obviously.

When Panfilo was nine years old, his father, Manfredo, remarried. His bride gave birth to a boy, whom she named Lorenzo. "Why would you name the boy 'Lorenzo?'" protested the father. "It is so *effemminato*."

"What would you have him called?" she asked.

"Nothing so ridiculously *latino*. This is Puglia. How about 'Lothario?'" His wife scoffed.

"This may be Puglia. It's also the fifteenth century," she cried. "I'm naming my son 'Lorenzo.'"

Neither one would budge. His mother called the boy Lorenzo. Manfredo called him Lothario. Panfilo himself had been named after a character in Boccaccio's *Il Decamerone*, though his father had probably never read anything by Boccaccio, or by anyone at all for that matter. He had heard it from an erudite and completely accidental drinking partner. His usual associates were not the literary type.

Panfilo would be constantly reminded that his name meant 'friend to all,' as his father would gesture to the friends of his gathered around the table. "Or," he would ask, "are you calling me a liar?" Panfilo would refuse to move until his father would sneer menacingly, "You will live up to your name. It's Greek and Greeks are servants. Get us another bottle: now."

Boccaccio was some kind of a hero to him, less for anything he did than for the fact that he was a bastard. Manfredo himself was named after a bastard king of Naples. As Panfilo had once heard mentioned, his father was, in all likelihood, a bastard himself—though Manfredo never discussed this, even when completely *ubriaco*, which was more often than not.

At such times, he would lift his cup and say, "Long live the Baron!"

"Hear, hear," his friends would shout.

"Even though he is a Hauteville," Manfredo continued. He would put down his cup. "My ancestor came here from Normandy with Drengot." He would so emphasize the name that almost every time he leaned forward to spit it out, he would almost fall out of his chair. "He was one of Drengot's two hundred and fifty knights-errant." He would hiccup. "Hauteville would be nothing if not for Drengot."

"Hear, hear," his friends would shout.

"Hauteville," cried Manfredo. "The dear Baron di Hauteville— God keep him—owes me," he would say, beating his chest, "a debt of honor."

"*Salute!*" his compatriots yelled. "Long live the Baron's wife! The Mongolian Princess!" The men would cheer.

"Bless her Mongolian heart," Manfredo would say.

"Her Christian Mongolian heart," one of his friends would point out. "Long live the Baron's baby! Her Mongolian Highness!"

"Her half-Mongolian Highness," Manfredo would correct him.

"Her half-Mongolian Christian Highness!"

"Long live the Pope!" This would make everybody spit his drink.

"Which one?" asked Manfredo.

"*Benedetto*," somebody dared to whisper.

"Who said that?" asked Manfredo. "Even in jest, that is an insult."

"Lando!" cried the men. "He is hiding a smile." Manfredo would throw his cup, hitting Lando in the arm.

"You should be ashamed," he would say. "Go get me another cup."

"Long live *Papa Gregorio*," Lando would say, getting another cup. "The suzerain of our new Lady, *Regina Giovanna*."

"You mean our old Lady," interrupted Manfredo. "She's older than the warts on your mother's *culetto*."

"We should drink to our very own *Papa Giovanni*," said somebody else. "After all, he's Neapolitan."

"I hear he ran with his tail between his legs from *Costanza*," said Manfredo. "Neapolitan or not, that doesn't make him fit for a toast."

"I hear he's a pirate and a sodomite," said Lando.

"Good," cried Manfredo. "You have three things in common." Everybody laughed.

"That's not true," said Lando. "I'm not Neapolitan." Again, everybody laughed.

"I forget," Manfredo would say. "You're a dirty Lombard. Come here. Lick my boots."

"Queen *Giovanna* should do like the last Queen *Giovanna*," said somebody else. "If she opened a whorehouse for all three popes, imagine how rich she would be."

"Yes," sneered Manfredo. "Your mother, your wife, and your daughter would all have jobs." The laughter notwithstanding, the camaraderie invariably ended with a fight. Depending on how drunk he was, Manfredo would either fall on his face, or fall on his back. Either way, it was Panfilo's job to put him to bed.

His wife wouldn't touch him. She generally slept with Lorenzo above the side of the hall facing the garden. Manfredo would sleep on the daybed, whether or not it was outside. Since the room above the shop was usually rented, Panfilo, like a dog, would have to sleep in the center of the hall, curled around the fireplace.

Years passed. The good Baron di Hauteville tried, with his peers, to get the Queen to marry a Bourbon count. The forty-year-old monarch's chief minister—and lover, as was claimed—was being too pushy. The Bourbon proved worse; after marrying the Queen, he tried to get himself crowned. The barons revolted; the insufferable French left—only to reappear under a Valois Duke, invited by the Pope, who had excommunicated the Queen for not coming to his aid. She, in turn, adopted another Frank, the King of Aragon, as her heir.

The anxiety of these times was nothing next to the true terror in Panfilo's life. His own father was most of time both drunk and delirious. "Who do you think you're dealing with?" he would ask. "I used to rob Venetian slave-traders for a living. I would cut their throats and rape their precious cargo." He was talking to his son.

"If you ever look side-ways at my wife again." He would hiss and snarl, wagging his finger in his son's face. Though his breath could have melted a mountain-top, he never dared finish the thought.

"Coward," Panfilo would think. It was true that he desired his stepmother. She was young, blond, attractive, and possessed an enormous bust. Panfilo had witnessed her in various states of undress over the years. He was too young to be unaffected. Besides, his father was a bastard.

One day, with her tacit consent, he stared at her in the bath. It kept happening. Panfilo was convinced that they would make love. It was merely a matter of time. She was only setting him up. One night, as he stood enthralled by her nakedness, she turned her back.

Her husband had appeared. Panfilo was beaten within an inch of his life. Undaunted, the young boy remained. To spite his treacherous stepmother, he gave her no privacy. His father gave no quarter. Beaten senselessly on a regular basis, Panfilo gave up. He began wandering through the Puglian countryside.

Within days, he was robbed of the little food he had brought with him. Stealing eggs and grapes along the way, he made it to the port of Bari and found work on the docks. Not finding his crusty, Venetian employer very agreeable, especially after breaking some porcelain, he stole a bag of old hyperpryons and headed toward Naples. Though the Byzantine coins would not be easily recognized in the countryside, Panfilo was confident he could sell them to a banker for at least a few ducats.

Like a man pursued, he reached Troia in three days. By the time he crossed the hills to Benevento, he was completely *stanco*. Waking up in the morning in sight of Trajan's arch, he got up from the ditch into which he had fallen, dusted himself off, and walked into town. Deciding against continuing on to Naples, Panfilo found himself the first bank with hard currency. This proved fatal.

Unbeknownst to the boy, Benevento belonged directly to the Pope. His bankers were not unscrupulous. They asked many questions, the kind which Panfilo was not prepared to answer honestly if at all. When it was obvious that he was less than what he might have others think, he was placed in custody and all his possessions, be they legitimate or not, were donated to the Church.

In confinement, he was fed nothing more than bread and water. Told he would get nothing more until he confessed, Panfilo succumbed. He admitted to the robbery, to the broken porcelain, and to the fact that he had seen his stepmother naked—though he neglected to mention his resentment, his feelings of entitlement, and, of course, his continued desire to dispossess his father of his wife.

Given absolution, Panfilo was transferred to the custody of the *condottiero* Muzio Attendolo, nicknamed 'Sforza,' who, at that particular moment, was serving the interests of the Pope and the Valois Duke. Pressed into service, Panfilo prospered. Though he first served the knights' grooms on foot, he took to horsemanship, as Sforza's bastard son Francesco put it, the way a calf takes to a bull's teat.

Indeed, Panfilo's persistence in pursuing the art of horseback riding was born more of innate pride than talent. Witnessing other, more skilled compatriots fall from their steeds, he laughed—not ostentatiously like Francesco, but quietly, as if it proved, not that they wore heavier armor and were therefore richer, but that they might not be as good.

Francesco admired this. He saw a bit of himself in the tenacity that Panfilo naively expected others to fear. It was made all the more endearing by the fact that Panfilo was not very strong. Francesco, only a handful of years older, was already famous for bending bars with his bare hands. He had no need for a limp-wristed knight. Being somewhat enamored of the boy's beauty, Francesco made him one of his flautists.

Panfilo's pride was hurt. A flautist was not as prestigious as a trumpeter. At least it kept him close to the *condottiero*. It seemed like a safe place to be. Practicing music was better than the usual military drills. Panfilo worked while everybody else danced, but his hands were kept cool and clean. Panfilo threw himself into his new profession. He mastered the pipe and tabor, the fiffaro, and the eight-holed flaut.

Meanwhile, the great *condottiero* Sforza di Cotignola switched sides. The Queen found herself a new lover. Though her quarrel with the Pope over her succession still raged, her favorite, the King of Aragon, had become such an insufferable brute, locking up her lover and even trying to arrest her, that she had to escape his clutches, adopting his rival, the Valois Duke, as her new champion.

Not everybody was prepared for the consequences. Sforza found himself opposed to his most recent comrade, arguably the greatest knight of his age, Braccio Fortebraccio, who refused to renege his commitment to the King of Aragon. Stomachs turned.

Most of the time, the armies of the *condottieri* danced around each other waiting patiently (and lucratively) for their monarchs to settle things on their own. That way both sides made money. This affair, unfortunately, had dragged on for so long, people feared, this time, bloodshed would be unavoidable.

Astrologers agreed. They predicted neither Sforza nor Braccio would long survive the other. When Sforza departed Ortona with his army and headed north toward the mouth of the Pescara River, the headwaters of which concealed Braccio, the astrologers warned against it. Even the men were frightened when a standard bearer tripped and tore their precious *bandiera*. Sforza was undeterred.

Fortune does favor the brave, thought Panfilo, but woe to he who ignores a bad omen.

All the best river crossings at Pescara were blocked. Though it was a stormy day, Sforza directed his men to ford the very mouth. To prove to them that there was no danger, he rode out to the middle and waited.

As the men crossed, one of his favorite pages, a boy named Mangone, was pushed by the current to high water. Instinctively, Sforza rode out to save him. His horse slipped. In an instant, underneath the weight of Sforza's heavy armor, the loins of his horse gave way. Both man and beast were delivered into the arms of the cold current.

A moment passed before the men realized their leader had simply vanished. They groaned. Twice Panfilo looked and swore he saw the knight's gauntlet reaching out for help. Perhaps he had been valiantly freeing himself from his steed, who later emerged downstream. It was a sad day.

That summer, after reconquering Naples, the combined armies of Her Majesty, *Regina Giovanna*, His Holiness, *Papa Martino*, and the ugly Visconti Duke of Milan met the army of the fearsome Braccio between the Hill of San Lorenzo and the long-besieged city of Aquila. The allies were commanded by Braccio's former lieutenant, Jacopo Caldora. They outnumbered the knight three or four to one. Though they seemed to have every advantage, they were losing the fight.

On each side, soldiers wondered what was going on. It seemed as though Braccio might beat the odds. The astrologers were wrong. The omens were false. Chivalry would actually triumph. It was too good to be true. Braccio was wounded. His knights panicked. Their leader was thrown from his horse. The battle was lost.

Surgeons claimed Braccio would live. For three days, he lay in Caldora's tent, neither speaking nor eating, as if he were trying to die. Panfilo was brought in to cheer him up with light-hearted songs. Nothing worked. On the third day, he gave up his ghost.

Peace arrived in Naples. *Condotierri* moved north. Panfilo, sick of war and disillusioned with its bitter-sweet fruits, went south. He was in the mood for love. He possessed new skills in the art of music. He was young and handsome. More importantly, he was a veteran.

On the road home, he strolled through the orchards he played in as a child. He crossed the streams and the forests of his youth. Walking past the Cathedral, he came across two men standing next to a strange wooden contraption. "What kind of a siege-tower is this?" he asked.

"This," said one of the men, "is our Lady's chair."

"The Honorable Rosanna di Hauteville," the other man hastened to add.

"I've never seen a chair like this," said Panfilo. "It looks like a box with windows."

"The Baron asks us to carry her Ladyship to and from the Bishop's palace in this chair."

"As you can see," said the other man, "there are two poles for us to hold it. One of them has broken."

"Is she the Pope that she must be carried?" asked Panfilo.

"His Lordship," explained the first man, "cares very much for his daughter."

"His wife," added the other, "is a descendent of one of the finest families of the *Ilkhanato*."

"She possesses," said the first man, "among her many exotic treasures, a wash painting from the time of the Great Khan himself."

"It depicts," said the other, "beautiful young ladies in chairs such as this."

"Conveyed by their loyal servants," added the first.

"It is our master's wish," continued the other, "to prevent the Puglian soil—"

"Blood-stained as it is," interrupted the first.

"By the selfishness of Her Majesty, the Queen's, ministers," all three of them agreed.

"From contaminating our Lady's feet," said the first.

"By constructing," said the other.

"Such a siege-tower," said the first, "as you like to call it."

"And employing it," said the other.

"When occasion calls," said the first, "for her Ladyship to quit her chamber. If you don't mind, we require your assistance."

"The two of us can't manage on our own," said the other.

"With your help," said the first, "we can do it."

Panfilo smiled. "It would be my pleasure," he stammered, "to help the Honorable Rosanna di Hauteville, if she truly be here. How do I know you are not stealing the vessels of the consecrated Host from the Bishop's sacristy, or worse, his vestments?"

"You blaspheme," said the box.

"Curious: never in my life have I heard a box speak with a high-pitched whine." Panfilo turned to the servants. Tossing his head, he smirked, "It must be Pandora's box."

The sound of a curtain whisked open sent Panfilo's head snapping back. "If you are too weak to lift it, we will understand." Panfilo's mouth dropped. In the airy shadows hovered a beauty unlike any he had ever seen. The great broad forehead, the dainty eyebrows, the round chin and the thick lip of the Great Khan himself entwined like a child's wreath of laurel and wildflower with the thin, straight nose, the strong jaw and the large eyes of a Norman hero. It was stunning.

The Honorable Rosanna returned an impatient and useless stare of her own. The sheer white lace of her partlet swooped high around her nape, cupped her head like the sepals of a morning glory, plunged down either side of her chest and did nothing to mask the low-scoop of her sleeveless gray gown, where the gold artichoke pattern of her black *gamurra* peeked out alongside the embroidered edge of a white chemise as two frightened children would, scared of Rosanna's frame, bobbing as it was imperceptibly up and down with her deliberately steady breath like the shoulders of a tigress unsure of its prey, which Panfilo's eyes absorbed as if he had never seen a person breathe and needed, like a child newly expelled from between its mother's legs, shocked to find a world of air, a moment to learn how to jump-start its lungs and live.

Like a cat, Rosanna impassively turned her face forward. For a few secretly proud moments, she waited. Reaching the end of her patience, she turned back and muttered, "There will be no fee." Snapping shut the curtain, she added, "Charity is its own reward."

Panfilo, back to his senses, approached the window and rapped lightly on the frame. "Your Majesty," he whispered—his impertinence had only grown—"I would carry you up the Oxus River to Prester John's palace on the highest peak of the Hindu-Kush. Though I would place you before his lapis throne and feed you grapes, if I am even to carry you home to your chamber, I must ask of you one thing."

Rosanna pulled the curtain. Gracefully cocking her head, she whispered, "You are a shameless young man."

To be called 'a man' by a woman is no small thing, especially after knights have always called you 'boy.' It humbled Panfilo. He bowed in gratitude. Adopting a genuinely earnest tone, he mumbled, "If I may be so bold, Your Ladyship, to ask you for your curtain."

Panfilo smiled. Before Rosanna could question his demand or remark upon his impudence, he added, "To protect my hand, Your Ladyship." Gesturing to the broken pole in front of her, he said, "From the splinters."

Rosanna relented. Receiving the curtain, Panfilo wrapped it around the broken edge. Positioning himself close to the now curtainless window, he walked backward all the way to the Baron's keep. When they arrived at the courtyard, he had the gall to ask Rosanna whither were her chamber, that he might help her disembark straight into her bed.

"Your sauciness notwithstanding," replied the Lady, "I will reward you." Taking Panfilo through the garden, she pointed up to a stained-glass window flanked on either side by two fastigiate poplars. Rising like Macedonian guards, they made a distinctly imperial impression. "Beautiful," said Panfilo.

"Do you know what that is?" she asked.

Panfilo shrugged. "Your chapel?" It was an honest guess. A chapel would be worthy of the cost of such luxury.

"That," insisted Rosanna, "is my chamber."

Over the next few months of Panfilo's ultimately short life, he would wonder what was meant by that revelation. Was it the nature of her bedroom window she wished to relay or its location? "The glass," she had said, "is stained red after my name." Panfilo decided, having been dismissed rather coldly from her presence, it must have been the former.

"She is spoiled," he thought to himself. There were no glass windows at his cousin's hut, where he decided to throw his boots. Nor were there any at his father's house. Relatively speaking, it was not insubstantial. Situated on the outskirts of town, it had its own stable in front and a wide garden behind.

Despite its accommodations, Panfilo's father had always spent more time in apartments along the main road or at his brother's farm. Both were places of ill repute. All Panfilo had to do was make sure his father's horse was gone. At such times, he could freely visit the site of his erstwhile childhood.

The first time he returned, he could hear a flaut being played in the hall. Going around through the garden, he walked onto the back porch. In the kitchen, he could see his stepmother kneeling on the floor, grasping her enormous breasts. She was squeezing milk into a deep bowl. He cleared his throat. His stepmother looked up. Staring blankly, she made no attempt to lift the chemise gathered around her ample waist.

Her face was older, thought Panfilo. She had gained weight. Her breasts were bottoming out with age. A small scar graced her upper lip. If anything, she was even more beautiful than he remembered. Her nipples were thick like short cinnamon sticks. There was no doubt they would taste just as sweet.

Panfilo left her without saying a word. He went to recline on the day bed in the garden. The skylarks bombarded him with noisy twittering—nature's version of men shooting crossbows and hand cannons. Panfilo thought of how angry he had been with his stepmother. When she showed up with food, the feeling dissipated. She sat on the edge of the bed. Panfilo stared at her bosom. He wanted to unlace her brown bodice and reach inside. "Boy or girl?" he asked.

"Girl," she replied, sighing. "I tried to wean her off months ago. For some reason, I'm still full." She patted her teat. Panfilo fought the urge to volunteer his help.

He munched on his bread. He asked, "Where is she?"

"Inside." She gestured toward the hall. "With your brother."

"Was that him playing the flaut?"

His stepmother laughed. "We heard all about your exploits." Panfilo looked askance, wondering what she knew. "Lorenzo admires you."

"Don't tell me he's going to join the *condotta*."

"Not at all. He plays for the Bishop nearly thrice a week. He's very good. Sometimes he even plays for the Baron."

This interested Panfilo. "I think I saw him on the road to the Cathedral," he mentioned. "You should be more careful. There have been reports of brigands."

That day Panfilo went to the Bishop's palace. He secured a meeting with the concertmaster. Though his playing was impressive, he was told there was no room. The concertmaster said, "We have all the flautists we need."

The next time Panfilo spied his brother walking down the empty road, he hid behind a rock and wrapped a turban across his face. Once his brother had passed him, he pushed him down with great force and robbed him.

Visiting his stepmother, Panfilo saw that she was troubled. Peeling artichoke in silence, she sat sniffling with her shoulders hunched. Genuinely bothered, though it must not have come as any surprise, Panfilo found his brother. He asked him, "What has our father done?" Lorenzo looked confused.

"What do you mean?"

"What has happened to make your mother mope?"

"I was robbed." Panfilo attempted a look of mild stupefaction.

"Are the highways so empty that robbers stoop to throwing down boys?"

"How did you know I was thrown?"

Panfilo betrayed nothing. "I can see the bruises on your face. I assume they didn't have to hit you. What did they take?"

"My flaut," said Lorenzo. The words had a little more spirit than Panfilo expected. Lorenzo continued, "It won't stop me. The concertmaster let me borrow one of his."

"Where is it?"

"He won't let me take it home."

Panfilo guffawed. "How will you practice?"

"He's showing me how to make one. It won't be perfect. I don't mind."

Panfilo was not amused by his brother's sanguinity. Joining his sulking stepmother on the day bed, he started sulking himself.

"Did your brother tell you what happened?"

Panfilo nodded. After a while, he murmured, "It's a shame."

"As grateful as I am for the Bishop, I'm afraid for the boy. He takes home a few *carlini*. If that robber had gotten to him on the way back, he might have had his fill. What if he tries again?"

"I wouldn't worry. If that robber means to sell the flaut, he's half-way to Bari by now."

"I know I don't deserve to ask you this." His stepmother put down the artichoke. "Can you watch him? I hate to admit this. I need the money. Otherwise, I would buy him a new flaut."

Panfilo agreed. It wasn't easy to keep his promise. His brother could barely keep the snot from piling on his upper lip. Every time Panfilo had to stand back and watch the concertmaster pull out his purse, pure envy pervaded his heart.

One night, some fellows of his called for his stepmother. "Come quickly," they said. "Take charge of your husband. He is threatening the whores at Lando's house." Manfredo was not at Lando's house, nor was he at any of the other places to which his wife was led.

Panfilo, meanwhile, with the stench of spirits on his breath, went to his old home. Assuming the voice of his father, he shouted, "Lothario! Come here and set the kettle." As Panfilo stumbled about the dark hall, his brother tended the fire.

Coming up behind him, Panfilo pretended to mistake his brother's head for the cauldron. He sprinkled pepper in his hair. Lorenzo brushed it off. He put a cover on top. Lorenzo removed it. Taking the hot tongs, he seized him by the ears.

Hell has not heard such cries. Nor had Panfilo anticipated, despite being on many battlefields, the strong smell of sulfur coming from his brother's hair. It was nauseating. Leaving him to writhe around, Panfilo fled outside. In the darkness, he found where he had left his father passed out in a wheelbarrow. Dropping him onto the day bed, he left.

His stepmother had no choice but to blame Manfredo. Over the next few weeks, Panfilo was kind enough to take over his brother's duties, only as far as concert playing was concerned. "Until he recuperates," he told his stepmother. He gave her a handful of *carlini*.

"Thank you," she said. The look of gratitude on her face was priceless.

Lorenzo never spoke. In order to communicate, he gestured. When he was thirsty, he mimicked holding a cup to his mouth. When hungry, he rubbed his belly. When he was out of bed, he didn't come when called. He didn't say anything.

Panfilo took him to the concertmaster. Though Lorenzo could read notation, he couldn't stay in tempo with the others. The concertmaster shook his head. "I'm sorry," he said. He had to take back his flaut.

Panfilo permanently replaced his brother. Continuing his contributions, he felt more bold. When his stepmother leaned in to kiss him, he pulled her by the hips and held her against his stiffness. She allowed him to kiss her neck. When the moment was right, he followed her up the ladder.

In his father's chamber, he unlaced her bodice and slipped her out of her dress. Standing in her white chemise, she breathed heavily as she untied his belt and removed his doublet. With the growing calm that comes with commitment, she unfastened his hose and breeches and watched them pile about his feet. Lifting up her chin with his finger, Panfilo kissed her gently.

The first few times they made love, they were quiet. Their passion soon emboldened them. Lorenzo couldn't hear anything. His sister was too young. As long as Manfredo wasn't expected, they could make the whole house creak. When he licked her, she would moan. When he pricked her, she would whimper. When he sodomized her, she would scream.

Manfredo interrupted this once by banging on the trapdoor. "What's going on?" he shouted. His wife was so surprised, she tensed her muscles. She screamed even louder. "I come home to pick up a bottle of wine and you're giving birth?"

"It hurts," she cried.

"What?"

"My *culetto*," she answered, honestly.

"It's those rotten cucumbers," replied Manfredo, as if he were actually sober and concerned. "If I didn't drink like a fish, I'd be sick too."

The lovers relied on luck. On more than one occasion, as his father climbed the ladder, Panfilo had to leap quickly onto the porch, praying that nobody saw him. Lorenzo, who had taken to long walks, would return by way of the garden. It was most inconvenient.

Panfilo had to be careful. Sometimes Lorenzo was passing through the kitchen. Once, he almost jumped right on top of him. He had held himself up at the last moment, scratching up his back side. Dropping right behind the boy, he was afraid he would turn around. He didn't.

Nobody cared what Lorenzo did. When a cherry tree was chopped down in the Bishop's orchard, nobody suspected him. "Who would do such a thing?" asked the concertmaster. Panfilo shrugged. He had his own business next to the Honorable Rosanna's litter. Every time she came to the Bishop's palace to hear a concert, Panfilo escorted her home.

"I would be your servant," he whispered.

"Do you know what your name should be?" she asked. Panfilo shook his head. "Sambao," she said. "It means 'The Three Treasures.'"

"What are they," asked Panfilo, "that I might give them to you?"

Rosanna smiled. "To the Buddhist, they are what we call God, the Gospel, and the Church; to the Taoist: charity, modesty, and temperance. To the witch doctor, they are the soul, the seed, and the breath of life. For the servant, they are kept inside a little box in the master's silver casket."

"What kind of trinkets could they be?" asked Panfilo, drawing nearer.

Rosanna smiled like a fox. Leaning forward, she whispered, "They're dangling between your breaches."

Panfilo laughed. "You're going to need a bigger box, Your Ladyship. You might have to keep them in your chest."

One bright afternoon, Panfilo's stepmother lay naked in her husband's bed. Her tired stepson lay next to her. He was listening to the noisy skylarks. She cuddled up next to him. She started nursing him back to life.

Panfilo was preoccupied. With a slightly mournful whisper, his stepmother said, "We found out who cut down the cherry tree." Panfilo thought he could hear the song of a river nightingale.

"He's so far from the reeds," he mused. "Yet he sings without a care in the world."

"It was your own brother."

Panfilo took a moment to respond. "Lorenzo?"

"He made himself a flaut, poor thing," his stepmother said. "He carved it all on his own. It was beautiful." The skylarks fell silent.

"Where is it?"

The woman sighed. "Your father heard him playing it."

"He sold it."

"For a case of *rosolio*." Her voice was so painfully full of defeat.

"Imagine," said Panfilo, "if he saw you playing my flaut."

Panfilo's stepmother huffed. "He wouldn't recognize me."

"What if you get pregnant?"

"I'll say I raped him in his sleep." She felt a burst of confidence. She climbed on top. She reached back. The instrument was ready. She put it away. Bobbing up and down, her breasts, as usual, started leaking milk. She stared at the lovely young man. She grinned. "You'll," she huffed, "be my witness."

Panfilo heard a hawk cry. He considered the poor nightingale. What was he doing so far from the riverbank? He smiled. He loved watching his mother's belly dance the tarantella with her breasts. Throwing her down, he penetrated her from his knees. Thrusting as fast as he could, he made her whole body jiggle.

When they were finished, Panfilo's mother grew sad. Tears welled in her eyes. "He wept bitterly," she whispered.

Panfilo took note of the fact that Lorenzo was eager to play. Such desire is easily exploited. Meanwhile, his conversations with Rosanna progressed to the Baron's garden. Among the olive and maple tree, she regaled him with stories of her Mongolian forefathers.

"The natives of Maragha," she told him, "hate the name Genghis. They see him only as a butcher of their people. They don't remember that their own Shah killed his ambassadors. That is the world we live in." Panfilo would nod his head in sympathy.

"Genghis had a hard life. When he was nine years old, he was sent to serve the family of his betrothed, all for the sake of an alliance. When his father was poisoned to death, he went home to stake his claim. His tribe would not be ruled by somebody so young. They abandoned his family.

"He and his mother and his brothers had to fend for themselves in the wild. Imagine that. When they say he killed his own half-brother over hunting spoils, I say, perhaps his brother deserved it." Panfilo kept nodding his head.

"Genghis was kind. He served the Christian Mongols of my mother's tribe. As he grew in power, their jealousy overcame them. His blood brother abandoned him. The Christian chief refused to give his daughter in marriage. That was considered a great insult.

"Genghis defeated them. Though his blood brother had fought against him, he offered to reestablish their friendship. That is magnanimity. His brother refused out of pride. That is sin."

Rosanna's interest in telling Panfilo these stories was not unnoticed. The Baron recognized him as a musician and commended his skill. He asked him for a favor. "The Baroness," he explained, "has copies of music from the Cathay courts. Some of them are labeled with two *carattere.*"

Using a staff, he began to draw a picture in the dirt. "This," he said, "is a thread next to a type of dowel; never mind why: it means red."

Below it, he drew another one. "This is a tree next to a flagpole. On either side are two women, one of whom is lactating. Never mind why: it means tower.

"The baroness claims that 'red tower' refers to young noblewomen who lived in beautifully accommodated chambers. The songs were meant them. She longs to hear them played. Our daughter has never been inclined to apply herself. She seems to have taken to your company. I was hoping you might teach her."

Panfilo blurted out that he was honored. Graciously, he accepted.

The instruction first took place in the open air of the *loggia*. Citing the noise of the courtyard, Rosanna had it moved to her chamber. Panfilo knew if music did not echo through the walls for even the slightest moment, somebody would investigate. The Baron's room lay through but one set of doors.

As for the rose window, removing the panes would require patience. It was not available in case of emergency.

"Do you desire me?" asked Rosanna.

Panfilo removed the flaut from between his lips. Eying his cunningly artless pupil, he said, "Whatever do you mean, Your Ladyship?"

"Do you want to make love to me?" she asked.

Panfilo gulped. Collecting himself, he smiled delicately. "You are a maiden," he replied. "Am I an Arab or a Frank, that I should love bloodshed? I am a Norman. I love my women strong and experienced."

"Give me your flaut." Handing it over, Panfilo watched his young charge lift her robes to her milky-white thighs. Spreading her legs wide, she dipped the flaut beneath her hems, nudging the fipple into her sheath; she pushed down on her mound and out came a sound, while the concertmaster sat gritting his teeth.

"It's a good thing," said Panfilo, clearing his throat, "this particular type of wood is resistant to moisture."

Once the flaut was out and the hems were on the floor, Panfilo breathed easy. He took the instrument. He sniffed it. He said, "It smells nice."

As soon as the lesson was over, Panfilo ran to his father's house. Panting like a chipmunk caught in a cat's throat, he asked his brother, "Do you want to play?" His brother said nothing. Panfilo remembered he was deaf-mute. He mimed playing a flaut. Lorenzo didn't understand. Panfilo mouthed the words. Lorenzo shrugged. "Alright," said Panfilo. "I'll show you."

The next time Panfilo gave a lesson, he hid his brother in the Baron's garden. During practice, he removed the panes from the rose window. Lorenzo climbed up a poplar into Rosanna's room. He was directed towards the instruments. Panfilo placed him with his back to the bed. He instructed him to play the pipe with one hand and the harmonium with the other.

The noise was loud enough to mask the involuntary sounds emanating from the bed. Everything was perfect, except Lorenzo kept stopping at the end of every page. Panfilo would have to tear his mouth away and quickly cry, "Don't worry. Keep going. You're doing well." Tucking his own flaut into his breeches, he would stride up to his brother, threaten him with violence—a slap in the face was usually enough—and as soon as Lorenzo put the pipe back into his mouth, Panfilo would rush back to Rosanna's bed and try to remember where he left off.

Panfilo wasn't stupid. When a cherry tree in the Baron's orchard was mysteriously chopped down, he knew exactly what it meant. It was a threat to his control. He searched for the evidence everywhere— from his father's house to the Baron's keep. There was no sign of it. He shadowed Lorenzo for days. He only left him alone to give Rosanna her lesson.

Lorenzo stopped climbing the poplars. He would fish out from the Baron's fountain the bottle he had made. The outside was waxed instead of the inside. It was shaped to fit the cherry branch he had chosen. Though Panfilo beat him badly for it, he wouldn't stop coming back to carve it.

Panfilo was worried. He told Rosanna, "He's up to something."

"Never mind him," she said. "I'm more concerned with my father. He wants to marry me off. I'm not going to let him do it. Do you understand? I would rather live like a peasant in Greece with a man I love, than be sold to a prince for a pound of pennies."

Panfilo and Rosanna declared their love for each other. They decided to elope. To prevent suspicion from taking hold, not least of all in Lorenzo, Panfilo convinced Rosanna to keep things the way they were, until he could make arrangements.

Meanwhile, Lorenzo finished. In the Baron's garden, he started playing the song he knew so well. The Baron heard him. He approached. He asked how the boy had come to learn the tune. "It is a family heirloom," he said. "Have you been listening at the window?" The boy said nothing. "I recognize you," said the Baron. "You once played for the Bishop."

The Baron took the boy to the Bishop's palace. He told the concertmaster, "This boy is superb. Why does he no longer play for you?" The concertmaster's face fell.

"I'm sorry, My Lord," he said. "The boy is deaf."

The next time Panfilo gave a lesson, Lorenzo climbed up the poplars and went to work. The Baron opened the doors to his daughter's chamber. He saw the pitiful figure of Lorenzo, playing a pipe with one hand and a harmonium with the other. The boy noticed him. He stopped.

The Baron motioned him to continue. Breathlessly, he approached the four-poster bed. Panfilo lay alongside his daughter's legs. Anything more and he might have killed him outright.

Panfilo sensed something. He turned his head. The room was empty. It wasn't until Lorenzo played the final note that the Baron returned with his kin. They dragged the young man away. Rosanna wept bitterly

The Baron knew that an open accusation would destroy his daughter's reputation. An Inquisition, though risky, would probably prove effective. Panfilo was eager to face it, until his stepmother visited him in jail. She was sporting a growing belly. Panfilo feared his father would betray him. He agreed to be banished.

Panfilo might have walked away with his life. Instead, like a true Christian knight, he honored his commitment to his Lady. Breathlessly, Rosanna was waiting. Together they crossed the mountains of Matera, shadowing the road south to Catanzaro. At port, they secured passage aboard a Venetian ship. The first mate claimed they were headed for Crete.

When the morning sun pierced the starboard hull, Panfilo knew something was wrong. He asked the other passengers where they were headed. "To Venice," they said. He checked the cargo. It was full of porcelain. "I knew that mate looked familiar," he told Rosanna. "I took something from his uncle."

"What are we going to do?"

"We're close to shore. If we take one of the broken oars we can swim for it."

Rosanna shook her head. "I'm not going into the water." Panfilo found all the broken oars. When night fell, he lashed them together and crawled over the side. Holding onto the ladder, he slipped his makeshift raft into the sea. Rosanna climbed aboard. Shoving off, Panfilo kicked his way toward land.

A few minutes after sunrise, Rosanna noticed a *barchetta* in the distance. Panfilo was relieved. He couldn't feel his legs anymore. When the fisherman came alongside, Panfilo knocked him overboard. Putting Rosanna into the small boat, he started rowing east. "With the wind at our back," he said, "we can make it all the way to Albania."

Rosanna cried, "Are you mad? Durazzo has fallen to the Turks."

"Durazzo is a long way to the north," explained Panfilo. "If we're lucky, we'll be dragged south to Corfu."

Rosanna was hungry. She said, "Catch me a fish." Panfilo laughed. "We'll have kippers and biscuits as soon as we get to the island."

"What about waffles?"

"I'm sure the Venetians have waffle irons."

"Do they have swanmeat?"

"I suppose they will."

"Porcupine pie?"

"Why not?"

Before long, they spotted a *galeotta*. Rosanna was overjoyed. "Perhaps they are heading to Greece," she said.

They were pirates. Taking them aboard, they put their hands on Rosanna. To prevent her from being raped, Panfilo confessed. He told them to return him to Bari. They would receive a handsome reward. Rosanna begged them not to do it. They wouldn't listen.

Rosanna entered a convent. Her father said it was the only way to save her lover's life. She knew it was a lie. Panfilo was sentenced to death. To Christ, he confessed his true crimes. To Church and State, he dedicated these last words:

"If I a brigand be,
    "Then so be all of ye.
"For though I robbed and sinned,
    "I did it like the wind.
"I never left my stench,
    "Upon a church's bench.
"While you Lords sit and pray,
    "You do it every day,
"Thinking yourselves so wise,
    "Deserving every prize,
"For having such clean feet,
    "And farting out your meat."

The people thought him quite brave. He was even hanged by an iron chain instead of a rope. He might have gone down in history as a great partisan, were it not for one troubling thing.

Moments before he was hoisted, Panfilo saw his brother approach the foot of the gallows. Putting his hands upon the floorboards, he gazed up with what seemed like total admiration. Panfilo snorted. "If only he knew," he thought.

From a distance, a guard shouted, "Get away from there!"

Before Panfilo could explain his brother was deaf, Lorenzo looked to the guard and stepped back.

The young man's eyes dimmed and brightened. He cried, "Wait!"

It was too late. The chain was up. It clinched his throat.

The people wondered why Panfilo hadn't been prepared. Was he really a coward? Not being able to figure it out, they soon forgot. Something more memorable occurred. His brother miraculously regained his speech and his hearing.

The boy had known to keep quiet. When he watched the masked robber walk away with his flaut, Lorenzo noticed something peculiar about him. It had been a bittersweet revelation. There was indeed something to be admired in such audacity.

A brigand conceals his face. Rarely does he think to disguise his gait. Lorenzo, like his father and his mother, led with his shoulders. Panfilo, more than anybody else, led with his loins.

Grand Horizon

by Betty Hargrove

When Bo stepped off the spacecraft, five of his shipmates were still defrosting. The other six had gathered at the foot of the ramp. Two of them were having a heated exchange.

"We should stay here," said a woman. She had strong features.

"What if there's a beach with litchi over that next hill?" asked a man of average build.

Bo had trouble concentrating on the argument. The man of average build was standing between two women. One was young. She had square shoulders. The other was middle-aged. Her breasts were enormous. She wore—like everybody else—a standard issue People's Liberation Army uniform. Her physique defied standards. The brown, woolen skirt mushroomed her belly. The top button of her white shirt was fastened; the bottom one, less so—the three in between had already popped.

Bo stared.

"This is an alien planet, Fang," said the woman with the strong features. "How do you know a giant serpent isn't waiting there to eat you?"

"I don't believe in giant serpents," replied Fang. He turned to the woman with the square shoulders. He added, "Except for my own." The woman giggled. Bo glanced at her. He noticed she also had square hips. He turned back to the breasts. Their owner tried to give him a dirty look. He didn't see it. She put her hand on her hip. That was a mistake. The fabric stretched. Bo's eyes bulged.

"A river runs through here," continued the woman with the strong features. "The plain is large enough for all our needs. We should immediately begin preparing rice beds and building levees—unless the three of you want to starve."

The fabric, thought Bo, was framing the cleavage in the shape of a teardrop, literally, as if the seam had split—or, had been torn apart—from the pants of a young, supple woman bending down to pick up, let it be, a child.

"The beds are going to take at least a month," said Fang. "Why can't we explore?"

"We have to build," said the woman with the strong features. "Our common needs take precedence over your curiosity."

Any second now, thought Bo, the stress on that last button would overcome the tensile strength of the threads. The whole thing would crash.

"Jyrgal and Hui will help with the beds," continued the woman with the strong features. "Till the fields. Mark them out. Don't forget. There's twelve of us."

"I know how to count," said Fang. "I didn't manage a hotel for nothing."

Bo turned his gaze to the woman giving orders. He wondered what made her so intrepid. The man named Fang had an understandable attitude. The woman's reluctance to accommodate it confused Bo. He watched her walk along the ship to the rear hatches. The passengers she called Jyrgal and Hui followed.

Jyrgal looked Turkish. He was probably a man from the western provinces. Hui was a woman. If she were from the Hui people, mused

Bo, it would all make sense. As minorities, they had felt compelled—not perhaps to support the woman, but surely to oppose Fang, a man who, at first glance, epitomized the mainstream. Bo huffed. Billions of miles from home, politics were already being played out.

A man came down the ramp. He looked up. "My God," he cried. "It's beautiful." Bo nodded. A luminous nebula stretched above them. It filled more than half the sky. "I thought I was warm from the de-freezing process," said the man. "I doubt it ever gets completely dark around here."

"There are four stars," said Bo. "I checked the computer."

The man squinted. He tried to count them. It was hard to make them out.

Bo looked to the right. A meadow stretched for about half a mile. It thinned into desert. Mountains rose in the distance. In front of the ship, gentle hills dominated the landscape. To the left, a river ran next to a thick forest. Beyond that were more mountains. Bo walked to the bank. The man followed.

Their bare feet sank into the soft ground. The man said, "This river runs parallel to the equator."

Bo asked, "How can you tell?"

"There's moss on this side. There isn't any on the other. Wet, cold air comes from this direction."

"I suggest," said Bo, "if you like it warm and dry, to claim a field as soon as you can. There's no telling what those others will do."

The man shook his head. "I like it damp. I find it refreshing."

"So do I." Bo plopped himself onto the grass. "I'll pitch my tent right here."

"I'll be your neighbor. We lucked out with this valley. Who knows what the rest of the planet is like?"

"If you're curious to find out," said Bo. "I'll help you convince a certain somebody it's alright to look."

The man laughed. "That's what got me here in the first place."

"What did you do?"

"I spied."

Bo knit his eyebrows. "On women?"

"No. Industrial designs."

"I'm surprised they chose you."

"It wasn't political or violent. That ruled a lot of people out. What did you do?"

"I pirated software."

"Must have been a lot."

"Enough to get life." Bo extended his arm. "What's your name?"

"Chung," said the man.

They shook hands. "I'm Bo."

A middle-aged woman approached. She looked attractive. From a distance, she said, "I'm Li. How's the water?"

"We haven't tried it yet," said Bo. "Help yourself."

The woman reached the bank. She crouched to her knees. Bo and Chung shared a look. Bo smiled wryly. He said, "What's a girl like you doing on a planet like this?"

The woman huffed. "You think I'm not worthy of it?"

"I'm surprised they would punish such beauty."

The woman countered his smile. She said, "I must be innocent." She sipped.

"How does it taste?"

"Try it."

Bo leaned over. Chung said, "We shouldn't take risks. We should test things first."

"It's not bad—tastes heavy."

"It's probably limestone. You didn't look at the probe's hydrology file?"

"I saw the chronometer," said Li. "It says we've been traveling for almost one million years."

Bo laughed. "That sounds like a while."

"If you ask me," said Li, "gene therapy was only yesterday."

"What about the rest?" Chung gestured towards the ship. "Have they defrosted?"

Li nodded. "You can see three of them in front of the ramp: there's a boy named Yang, a girl named Yi, and an old man named Zhang."

"They're pointing in the direction of the hills," said Bo. "They must like higher ground."

Chung scoffed. "That doesn't sound like Zhang. He's a kleptocrat."

"How would you know?" asked Li. "What if he's innocent?"

"I bribed him myself."

"Those three are greedy. The boy said he stole from a malfunctioning ATM."

Bo jeered. "I remember him. The people's government thought it was making an example. I'm surprised he's here. He should have lived and died a million years ago like everybody else."

"What about the girl? She took in hundreds of thousands with a lottery scheme."

Chung blurted out, "What did you do?"

Li blushed. She paused before confessing, "I embezzled."

"You're one to talk."

"It wasn't for me. I was trying to start a company."

"What kind?"

"Software." Bo laughed.

"Do you know everybody's crime?"

Li blushed some more. "I can't help it if I'm nosy."

"The one who thinks she's in charge," said Bo, "what did she do?"

"She managed a mining company. Her name is Yuan. I think she was held responsible for a collapse. She didn't want to talk about it. The Turkish man was funny. He defended himself. He said all he wanted to do was run a site for people to post things. They charged him with sedition. The woman named Hui: she's an artist. She forged documents. The three of them are like best friends already. They told me to tell you to start digging irrigation ditches. The fields, they think, ought to be further from the river."

"They like it warm and dry," said Chung.

Li pointed to a rocky area behind the ship. "A man named Fang is over there. He thinks he's surveyor in chief. He and his lady friends found a hot spring. They're claiming that entire side for themselves. If I were you, I would wait. They'll dig the ditches, if only to preserve their stakes."

"I heard him say he managed a hotel," said Chung. "What was his crime?"

Li giggled. "He organized an orgy—for three hundred Japanese businessmen. Mei was in charge of the girls."

"Is that the one with the square shoulders or the enormous breasts?" asked Bo.

"The breasts. The other one is named Ting. She ran a pornography studio. I think the models she was using were trafficked."

A wisp of steam rose from the rocks. Bo felt the urge to check it out. "Excuse me," he said. He left Chung and Li behind. He climbed the rocks with his bare feet. He heard the sounds of splashing. Two women laughed. A man said, "That bean counter wanted us to till fields." It was Fang. "I showed her. We marked out the best spots for ourselves—right next to a hot spring. We should open a resort. Charge the others admission."

"What would they pay us with?" asked one of the women.

"Rice. Why should I waste my time rotting my ankles? I could be here, rotting my entire body."

Bo poked his head over the edge of a rock. A few meters below, Fang lay naked, neck-deep in a pool of steaming water. Mei swam next to him. Ting sat on the edge, soaking her feet.

Fang suggested they cool off on the grass. Mei agreed. They climbed out.

"I'll be here," said Ting.

"Don't be afraid," said Mei. Her breasts dripped like immense cloth sacks straining a whole week's worth of doufu. They sagged below her belly button. "Jump in." She turned to follow Fang up the side of the rocks.

Bo watched. Mei struggled to climb the boulders. Her breasts jiggled like a giant donkey's balls. Bo realized it was too bad for her there wasn't less gravity here than on Earth. He suddenly imagined what might have happened if there had been more.

Mei disappeared over the opposite edge. Ting was left alone. Bo revealed himself. He watched the woman gasp. He slowly climbed down.

"What's your name?" he asked.

"Ting,"

Bo nodded. He stripped off his clothes. He got into the water. It was hot, but pleasant. "What's the matter?" he asked. "Do you only like to watch?"

Ting smirked. She started unbuttoning her shirt. She didn't have time to take it off. Bo pulled her in. She yelped. She thrashed her arms about like a baby. Bo held her up by her bottom. He laughed. "Can't you swim?" he asked. He didn't wait for an answer. He kissed her on the mouth. Ting kissed back.

They weren't alone. Physical intimacy was the first order of business for almost everybody. Fang did it with Mei. Yang the ATM thief did it with Yi the lottery cheat. Even the old man got busy. Bo was surprised to learn he did it with Li. "What happened?" he asked Chung. "I left you two alone. Why didn't you take advantage?"

Chung shrugged. He said, "I'm a Christian."

"What does that mean?"

Chung bobbed his head. "I'll wait until I've committed myself."

Bo was confused. Within a few weeks, he discovered the wisdom of Chung's words. He realized he had been too hasty with Ting. He was growing tired of her square figure. Often he found himself staring in the direction of the desert. A tent stood across the way. It was Yuan's tent. Bo would watch her in the mornings as she emerged from her abode, stretching, walking around—sometimes she would bend over to pick something up. Bo imagined what life was like on the sunny side.

All of a sudden, she was gone. Jyrgal had taken her place. Bo curled his lip in disgust. He wondered. He learned discreetly from Hui that they had switched fields. She couldn't tell him why. Bo came to understand he missed seeing Yuan. He admired not just her rounded figure, but that strangely solicitous spirit. He cursed the spaceship for now blocking his view. He decided he would have to pay her a visit.

Bo walked along Chung's field. He saw his friend washing clothes in the river. He waved. His friend waved back. Bo approached the front of the ship. In the distance, he saw Zhang and Li. He waved to them. They didn't see. He passed Yang and Yi's fields. He wondered whether Yang were in Yi's tent or Yi in Yang's. He thought, somebody should tell them to put their tents together—on the other hand, he concluded, they might not be ready for that.

At the end of the irrigation ditch that he himself had grudgingly helped to build, Bo found Yuan laboring in her field. "Good morning," he said. Yuan looked up. Bo smiled. "It's a nice day for a walk." He gestured towards the desert. "Would you care to join me?" Yuan looked at the landscape. She thought about it. She put down the rice plant she was holding. She wiped her hands. She looked at Bo. She nodded.

Bo stepped gingerly into the field. Together, they walked.

"I have to say," said Bo, "I miss seeing you in the mornings." Yuan laughed.

"I'm sure you have more immediate attractions." Bo knew she was taunting him. He ignored it.

"Why did you move? Did Jyrgal want a better view of Mei's breasts?" Yuan slapped Bo playfully on the arm.

"Don't say that. Jyrgal devotes himself to Hui. He's teaching her the ways of Islam."

Bo laughed. "Which way is Mecca?"

Yuan shook her head. "You know that sort of thing isn't important."

"My neighbor is a Christian," said Bo. "That's why he's still single. What's your excuse?"

Yuan looked to the ground. She shrugged. "I follow the path of Buddha."

"Is it a lonely path?"

"It doesn't have to be."

Bo smiled. "I think you would look good with your head shaved."

Yuan chuckled. "There's no time to read sutras. We have to work."

Bo huffed. "You'll bury us with all your work."

Yuan's face fell. Bo realized his mistake. "I'm sorry," he said. "Li told me why you were sentenced. I should have been more careful."

"No," insisted Yuan. "I'm the one who should have been careful." They walked in silence. Eventually, Yuan said, "I was the managing supervisor. The investors wanted to expand operations. The people wanted work. I overlooked the risks."

Bo nodded. "There was pressure from everybody. It wasn't your fault."

"I failed the holy Dharma."

"Don't be ridiculous." Yuan shot Bo a dirty look. He was surprised how much it unnerved him. He tried unsuccessfully to hide his feelings. He spluttered, "Buddha will forgive you—so will Allah, His son Christ. As for my forgiveness, it will come at a high cost."

Yuan raised an eyebrow. In a mocking tone, she asked, "What would that be?"

"You must forgive yourself. More importantly, you will have to tell me why you moved." Yuan laughed. She shook her head.

"If you must know, I didn't see eye to eye with Mei."

Bo giggled. He said, "Neither do the men."

"You are awful. You're keeping me from my planting."

Bo stopped Yuan. He held her by the arm. He said, "There is no work without rest." She turned to face him. Bo gazed into her eyes. "Maybe we can do both together."

Yuan hung her head. She stared for a moment at the cracks in the ground. Suddenly, she looked up. Slowly, she pressed her lips together. She started slightly to nod. Bo took her by the hand. They turned towards the fields.

One day, Bo realized a woman was crying in Chung's tent. He crossed his friend's field. He peered through the entrance. He could see Chung consoling Li. Bo made a sound. Chung came outside. He frowned. He said, "Li went for a walk in the hills. She caught Zhang with Yang."

Bo's eyes went wild. "The boy?" Chung nodded. "The old man?" Chung nodded. "They were?" Chung nodded. Bo laughed. "Six men. Six women. I guess they're lucky to have each other."

"Li's not lucky."

"She's lucky to have you. Take her. Teach her about your Christ. She's not a child like Yi. She's smart. She'll listen."

Chung thought about it. He realized it was a good idea. He asked Li to marry him.

"What?" she cried. "I'm pregnant with Zhang's child. How can you stand to look at me?"

Chung explained, "All I need from you is faith. Swear yourself to me. My God will take care of us." Li felt she had no reason not to do it. Chung saw only one problem.

"Who will marry us?" he asked. "I can baptize her. I can't officiate my own wedding."

"Ask Yuan," said Bo. "She follows the Dharma. She will understand your ways."

"My friend," said Chung, "could you ask her for me?"

Bo hesitated. Yuan might be bothered by the request. If Bo were to

51

ask himself, it would make it easier for her to refuse. He would have to come prepared. "Alright," he said. "I'll try."

"No," said Yuan. "I've never been a member of the Sangha. I wouldn't know what to do."

"You will find it in yourself," said Bo. "I know that. Out of all of us, you are the strongest. You were tested. We indulged our weaknesses. You alone faced a challenge. In failing, you learned the difficulties of overcoming pressure."

"What about Jyrgal," asked Yuan, "or his wife, Mei? They are far more deserving than me."

"They listened to you. They know you are meant to be our leader. The rest of us haven't been paying attention. If you officiate this ceremony, it will help establish your authority. I will defend it."

Yuan gave Bo a stern look. She held the gaze as she slowly turned her head. She said, "Why?"

Bo blinked. He already knew the answer. He gulped. He whispered, "I love you."

Yuan was shocked. She looked away. She dropped her head. She kept it down. After a moment, she turned it half-way back. After another, she nudged it closer. She said, "I'll do it."

The marriage was organized with exquisite care. Decorations were placed aboard the spaceship. Incense was burned. Prayers and offerings were made. Jyrgal and Hui sewed the couple's tents together. Fang made furniture. Ting and Mei decided to sheer some of the defrosted sheep.

Everybody was participating. Yi had to avoid Yang. Zhang was coerced into helping. As soon as the celebratory fires were smoldering, he disappeared. The grazing animals went with him. Yang was observed packing Zhang's things. He explained pasturage was getting scarce around the ship. It was necessary to take the herds into the hills. He struck his tent and left.

Yi found solace in Mei's arms. At first, it seemed natural. The two had worked closely on the textiles, Ting having abandoned them in favor of helping Fang. It was later discovered Fang had, in fact, been neglecting Mei and sleeping with Ting. Yi and Mei were now both jilted lovers. It wasn't long before they were whispering in each other's ears, holding each other's arms, staying overnight in each other's tents.

When Yi was seen moving intimate apparel into Mei's tent, the rumors began.

"I wonder what it's like for them," said Chung. "Yi is shorter. Mei has the larger breasts. Who feels more like the man?"

"Good question," said Bo. "I would say, as Yi is shorter, she feels more like the woman. Mei's breasts being overwhelmingly large, it offers her the kind of dominance that could translate into masculine feelings—not to mention the fact that she's older."

One misty morning, Bo saw the two in the distance. They were walking hand in hand. They were heading for the hot springs. Bo dropped his spade. He sneaked into the boulders. He tiptoed up the side of the pit. He peered over its edge in time to see the women strip. Bo grinned. When the two embraced, Yi's fleshy body burst Mei's breasts apart like pound cake exploding in a hot oven. They leaned their heads back to kiss. "By all that's holy," thought Bo, "they are in love."

Mei held Yi's hand as she slid her into the water. They splashed and giggled. At one point, Mei gripped her lover's bottom. Yi stood on her tip-toes. She rested her arms on those experienced shoulders. She gazed into those wrinkly eyes. Bo clutched his head. He thought, "How did this happen?"

The fog lifted. On the opposite side, Bo caught sight of another face in the rocks. It was Fang. What a dirty man, thought Bo. Fang spotted him. He scowled. Bo turned away in spite. To his left, he saw another man. It was Chung. Shame on you, thought Bo. Chung's eyes went wide. He ducked. "Whom had he seen?" thought Bo. It wasn't him. He looked to the right. It was Jyrgal. He, too, was peeping. Bo shook his head.

He went back to his tent. Yuan showed up with a flush of tea leaves. "I transplanted some more into the field," she said. "Things grow quite quickly around here."

Bo was too busy pouting to pay attention. "She's like a little girl," he said. "She stands up on her toes. She pecks Mei on the lips as if she's her mother—except they're naked, holding each other by the bum."

Yuan shook her head. "There's no accounting for love."

"It's not healthy—not for this community. Li can't be the only woman pregnant. Every man needs to do his part."

"How do you know Mei isn't too old?"

"That's my point. Somebody ought to be testing. Her unique qualities have to be passed down."

"Is that what this is about?"

"Don't be jealous. I want what's best for all of us."

"Genetic diversity?"

"If Fang can't do it, somebody else ought to try."

"Like you?"

"Don't tempt me."

"You're obviously obsessed with her unique qualities."

"I like your breasts best of all."

"Don't patronize me. If you want to play in the hot spring, go ahead."

"Don't be bitter." Bo changed the subject. The next time he brought it up, he was with Chung. He was gratified to learn his neighbor was of a similar mind.

"I would do it myself," he said, "only my religion prevents it. Why don't you try?"

Bo shook his head. "Yuan claims she wouldn't care. She's lying. She's been mortal enemies with Mei ever since she saw her pee into the irrigation ditch. That's why she changed fields. She wanted uncontaminated water from the other side."

"Why don't we ask Jyrgal? Muslims like having more than one wife."

"By the time we get around to making a still, he'll have two women nagging us."

"What about Fang?"

"He tried and failed. If we asked him, it would remind him of his shortcomings while simultaneously pumping up his ego."

They dropped the matter. Life continued. Mei and Yi stopped hiding. They would kiss each other in front of everybody. Bo and Yuan encountered them on their walks. "They're happy," Yuan would say. "That's good." Yi was growing a belly. Mei went around calling herself the father.

"It's obviously Yang's child," said Bo.

"Aren't you satisfied? This is what you wanted."

"I would be," said Bo, "if we had one of our own."

Yuan never liked hearing those words. Every time Bo uttered them, she would turn away. He would embrace her from behind. He would murmur, "All the women are pregnant now except for you and Mei." He would stroke his head along her rounded shoulders. "Can't we make love?"

Yuan would insist she wasn't ready. "Wait," she would say, "for the first harvest. It will be a cause for celebration."

One day, Yuan was washing her clothes in the river. The water was unusually full of silt. She tried wading further out. The current there was strong. She hit her ankle on a rock. It started to hurt terribly. She hobbled her way back towards the bank. A bit of laundry slipped from her hand. Foolishly, she tried to grab it.

Chung heard her cry. He ran to the bank. He saw Yuan struggling in the distance. She disappeared behind a bend. Chung knew it was madness to follow her by himself. He found Bo in Yuan's field. He was planting tea. "Bo," he cried. "The river is dragging Yuan away."

Bo raced to the water's edge. Yuan was nowhere to be seen. Chung came up behind him. He said, "She was near the bend when I saw her."

Bo ran to his tent. He grabbed a spear he had fashioned in case of animal attack. He followed the bank. He encountered a forest. Roots stretched over the ground. Branches slapped him in the face. Bo was forced to slow down. He feared the worst. There was no telling how far Yuan would go. "Stay alive," he kept repeating to himself. "I'm coming."

On the surface, the river was calm. Thoughts of rapids and waterfalls injected themselves into Bo's mind. He imagined Yuan drowning. He shook his head. He solemnly vowed never to return without her, no matter how far he would go. If the river drained into a massive whirlpool, he would jump into it. He would die in its murky depths looking for her body.

Bo noticed the river growing narrow. It was getting deep. If it emptied into a lake, he thought, Yuan would be saved—unless there were a lake monster. Bo rubbed his eyes. It was useless to worry.

The hills flattened. The forest thinned. The river widened. "If it's shallow," thought Bo, "Yuan may have climbed out. I don't want to miss her." He kept glancing to the other bank, hoping he would spot Yuan wringing out her skirt in gentle frustration. There was nobody.

Bo stopped. He went to the river's edge. He gazed into the water. It was as clear as day. He could see the bottom. "This water would reach my chest," he thought. "Surely Yuan is safe." He kept running. The bank got low and sandy.

Bo tried again to ascertain the water's depth. As he approached the edge, a rumbling came from somewhere downstream. Bo couldn't see what was causing it. The sound grew loud. He squinted. His eyes widened. A massive wave was rounding a bend. It was climbing the river. It passed Bo as it dissipated into a gentle swell. He thought, "A tide."

Bo turned the bend. Sandbars glimmered in the distance. They were at the corner of yet another bend. Bo ran. He could hear the sound of waves. He approached the sandbars. He could see something stuck against one of them. He neared it. He crouched. It was laundry. Bo looked.

An ocean spread wide, rippling multitudinously, pinned seemingly by the marbled plumes of the nebula. Bo's heart leapt. Yuan had to be here. She had to be alive. He approached the sea slowly with reverence. Water splashed his ankles. It got deeper. All of a sudden, Bo fell into a deep trench. He had to swim onto dry land. Ahead of him stretched a vast coast. In the other direction, another river cut into the shoreline. It disappeared between low-lying hills.

Bo turned. There she was, sitting cross-legged like Buddha against the side of a dune. Bo sighed. He ran as fast as he could. He threw down his spear. He dropped to his knees in front of her. He panted. Joy swelled his face. He waited. Yuan sat motionless. Her eyes were fixed on the grand horizon. Her face betrayed nothing. She said, "Is it not beautiful?"

Bo nodded. He understood they were looking at two completely different things. He fell onto his back. He lay, regaining his breath, hoping it expressed to some extent the dread he had felt chasing Yuan down the river or the great devotion that had compelled him.

He suddenly thought of the moment he confessed his love for her. It was then that she had agreed to perform the ceremony for Chung and Li. Those things were somehow connected. She had dwelled on her decision. She was fond of mentioning how happy she was to see Chung and Li so full of life. Other times Bo would catch her staring at their tent, frowning, giving him a dirty look, as if it were his fault she had married them—as if he had pressured her into doing something wrong.

Was it him? he thought. Was it his love for her that she frowned upon? Bo huffed. She couldn't possibly consider herself that unworthy. He turned to look at her. She was still sitting stoically, as if she were teaching him not to be bothered by her—as if it were a crime to love her and a punishment for her that she be still alive.

What selfishness, thought Bo. He chastised himself. Was he any better? He recalled how poorly he had treated Ting. He complemented his impetuousness in pursuing her with a marked listlessness in retreat. He had abandoned her slowly, drawing it out over the weeks he had visited Yuan in her field. How embarrassing it must have been.

Bo shrugged. "It serves her right," he thought, "for having such square shoulders." He turned to look at Yuan. She was so stubborn. She was still staring into the distance. What did she think? that she had failed Virtue? as if it were some hurt friend who moved away, whose forgiveness she was now fruitlessly condemned forever to seek?

Bo rolled himself to the waves. He let them knock his body about. This is the way, he thought. This is how you let go. If he could stop trying to rationalize Yuan, she might be able to stop irrationally punishing herself. To embrace each other, they would have to stop embracing their own natures.

Something plopped. Bo's head darted. There was nothing there. He could have sworn he had heard a plop. Since emerging from the ship, Bo had seen no bird, no insect, no reptile in the desert, nor rodent in the ground. What if, he suddenly thought to himself, smiling at his own audacity—there were fish?

Bo took up his spear. He walked down the shore. He searched in vain for a cove or a tidal pool. The water was too high for mud flats. He would have to wait for the tide to go out. He headed back to Yuan. He walked along the tree-line. He came across a sinkhole. It was as wide as Bo was tall; twice as deep. Tides, he thought, must have caused an underground cave to collapse. The walls were steep and rocky. The floor was moist. "If only there were wildlife," he thought. "We could make a trap."

Bo noticed the tide turning. He walked past Yuan. He approached the mouth of the other river. As he climbed over a low ridge of sand, his eyes began to bulge. An army of molting crabs held court in the ankle-deep water. "By Heaven," he said. He turned to Yuan. He cried, "Here is a gift."

Bo speared three of the largest crabs he could find. He brought them to Yuan. She refused to look at them. Bo went about making a fire. By dusk, he had cooked two of the crabs. He ate them with pleasure. Yuan sat motionless the entire time. Bo thought, "Hunger will move her."

In the morning, she was still sitting cross-legged with her hands in her lap. Bo went to her. "Come," he said. He held out his arm. "Have breakfast."

Yuan looked. It seemed as if she were waking from a dream. She took hold of Bo's arm. She struggled to get herself up. She fell. Bo laughed. He smacked her legs. He gripped her by the torso. He lifted her to her feet. "Is this what they call enlightenment?" he asked. "Your legs are like rocks."

Yuan sat in front of the fire. She devoured the last crab. Bo came with more. "Have as many as you want," he said.

Yuan licked her fingers. She gazed into Bo's eyes. She whispered, "Thank you."

Bo unbuttoned his standard-issue Liberation Army shirt. He threw it into the fire. He unzipped his standard-issue Liberation Army pants. He showed them the same courtesy. His standard-issue underwear fared no better. Standing naked, he smiled. What a liberating impulse, he thought to himself. He turned away. He lay quietly in the sand.

Yuan stared at the burning cloth. She was struck by how readily Bo had disposed of it, after she had risked her life to grab a little piece. Yuan breathed deeply. She fingered the buttons of her shirt. She decided it was time to let go. Bo listened. The fire crackled.

They spent the next few days enjoying each other's company. They walked along the shore. They caught crabs. They played in the waves. For the first time, they made love.

The next morning, Yuan whispered, "I'm anxious about our fields."

Bo said, "Don't worry. Chung and Jyrgal will take care of them."

"The rice may have already turned yellow. What if they take our crop?"

"We can go now if you insist."

"You go. Bring me some clothes. I don't want the others to see me naked."

Bo left. By midday, he was near his field. He could see his rice was gone. Chung's crop was still standing. Bo grimaced. He walked through the stubble to his tent. He put on some clothes. He paid Chung a visit.

"My God," cried his friend. "You're alive."

Bo looked at him sternly. He said, "Where is my rice?"

Chung breathed a heavy sigh. "You wouldn't believe what's been happening. Since you left, Fang and Ting have been running amok. They've been trying to take over. They claimed your field for their own. I threatened them. They backed down. They went to Yuan's field. They told Jyrgal they were doing it on behalf of Yi. She and Mei joined their gang. The four of them harvested their own fields as soon as they could, so they could move on to the rest.

"They took Yang's crop. Zhang didn't argue. Jyrgal tried to stop them from taking Yuan's rice. He attacked Fang. Ting retaliated against Hui. She fell on her belly. She lost her child." Chung paused to let the news sink in. "They threatened to do the same to Li. What was I supposed to do? I had already given you up for dead. I let them take it. I couldn't risk it. My wife isn't as young as Hui."

"I understand," said Bo. "Where is my rice?"

Chung bowed his head. "They keep it on the ship. The four of them moved in. Fang treats it like his own imperial palace. He calls Ting his consort; Mei and Yi, his concubines. He bullied Jyrgal into adding his rice to the pile. He filled in the irrigation ditch on the end of Yi's field. He blocked your sluice gate with rocks. My crop is the only one left standing. I'm afraid if I harvest, they'll come and steal it while I'm asleep."

"When do they leave the ship?"

"Hardly ever. Yi comes to the river to get water."

"Does she wash clothes?"

"Yes."

"Where?"

"The same spot Yuan used. Is she alive?"

Bo nodded. He left without saying another word. He went back to the beach. He told Yuan the news.

She asked, "What are you going to do?"

Bo grinned. "I'm going to build a jail. You will be my jailer." Bo gathered dead trees. He stripped them of their branches. He arranged them according to their knots. He lashed them together. It would serve as a ladder. He slid it into the sinkhole. He leaned it against the side. It worked. Bo lashed more trees into a lattice. He covered the hole with it. He weighed it down with rocks.

He asked Yuan, "Will you be alright? I'm not sure when I'll be back."

"Don't worry," she said. "Just bring me my prisoners."

Bo went to his tent. He waited. Eventually, Yi appeared with her laundry. Bo sneaked upstream. He put rocks in his pockets. He tore off a reed. He stuck it in his mouth. He waded into the water. His body disappeared beneath it. He crept silently along the riverbed.

At long last, like the wisps of a ghost, Yi's calves flickered into view. Bo took one last breath. The reed slipped from his lips.

Yi dipped her articles into the water. She spread them out. She hummed quietly. She saw the reed floating on the surface. She watched it for a moment. It might have been a curious thing for a more insightful person, considering the lack of apparent wildlife. Only one thought crossed Yi's idle mind, if a thought it could be called. Articulated into words, it would have amounted to no more than, "There goes a reed."

Bo leapt from the water. Like a sow sensing a crocodile's breath, Yi knew it was too late. All she could do was cringe. An arm went across her chest; another supported her waist. She was pulled off her feet. Falling backwards into the water, she was pressed against a man's chest. She gurgled all the way down the river.

Mei was vexed. She looked everywhere for her precious Yi. She asked Chung if he had seen her. He turned away. He seemed to be fighting back tears. He murmured, "I think I know what happened. Yi was kidnapped by creatures native to this planet. They took Yuan; doubtless Bo as well. One of them visited me. He talked to me through his hands."

Mei shook her head. "Why haven't you told us?"

"I was afraid. I didn't want you to know what I did. Li was having nightmares. She would dream Jyrgal's dead baby was digging itself out of its grave, crawling to our tent, coming to ask if our child were ready to play. She begged me to do something. I unearthed the corpse. I threw it into the river." Chung buried his face in his hands. He peeped at Mei through his fingers. She seemed suitably horrified.

Chung continued. "The next day, it came. It was covered in mud. It wore a hideous mask of claws. It showed me what it wanted with its hands. I realized it had found the child. It had eaten it. Now it hungers for more." Mei shook her head. She couldn't believe what she was hearing. Her gut told her it had to be true.

Chung said, "If Yi gives birth, the creatures will take her child. They will eat it. They know about the bellies. Yuan must have told them. The one who came was looking for my wife. I scared it off. I followed it down the river. I saw the cave where they live. It's on the shore of a vast ocean. Yi must be there. You would never free her. Guards were everywhere with spears."

Mei wailed. She pulled her hair. She cried, "What will I do?"

"Barter for her life. It's the only way. Trade Yi for another belly."

"Whose?"

"Ting's. She's the one who murdered Jyrgal's baby. She should be the one to suffer."

"That's right," said Mei. "How should I do it?"

"I will help. I will go to the creatures. I will arrange a trade. All you have to do is bring Ting to the beach."

"She would never go. Now that Yi is gone, both she and Fang are too scared to leave the ship."

"Trick her. Tell her you found Yi on a beach populated by natives. They showed you an underground pool with miraculous power. They warned Yi not to bathe in it as long as she were pregnant. It would give her child superhuman strength. It would burst through her belly.

"Tell her, when they weren't looking, Yi dipped in her toe. All of a sudden, she could feel the child kick. It nearly tore her apart. She's recuperating now with the creatures. Ting will believe you. She will want to put her whole foot in. Tell her not to mention anything to Fang. He would only fear such a child."

Mei gathered her courage. She feigned excitement. She ran to tell

Ting the news. Ting was, at first, suspicious. Her vanity soon got the better of her. They went to the beach. They encountered two creatures covered in mud. A chain of crab legs dangled over each of their eyes. Each of their heads was covered with a crown of claws. Ting whispered, "I don't like it."

Mei reassured her. The women approached the pit. Ting peered through the lattice. Bo grabbed her. Yuan pulled off the cover. Bo positioned the thrashing woman over the hole. She slipped gradually through his arms. She fell to the bottom. Yuan covered the hole. Mei cried, "What about Yi?"

Ting shouted from the pit, "She's here, bound and gagged. Damn it. What have you done?"

Bo removed his mask. Mei staggered back. She fell to the ground. Bo grinned. He nodded towards the pit. He said, "They're my prisoners."

Mei whimpered. She hit the ground with her fists. She sniveled, "Let my Yi go."

Bo laughed. "You think I would do it for nothing? Give me what I want."

Mei sniffed. "What?"

"A baby."

"Whose?"

"Yours. Go sleep with the old man or the boy. I know they're both capable. I don't care if you have to smother them with your breasts. You won't get Yi until your traits are being passed down."

Bo took Mei into the hills. He threw her at Zhang's feet. He went back to the settlement. It wasn't long before a thirsty Fang was forced to leave the ship. Bo was waiting with his spear. He had Chung escort the prisoner to the pit.

"Hear ye, hear ye," said Bo. "Henceforth, our world—from the hot springs to the shores, from the desert to the river—shall be named after Yuan, our leader."

Bo fashioned posts to mark the edges of the realm. On each he carved two characters: a picture of a head poking through a robe, meaning "Yuan," and a picture of another head over a foot in the crossroads, meaning "way."

Yuan didn't like it. She thought it was overbearing. She told Bo to add the foot in the crossroads to the first character, making it mean "far." She told him the sign should read, "Farway."

"Brilliant," said Bo. "Your name is still there, but disguised."

Yuan proved a decisive leader. She felt her first task was to assign somebody to mind the shore. His job would be to collect crabs and feed prisoners. Bo asked Chung if he were interested. Chung declined. The burden fell on Jyrgal. He was in no position to argue.

Bo was convinced Jyrgal could be trusted. After all, the prisoners were responsible for the death of Hui's child. Circumstances proved Bo wrong. Jyrgal took pity on Yi. She seemed innocent. Day after day, she begged to be released. She told Jyrgal she would be good. She would help Hui gather firewood. Jyrgal took matters into his own hands. Without informing Bo or Yuan, he let Yi go.

One day, Yi left Hui in the forest. While Jyrgal was catching crabs, she released Fang and Ting. The three of them threw Jyrgal into the pit. They went back to the settlement. They knocked on the hull of the ship. Bo appeared at the top of the ramp.

"We're tired of sitting in jail," they cried. "We want better."

Bo asked, "Where is Jyrgal?"

"We threw him into the pit."

"And Chung? He was sent to bring us crabs."

"We hid from him as he came down the river."

Hui appeared. She looked panic-stricken. She claimed Fang and Ting had murdered her husband. The others insisted it wasn't true. Hui swore she had seen them do it.

Bo waited for Chung. When he arrived, he testified he had found the shore empty. "I checked the pit," he said. "I saw somebody there. I didn't think to make sure who it was. I know now it must have been Jyrgal. I went to search the coast. When I came back, the pit was uncovered. Jyrgal was on the bottom—dead. I assume he fell trying to get out. His head must have been split open by a rock."

Bo asked, "Are you sure he was alive when you first passed?"

Chung nodded. "I saw him move."

Yuan appeared at the top of the ramp. She ordered Hui be thrown into the pit for lying. Chung seized her. She told Fang to construct a bier to bring Jyrgal's body back to the settlement. "We will bury him in his field," she said. "His grave will be a constant reminder to us of the preciousness of life."

Hui cried, "My husband is dead. Am I to sit in the pit where he was killed while you bury him without me?"

"I will not tolerate falsehood," said Yuan. "If Chung had not witnessed Jyrgal alive, what would I have done to his supposed killers? I understand you seek vengeance for your child. I sympathize with your loss. I cannot excuse your crime."

"You lied to Mei," said Hui. "Otherwise you would not be in power. Now you don't tolerate a lie? You're a hypocrite."

"I did not bring false accusations," said Yuan. "Carry out the sentence." Chung dragged her away. The others watched. After a moment, they dispersed.

Bo admired Yuan's strength and her wisdom. He told her this is what he meant when he said she would find it in herself.

"I will not keep Hui there for long," said Yuan. "I love her. I understand her pain."

"There is no need to explain yourself to me." Bo kneeled in front of her. "I am your servant. I trust you."

Yuan caressed the back of Bo's head. She whispered, "I know." She gazed at the paddies they had made. The hills stretched into the distance like the breasts of sleeping giants. To her, they represented the men who perished under her care. They were the men who judged her for it. They were the men who sent her to this land, so far removed in time and space from everything she had ever known.

Yuan closed her eyes. Those men were gone. The joy, the anguish, the hope and the sorrow they inspired had followed her through the cold dimensions of space. She had once thought she had no choice but to cling to them. Now she could sense them fading away.

Chung arrived with happy news. Li was delivered of a baby boy. "Congratulations," said Yuan. She smiled. There were now twelve again.

Bo rubbed his face in Yuan's belly. "There will soon be more," he said. He looked up. Yuan caught his beaming eyes. "Crying, eating, smiling, laughing, learning what it means to be sentenced to life." Bo looked at the hills. Billowy clouds of lustrous gas gleamed above them. With any luck, he thought to himself, one in particular would have her mother's unique qualities.

Clutch Bag

by Ted McConkey

Junior's favorite sport was sex. The people at his father's company, J.N. Vandenhoff, thought it was golf. Many of the upper managers who weren't vice presidents (nor had permanent seats on the executive jet) liked to talk to him using golf metaphors, thinking it might get them invited to the next round. Usually, Junior had no idea what they were saying.

He didn't like to talk during golf. It didn't matter if he were playing George Price, the Vice-President for Export, or Mark Upshaw, the Vice-President for Sales, or Dick Stockton, the Vice-President for Development of Petroleum-based Products. None of them had been made Vice-Presidents because they were qualified. They were good at having fun. They told bawdy jokes. Above all else, they let the boss's son win.

Junior admired golf. It took an amount of discipline he lacked in regard to women. He noticed similarities between the sports. In each case, though it was possible to play with teams, the goal remained essentially one of individual accomplishment. A man had to use his club to get the ball, or the contents of his ball, into the hole.

The best place to practice such skills was on Long Island. Beyond the boundary of New York City lay what Junior liked to call, 'Country Club County.' It had a permanent population of women whose most active pursuit was sipping martinis on the verandah. As their husbands were away on business, it was Junior's responsibility to give them exercise.

Having consumed his fair share of amateur sport in college and high school, Junior considered himself a suitably hardened veteran. He adopted a professional mindset. Taking women in their thirties to be his average, anybody older was a par four and up; anybody younger, a par two. Obviously, a woman under twenty was a hole in one.

His first group tournament involved a par four and a par five. The quinquagenarian wasn't Junior's favorite. The other one had two marvelous pairs of hazards on either side. Sandra was her name. The thought of her sitting on those black pantyhosed bunkers made Junior's head swim. As much as he thought he was in love, his career got in the way. He was soon attracted elsewhere by extremely large purses.

There was the short, elegant course with the gorgeous bunkers in front. Junior was kind enough to hold her umbrellas. There was the course he met at the opera. She was a standing ovation. The one at the cosmetics trade show took him home. It bothered him to see the pictures of her family smiling at him.

He found himself a divorcee. She had wonderful, large saggy bunkers. Her face said par three; the back of her legs said par five. Junior took the average. He might have stuck with her long enough to learn the truth, except Sandra returned.

She was the type of girl his mother would want him to marry. She was rich, sophisticated, charming, articulate, white, Protestant, not to mention sexually adventurous. It didn't matter she was in her forties. The problem was she was already married.

"You're what?" asked Junior, panting.

"I'm married," she said, looking for a cigarette.

Junior shouldn't have been surprised. Middle-aged matrons

masquerading as sex maniacs do not marry men who have not yet come into their inheritance. Everybody knows that. Seeking refuge among women he would never want to marry, Junior's career took a significant slide.

He went from grandmothers to hippies to the morbidly obese. Junior even stooped to buying prostitutes to see what he was missing. Tired of overpaying for cheap sex, he found himself a pair of oddly shaped female swingers. Suzy was large. Linda was small. One was all flesh; the other, just bone.

When Linda wore her glasses, she resembled a man named Jeremiah Myklebust. He was J.N. Vandenhoff's chief accountant. His wife, Deborah, equally outstripped him in terms of proportion. Junior felt strangely comforted. With Suzy and Linda, the familiarity of their bodies gave him a warm feeling. It was almost as if he were going to the office.

Suzy and Linda were not the only chronic habits in Junior's life. The circle of perverts was quickly closing in on him. There were only so many willing to tolerate his appetite for casual sex. On the bright side, some of them looked younger than he remembered. Though now in her sixties, the woman with whom he had first shared Sandra looked stunning. "It's the bangs," she said. "I didn't have them before."

Junior tried to get serious. He started dating an unmarried thirty-year-old black professional. He had to keep it a secret. His mother would not have approved. He might have been written out of the will like his older brother. He had married a Catholic.

When the relationship failed, Junior tried to figure out what went wrong. The vice-presidents were all divorced. He talked to their ex-wives. The former Mrs. Price complained her husband was never right. The former Mrs. Upshaw claimed her husband couldn't keep "it" down. The former Mrs. Stockton said, throughout her entire marriage, Dick lay there flat.

Junior's father died. In his will, he left Junior and his mother, Dorothea, joint ownership of the company. "We need to find you a wife," said his mother. She introduced him to the daughters of her country club friends. Her favorite was Jacqueline Carter-Granville. She was in her twenties. She was pale-skinned. She had lovely legs.

Junior was otherwise employed. He had a newfound urge to fulfill his fantasies. He frequented fetish clubs. He liked Asians who only shaved their heads. He paid black girls to wear pink wigs. He visited Thailand.

No longer did Junior have the stamina to do these things himself. He needed the help of his new company pilot, Scott Prescott. He was always fresh. As soon as Junior spent himself, he could watch Scott perform for hours on end, lying butt-naked, chain-smoking Macanudos, sandwiched between a group of lovely, underage Mexicans.

To expedite their affairs, the two borrowed codewords from golf. 'Scotch foursome' meant they would alternate women. If Junior yelled, "Greensome," he was keeping his own. 'Scrambling' involved sharing one girl. As a matter of courtesy, she would have to attend the other player's flagstick. If there were very little green, a 'flop shot' would be called, which Junior enjoyed watching land either on the face or on the back.

As proficient as he was, there was something odd about Scott. He almost worked too hard, the way some nutjobs perpetually address the ball even though the hole is only two inches away. "What's the matter," asked Junior. He playfully tickled the bottom of his wingman's clubhead. "Can't you find your shot?" Scott grimaced. Junior realized his palm was sticky. Things turned awkward.

One day, Scott found the courage to break the ice. They were scrambling Sienna Watanabe, an Asian-Australian they had met in a Los Angeles fetish club. She had told Scott not to be afraid. "Be yourself," she had said, caressing his cheek.

While Junior was on his back, chin-deep in green, Scott carefully took the club from Sienna's hands. He spread his lips the way a caddy parts the fabric of a headcover sock. He pushed all the way down.

"My God," said Junior. "Sienna, how do you do that?"

Sienna lifted up her leg and turned around. Kissing Junior on the lips, she whispered, "Magic." She went to get her cigarettes.

Junior realized what was happening. Any incipient anger he might have had went out like a match in a thunderstorm. This was too good. "Scott deserves a reward," he thought to himself. "He's been working so hard." The longer he enjoyed it, the less he felt he had to justify it.

Soon after this revelation, Junior had an incident. He found himself being aroused by a young caddy's very hairy chest. Giving the boy a look, the boy returned the look. Junior followed him into a closet. After so many years of casual heterosexual and group sex, it had come to this.

Junior shook his head. "I have to get married," he told himself. The feeling was genuine. If there had been a hall of fame for perverts, he would already have been inducted. At long last, after a glorious career, John Nicolas Vandenhoff retired.

Junior wasn't sure how to find a wife. There were mail-order catalogues. The pictures were nice. The process seemed suspicious. He certainly wasn't going to rely on his mother. She was still pushing Jackie. "She's such a lovely girl," Dorothea would say. "Why don't you marry her?"

Junior tried looking through the company's personnel files. He wanted somebody young, experienced, with a mature sensibility and a drive to explore new things, which for Junior meant the possibility of settling down. Federal tax exemptions and social security numbers did not provide as much insight as he had hoped. The names were nothing special.

"Michelle Brown. Amy Johnson. Kimberly Jones. Jennifer Smith. Melissa Williams." Junior stopped. He had skipped an unfamiliar-sounding name. He went back and checked the sex. It was a woman. He carefully sounded out the name, "Naledi Mbete." She was a new hire from South Africa.

"A Bantu woman," thought Junior, "in my company. She must be worthwhile." He checked the department listing. She was a secretary for Anne Fenton. That was going to be a problem. Anne was the most successful woman in the history of the company. She worked for the general commercial manager, Randall G. Fitzwater III.

Randy was always talking to him in golf metaphors. Anne was also ambitious. Instead of golf, she used the feminist approach. If either one of them caught wind of what he was doing, they would gossip. If the chief operations officer found out, he would tell Dorothea. That would be a disaster.

Junior decided to rummage through the office after hours. There being nobody to ask for directions, it took him a while to find the elevator. He got lost on the second floor. Stumbling eventually into the minerals department, he searched the vicinity for photographs. He kept seeing the same African beauty. "This must be her," he thought to himself. "She's quite a fox."

Thankfully, there were no prominent photos of her with a young man. She was pictured in academic garb, standing next to a pleasant looking older couple, and even caressing a horse. "She likes horses," thought Junior. "I should invite her to my stud farm."

In one photograph, she had her arm around Jeremiah Myklebust's wife, Deborah. "She's got long arms," thought Junior. "I like that." He realized this was a golden opportunity. If she saw the Myklebusts socially, Junior could finagle his way into her company. All he had to do was make friends with Jeremiah.

It was easier said than done. Junior didn't have anything in common with the spindle-shank accountant. His mere presence in front of Myklebust's desk made the man visibly uncomfortable. Junior tried to break the ice.

"That's an impressive stack of invoices, Jerry. It looks like you need a break. How about I take you golfing?"

"Thank you, Mr. Vandenhoff, sir."

"Please. Call me John."

"Thank you, Mr. John Vandenhoff, Junior, sir—um—I don't golf."

"You must do something. How do you keep so fit?" Jeremiah snorted.

"Thank you, sir. I mean, John, sir. John, I—um—I don't exercise."

"Don't be modest. You must do something to keep your edge."

"I suppose. Once in a while, I do a little Sudoku."

"Is that some kind of martial art?"

Jeremiah snorted again. "You don't know?" Junior shook his head. "It's in the newspaper." Jeremiah took a moment to gulp. "It's a number puzzle."

Junior nodded. "I see," he whispered. Giving the man a weak smile, he added, "Carry on."

That was easier said than done. Junior didn't have anything in common with that spindle-shank accountant. He had a hard enough time justifying his presence in front of his desk.

"Come on, Jerry. You've got to get out and exercise. Let me take you golfing."

"Thank you, Mr. Vandenhoff, sir."

"Please. Call me John."

"Thank you, Mr. John Vandenhoff, Jr., sir—um—I don't golf."

"You must do something. How do you keep so fit?" Jeremiah snorted.

"Thank you, sir. I mean, John, sir. John, I—um—I don't exercise."

"Don't be so modest. How do you keep your edge?"

"Well. Once in a while, I have time to do a little Sudoku."

"Is that some kind of martial art?"

"No." Jeremiah snorted again. "You really don't know?" Junior shook his head. "It's in the newspaper." Jeremiah took a moment to gulp. "It's a number puzzle."

Junior nodded his head. "I see," he whispered. Giving the man a weak smile, he added, "Carry on."

Junior would not give up so easily. A few weeks later, he showed up for the first time ever at a company picnic. He spotted Naledi seated with Anne Fenton and the Myklebusts. He casually approached. Without introducing himself, he solicited Jeremiah's help for a game of five-on-five basketball.

"You know George, Dick, and Mark." Junior gestured to the men in the distance. The vice-presidents waved.

"They're the vice squad," said Anne, sarcastically.

Junior ignored it. "R and D challenged upper management to a game. We need you for a point guard."

Jeremiah shook his head. "I'm not upper management."

"Yes, you are," insisted Deborah, as she munched on a chicken wing. "You're a chief accountant."

The man whimpered. "I don't know anything about basketball."

"It's easy." Junior attempted to explain the fundamentals. "George is your shooting guard. Give him the ball to kill time. Mark will be ready for the screen. If I'm not open, pass to Dick. What's there not to get?"

Jeremiah scratched his head. "What do I do with the ball?"

"You bounce the ball, idiot," said Deborah, tearing into a drumstick. "Once you do that, you throw it to one of them."

"Don't worry about defense," said Junior. "If you feel brave, go for a basket."

Jeremiah gulped. "What if it doesn't go in?"

"We'll take care of the rebounds." Junior clapped his hands. "Come on."

The man hesitated. "Don't be a twig," said Deborah, picking up a breast in one hand and a thigh in the other. "Go play basketball like a real man."

The game was disastrous. The vice-presidents kept ignoring their spindly point guard. When Junior passed him the ball, he would carefully dribble it. By the time it bounced back, it was already gone. Sometimes his own teammates took it.

"Way to call the fast break," they yelled. "Hey, Jerry. What do you think? Should we try a pick and slip, a pick and pop, or a pick and roll?"

Jeremiah said, "Is that like gymnastics?"

Junior called for the ball. As forcefully as he could, he passed it to Jeremiah. "Ow," he yelled, clutching his hand. "My finger!"

"Time out," said Junior. "That was my fault. Keep playing, boys." He turned to Jeremiah. "Let's put some ice on that thing."

Junior brought the man back to his table. He apologized to him again. "I wasn't trying to embarrass you. I wanted you to get your blood flowing."

Deborah murmured, "Angioplasty wouldn't help that."

Junior continued, "I want my employees to be as healthy as possible. It saves me money." He pretended to notice Naledi for the first time. Casually stretching out his hand, he said, "I don't think we've been introduced."

As Naledi lifted her arm, Junior took her hand. Without shaking it, he said, "I'm Junior. That's what my family calls me. It's short for John Nicolas."

Naledi smiled. "As in J.N. Vandenhoff?" Her accent made Junior's hair stand on end. He kept holding onto her hand.

"No. That was my father. My friends call me John." He finally gave her one, firm shake. He arched an eyebrow. "You can call me Nicky." Naledi laughed. Deborah smiled. Anne snorted.

"Thank you, Nicky." Naledi took her hand away. "I'm Naledi Mbete. It's nice to meet you."

"Likewise."

Anne was not about to cede the conversation to patriarchal advances. She returned to the subject of handbags.

"It's horrible. It resembles a suitcase. The corners are sharp. The strap is short. If it weren't black, you could mistake it for a carpetbag, the kind that looks like a pot of dead hibiscus. Imagine trying to lug that thing around."

"I would use it like a tote bag," said Naledi. "I would put my groceries in it. I might start a fashion trend."

"Don't tell me you would pay thousands of dollars to do it."

"You're right. You're supposed to hold it on your elbow. I would think it would be too heavy if you put all your things into it. It's not practical."

Junior was transfixed. As long as the women kept blathering, every inch of Naledi's body could be inspected, at least the part above the table. If the other half were anything like the top, there would be no problem. Meanwhile, at the bottom of his mind, Junior noticed she was a sensible woman. He liked that, too.

Anne agreed. "You can't put your make-up in it, your pocketbook and your cell phone and not expect to get tired. It's a regular everyday satchel masquerading as a clutch bag."

"That's why it's so expensive," remarked Deborah. "You're not expected to use it the way you would use a regular bag."

"If you're rich, you don't need a regular bag. That's the idea. When you make something impractical, all the rich people buy it to show off how impractical they can be."

Junior realized he needed to join the conversation quickly. Jeremiah wouldn't be of any help. He was quietly nursing his finger next to his wife.

Junior had to mention horses. He couldn't think of a way to do it now without sounding like a jerk. Middle-class contempt was already permeating the air. With every silent breath he took, he looked more ridiculous. He started up in his seat. "I'm sorry," he blurted out. "What's a clutch bag?"

Anne took a moment to absorb the question. "It's a small bag," she explained. "You take it to parties."

"It carries your most important things," said Naledi. "Whether it's your phone or your make-up."

"This is my clutch bag," said Deborah, squeezing her arm around her husband. Jeremiah squirmed.

Junior turned to Naledi. "I always wondered what those were called. It's a good name. I should give it to my horse. 'Clutch Bag to win.' It's got a nice ring to it."

"You own a race horse?"

Junior nodded. "A few."

"Are they thoroughbreds?"

"Of course."

"You realize raising thoroughbreds is a useless and despicable pastime. It causes needless suffering to the animals." Junior was speechless. Naledi kept going. "I don't mean to insult you. I just wonder if you know what you're doing. I care very much for horses. My uncle was a breeder."

As shocked as he was, somewhere in the bottom of his mind, Junior appreciated Naledi's passion. She was a principled woman. That was sexy.

Junior stuttered, "I know they're prone to many illnesses. It was my father's hobby. I tried to put an end to it. A lot of people rely on the farm. They convinced me to keep it. I'm eager to hear what you have to say. Perhaps you can visit the place. Show me what's wrong with it."

Everybody—including Junior—was somewhat stunned by his deference.

"I'm sorry," said Naledi. "It's none of my business. I shouldn't have spoken. I apologize."

"Not at all," insisted Junior. "I value your opinion." He couldn't believe what he was saying. He was being so strangely respectful. "What were we talking about? Clutch bags. I like the adjective. It lends a certain air of gravity. It's used a lot in baseball."

Junior wanted to ask Naledi if she liked baseball. It might have made him sound solicitous. "Do they have baseball where you're from? I take it you're not from Kentucky." Junior smiled. He thought, "Not bad." It was politely confrontational—the very essence of flirtation.

"I'm from South Africa," she said. Junior nodded. "I know we have a national team. I think we lost to the United States seventeen to nothing. They had to stop the game early."

Junior laughed. "I'm embarrassed to say how proud I am."

"Never mind," she said. "My sport is netball."

"What's that?"

"You don't know netball?"

"Enlighten me."

"Americans invented it. How could you forget? It's so much better than basketball."

"Explain yourself."

"Women played it before they took the men's game. It's a shame you abandoned it. Netball is a very democratic sport. For example, you can only hold onto the ball for three seconds. Everybody has to stay in her zone. There's no dribbling. You have to keep passing. It's all about out-maneuvering your opponent. It takes skill and endurance, not strength."

Deborah chuckled. "It sounds like the perfect sport for you, hubby."

"I suppose there aren't many slam dunks," said Junior. Naledi laughed.

"There aren't so many tall women. The only downside is that only two players can shoot. I like the version we played when we were kids, High Five. You cycle through the positions. I was always afraid to be the shooter. There's no backboard. You need finesse."

"Are men allowed to play?"

"Sometimes—if they're nice. They have a habit of breaking the rules. It's no surprise. They were designed for women playing in long skirts." Naledi smiled. She had a beautiful smile.

"It sounds like a golf handicap," said Junior. He almost choked on his words. Randall G. Fitzwater was joining the party.

The burly man slapped Jeremiah's back. "I heard you got shanked," he said. "I had to take your place."

Junior felt compelled to ask, "Did we win?"

"We took the R and D guys to the clubhouse. I whiffed a few shots. George was there with the wedge. They pulled a mulligan on the last point. Mark topped it on the block. They claimed it went out-of-bounds. Things got a little sprachled. If you ask me, they're a bunch of sandbaggers. They're setting us up for a Calcutta. We've got the pace for that break." He munched into a carrot. "Who wants to play badminton?"

That was the first thing anybody understood. Naledi was game. She convinced Deborah and Anne to play. Junior politely declined. Badminton would not serve his interests. Randy asked Jerry if he would play.

"Come on," said Deborah. "We need a shuttlecock." Jerry refused. He cited his jammed finger.

As soon as everybody else had left, Junior asked Jerry why he let his wife treat him so poorly. "You're not one of those masochists, are you?" He had met a few of those. They had watched him make love to their wives.

Jeremiah shook his head. Junior thought he heard him whisper the word, "No."

"Why doesn't she respect you?" Jeremiah shrugged. "You need to show her you're capable of great things." The man snorted.

"Like what?"

"Strength comes in many forms," said Junior. "We need to explore the possibilities." He looked around. He saw two girls playing frisbee. He turned back to Jerry. He smiled. He said, "I have the perfect thing."

Junior attempted to teach Jeremiah the fundamentals. Standing before him like a friendly drill sergeant, he gripped a frisbee using different techniques. With a clear, forceful tone, he explained, "This is an ancient game. It traces back to the discus-throwing championships of ancient Greece. There are many modern variations, including golf frisbee, ultimate frisbee, and even guts frisbee."

Jeremiah gulped. "I'm sorry," he interrupted. "Did you say, guts?" Junior threw as lightly as he could. Jeremiah cringed. The flimsy plastic bounced off his pigeon chest.

"Let's try something else."

Junior strapped Jeremiah into a go-cart. "Hold onto the steering wheel. Press down on the gas. Give 'em hell. Don't even worry about the brakes." He patted Jerry's shoulder. Giving the vehicle a quick kick, he ran to the side of the track.

Jeremiah put on his gloves. He put on his leather cap and his goggles. He watched the children zoom by. Taking one last breath, he gripped the wheel. "Here we go," he whispered. He pressed down lightly on the gas. Shooting off like a toy boat, he reached the first turn and crashed.

Junior rushed over. "What happened?" he asked.

Jeremiah lifted his goggles. "I think the power steering is broken."

Junior took Jerry onto his yacht. "The wind does the work for you," he explained. "All you have to do is sit back. Use your brain." He gave him the mainsheet. "This line controls the boom. We're downwind. We want to make sure not to sail by the lee. Otherwise, the wind will catch the clew and push it when we're not looking. I'll turn the rudder. You ease the line. This is called jibing."

Junior executed the maneuver. The boom began swinging across too quickly. "Slow it down," said the captain. Jeremiah tried to keep the sail in check. He was lifted out of his seat. Junior laughed. "Get back," he said. "We're not clear yet. Keep the line going."

The wind caught the lee. The boom swung back. Junior yelled, "Jibe ho!" It was too late. As Jerry stood confused, the full force of the boom hit him in the ass. He was overboard. It was a good thing Junior made him wear that ridiculously oversized life preserver.

Back on dry land, Junior kept trying. Jeremiah hit his foot with the croquet mallet. He could only get one inch off the ground on the climbing wall. He even almost drowned in the pool of balls.

"There's something we haven't tried yet," said Junior. "The mechanical bull."

"Oh, no," said Jeremiah.

Junior wouldn't listen. He lifted him onto the saddle and stepped back. "Are you ready?" He had the controls in his hands. Jeremiah cringed. Junior pushed him left, right, up, down, around. Nothing moved him. Eyeballs in or eyeballs out, Jeremiah couldn't be thrown.

Junior shook his head. It looked like the man was spinning around at six g. He might as well have been an astronaut. "I think we found it," he said. "We've got ourselves a champion rider!"

Junior stopped punishing the man. Jeremiah slumped in the saddle. "Good luck," he whispered, "getting me onto the real thing. I'm going to vomit."

Pleased with his success, Junior went back to the business of courtship. He called Sienna Watanabe. "Have you ever played netball?" he asked.

"Of course," said the Asian-Australian. "When I was a kid."

Junior asked for a favor. "I need you to join my company and start a league." Sienna was confused. "It's very important," he explained. She needed a reason. He had to tell her all about Naledi. "She can't know I'm behind it," he said. "Please. There will be benefits."

"Like what?"

Junior paused. He remembered the time Sienna had spanked him with a riding crop. "Do you like horses?" he asked.

The netball league became very popular. Naledi signed up. Scott was instructed to join. He brought with him some secretaries. Junior waited for Naledi to inform him of the opportunity. He pretended to be mildly interested. He let her talk him into it.

Everything was going smoothly until Jackie showed up. "You're not an employee," said Junior.

Jackie smiled. "I am now. I'm the COO's new secretary." Dorothea was behind this.

"I see," said Junior. "Welcome."

Jackie kept getting in his way. When he took Naledi to the horse farm, she tagged along. "Are you going to give me a horse for my birthday?" she asked.

"Are you going to take care of it?" Jackie grinned devilishly.

"I would love to take care of your horse," she whispered, licking her lips. Junior had Sienna show her around.

As fate would have it, the Asian-Australian had a thing for high-society debutantes. In Junior's book, they defined ordinary. For a professional like Sienna, they were a welcome change of pace—a challenge—a soft pie hiding behind a thick upper crust, no doubt spoiled by daddy's love, in need of mommy's punishment. The sight of a stern woman in boots, breeches, riding jacket and helmet was making the hussy sweat.

Jackie followed Sienna into what looked like an empty stable. She stopped. Sienna turned. "What's the matter?" she asked. "Don't you want to see my favorite ride?" Jackie stepped forward. Sienna led her to an empty stall. The poor woman leaned against the door. She looked confused. Suddenly, the handle of a riding crop pressed into her buttock. She tensed. She started to breathe heavily. The crop made small circles. It came around her hip.

Sienna stepped in front of young Ms. Carter-Granville. She poked the black rubber into her belly. It crept slowly down to the dardanelles. It insinuated itself into the soft hillsides. The hard edge pressed up and out. It tipped the bird's nest. Jackie fluttered in her denim jeans.

Sienna grinned. She brought the instrument up to the woman's chin. She pushed it up. Jackie yielded. Her lips presented themselves. Sienna slowly encroached. Their breaths mingled.

Sienna suddenly pecked Jackie on the lips like an eager, young sparrow. Her victim looked shocked. Sienna laughed. She watched Jackie run out of the stable like a little piglet. A smile crept onto the former fetish club performer's face. She whispered, "Let the games begin."

Jackie found Junior with Naledi in front of a three-year-old colt. Trying not to look flushed, she listened to him explain the inner workings of the racing world. He was stroking the horse's mane. "This is the one I named, 'Clutch Bag,'" he said. "He's my best horse. I hope I can win with him at Belmont."

Naledi pointed to the lumps on the horse's barrel. "Do you see this? They are botflies coming out from underneath the skin. Until the wounds heal, you won't have any way of strapping on a girth."

"You're right. I didn't see that. They must be new." Junior almost cursed.

"Without a girth," explained Naledi, "you won't be able to hold down a saddle."

"The stableboys have been sleeping on the job."

"If you want him to race Belmont, I don't think he's going to be ready in time." Naledi looked him in the eye. "Don't tell me you're willing to put the horse at risk."

Junior shook his head. "Of course not." He had no idea what was in store.

Dorothea had started to worry. Her favorite girl wasn't getting anywhere. She decided to see for herself what everybody was doing. Joining the netball league, she showed up in a baggy long-sleeved shirt and a pair of long sweatpants. There was a good reason for that.

Dorothea didn't like to talk about it. Her parents had been upstart middle-class Greek converts to an elite Reformed church on Long Island. Her long, thick nose matched perfectly with her high cheekbones and the thick lower lip of her almost symmetrically decahedral face. Her large, green peach-pit-shaped eyes melted many a man's heart. The only thing she hated were her legs.

They were a man's legs. They were two thick pegs that the drunkest, poorest pirate in the quietest corner of Tortuga would only have dared wear at night. They had no shapeliness whatsoever. If not for the fact that Dorothea could afford a fully staffed kitchen, she would have pounded meat with them.

One day, after a hard game of netball, Dorothea went to the girls' locker. She always waited until most of the people had left. She needed to make sure the private shower was unoccupied. With the water off, she started soaping herself. She realized she had once more forgotten to buy a new curtain. This one only came down to her knees.

A pair of giggling women came rushing into the otherwise empty room. Dorothea sat on the seat. She lifted up her legs, resting them against the wall. She didn't want anybody to see them.

It was Jackie and Sienna. They too had waited for everybody to leave. Seeing that the room was empty, they locked the door. They started doing naughty things. Dorothea peeped past the edge of the curtain. She couldn't believe it. The two women were doing it. She watched. She couldn't take her eyes away. She kept absolutely still.

Thirty minutes passed. The women started giggling again. Sienna whispered, "It reminds me of the first time I made love."

"Was it with a woman?" asked Jackie.

Sienna nodded. "I was so shocked. I laughed. I didn't know they could get so hard, like cherry tomatoes."

Jackie smiled. "In the time it takes to lick a stamp."

Sienna breathed a heavy sigh. She said, "It made me feel so powerful."

Jackie asked, "Is that how you got into the fetish thing?" Sienna shrugged.

"I don't know. I liked sex. I liked having fun. My job was simple. I always hoped someday I would find the right girl." She looked into Jackie's eyes. The debutante turned away.

She whispered, "I'm not like that."

Sienna breathed an even heavier sigh. "I know. I was looking for somebody older." A noise came from the private shower. It almost sounded like a plaintive echo. Jackie was frightened; Sienna, bewildered. Carefully, she approached the curtain. Gathering her courage, she jerked it open.

Jackie was so shocked, she ran away without her clothes. Sienna was mesmerized. Dorothea sat slouched on a tiny bench. Her hand lay between her hairy, outstretched legs. Her soft, sedimented breasts had run aground like Viking boats upon her belly. She could barely lift her head. Sienna stepped inside. For the sake of modesty, she shut the curtain.

A few weeks later, Jackie surprised the office by announcing her engagement to the chief operations officer. Junior was relieved—until Sienna whispered in his ear, "Your mother wants to speak to you."

He asked, "Why did she send you?" Sienna gazed into his eyes.

"Please understand," she whispered. "Your mother and I care for you deeply. I'm sorry it had to come to this. I had to tell her." Junior was confused.

Sienna brought him to see her. The kiss the women shared was something more than cordial. Junior couldn't believe his eyes.

"I've been informed," said Dorothea, "you have serious intentions to marry a black South African. Do you deny this?"

Junior squinted. He started shaking his head. He laughed. He said, "Are you having a homosexual love affair with a fetish club performer?"

"A former fetish club performer," said Dorothea. "Answer the question."

"You first."

"My private affairs are quite inconsequential."

"Not to me."

"Don't you understand? If you marry a woman like that, it would ruin us."

"In what way?"

"Don't be silly. How many playdates do you thing the mothers at the club will arrange with my black grandchildren?"

"I'll have them attend public school."

"Don't joke around like that. You're worse than your brother. At least Catholic schools discriminate. If I so much as hear you've gotten down on one knee to tie your shoe, I'll have Jackie tear into the company's finances. The IRS will freeze your assets. We'll see how your Bantu wife copes with bankruptcy."

Junior gave Sienna a painful look. She averted her eyes.

Dorothea clenched her jaw. "Well?" she asked. "Do I have an answer?" Her son stared blankly. She continued, "I understand you have feelings for her. I'm not asking you never to see her again. I simply want you to give me your assurance that you won't marry her."

"I can't," said Junior. "I love her."

"I see," said Dorothea. "I'll be sure to let Jackie know."

"Can't we settle this like gentlemen?"

"What do you mean?"

"Give me a sporting chance."

Dorothea cocked her head. Her mouth curved into a slight smile. She said, "I hear your girlfriend cares passionately for horses. Why don't we make a bet? If Clutch Bag wins the Belmont Stakes, you can marry whomever you please." The smile turned sinister.

Junior's days turned dark. From his empty corner office, he often sat and stared as Naledi talked in the distance with Anne Fenton or Randy Fitzwater, discussing no doubt particulate levels in the base or the market potential of whatever it was the company made. Sometimes she would look up and catch Junior staring at her. A smile would start to creep across her face as she slowly turned to look back down at the paperwork. Junior was left to wonder if she were somehow missing the despondency he was sure was etched across his face, or if she were misinterpreting it as a simple matter of desire.

Junior prayed. "Lord, I have committed, as you must know, acts which, by the local standards of my community, would probably be considered depraved. I fully admit my licentiousness, as You would no doubt call it, was practiced on a more or less biblical scale. I realize now my debauchery served no purpose other than my own self-gratification, though other people's pleasure was enhanced through my efforts. Never mind. I'm sorry. If You can find it in your vast, not totally congested heart to forgive me, I'm begging you, let me marry Naledi without punishing her for my transgressions. I love her." Junior broke down and cried.

That very moment, Jeremiah came in to see him. "I'm sorry to bother you, Mr. Vandenhoff—John. I was wondering—is this a bad time?"

"No, Jerry," said Junior, wiping his face. "Not at all. Please, come in. Sit down."

Jerry looked around in vain for a chair. Junior realized there wasn't one. He got up. "I'm sorry," he said. "I'm never here. I suppose somebody took all my furniture for themselves."

Jerry seemed puzzled. Junior walked around the desk and offered the man his own chair. Jerry said, "Your office is down the hall."

"What?"

"This used to be the COO's office, until, for some strange reason, his new secretary moved him to the one without windows."

"Never mind," said Junior. "What did you want to talk about?"

"I was thinking about what you told me. My wife and I have been getting along as usual. I decided I need to show her I'm capable of great things. Is there some kind of rodeo I can enter?"

Junior was shocked. It had to be, he thought. It was a sign from God. He smiled. The shock momentarily flashed back, as if he couldn't help doubting it. He smiled again. He was sure. He put his hand on Jerry's shoulder. He said, "My friend, we have work to do."

There was no way of keeping it a secret. Naledi heard from Deborah. Junior was training his accountant to ride Clutch Bag strapless. She stormed up to the longeing ring. She slapped Junior on the face. She cried, "How could you lie to me?"

Junior cringed. His face contorted. His head dropped. He started to weep. Naledi sat him on the grass. She embraced him. She cooed into his ear. Junior calmed down. "For twenty years," he spurted out between sniffles, "I lived the life of a dedicated pervert." He began cataloging his many conquests. Naledi listened. "I'm so sorry," he said. "I should have told you a long time ago. I assumed you knew. I figured Anne told you all the stories."

"She didn't know the half of it." said Naledi.

"I probably would have never confessed," said Junior, "if not for mother."

Naledi nodded. She said, "I'm glad she has a good influence on you."

Junior knit his eyebrows. "No," he said. "You don't understand. She's evil. She's convinced I'm planning to ask you to marry me. She'll stop at nothing to prevent it. She threatened to sabotage the company—my livelihood. I asked for mercy. She offered to make a bet. I could have my way if Clutch Bag were to win the Belmont Stakes."

Naledi shook her head. She whispered, "I'm sorry. I didn't know she had put you in such an awful position. If there's anything I can do to please her, let me know. I'll do it. Just promise me you won't put the horse at risk, no matter what your feelings are for me."

Junior clutched his brow. "There's nothing you can do," he said. "It's who you are. It's because you're black."

The next morning, Naledi was at the stableground. She yelled at the top of her lungs, "Get back on that horse, Jerry!"

Things were going well. Jeremiah was able to withstand at least a mile-long gallop. Another half-mile and he would be ready.

Junior bought a professional hip adduction machine. Within days, Jeremiah had mastered it. Junior attached ropes to his feet. Naledi pulled one way; Anne Fenton, the other. The mild-mannered accountant made both women fall forward. "Sorry," he said. "I—uh—I hope you ladies didn't bruise your knees."

Deborah scoffed. "Give me a chance," she said. She put Junior on the opposite side. She started to pull. It wasn't enough. She leaned back. Still, Jerry was bringing his legs together. She dropped all the way down to the ground. It was useless. She was being dragged—all her weight—her incredible inertia—feckless in the face of Jerry's crotch. She couldn't believe it. She refused to give up. She dug in her heels. She was losing ground. She turned. She started to tow like an ox. One hock went after the other and still she was going nowhere. She was out of breath. She turned back around. She could see Jerry's legs almost touching. This was it. This was her last chance. She heaved one final time. Jerry's legs snapped shut.

All present watched in horror as Deborah dropped like a slaughtered elephant. It took ten stableboys to carry her into the shade. Junior stood inspecting the impact crater. He thought to himself, "This man has a crotch of steel. How is it possible?" He dared not ask. Miracles in progress ought not to be questioned.

The day before the race, Jeremiah did it. Everybody cheered. He had withstood a mile-and-a-half long gallop with an unstrapped saddle.

His legs were like jelly. Stumbling around, he thought to himself, "My God. I did it."

That night, Junior slept at the foot of Jerry's bed. Nothing was going to harm his precious jockey. In the morning, Scott found him at the stables. "What are you doing here?" asked Junior.

Scott gave him a sponge. "Your mother sent me to sabotage your horse. I couldn't do it."

Junior smiled. He clapped Scott on the shoulder. He said, "You're a good man, Scott. I'm sorry things didn't work out between us."

"It's alright," said Scott. "I want you to be happy." He shook Junior's hand. He said, "Good luck."

Junior was going to need it. Dorothea had a back-up plan. When nobody was looking, she fed Clutch Bag half a peck of whiskey-soaked apples. "Suck on that," she whispered. When Junior led the horse out for his morning exercise, he wobbled.

"That's odd," he said. "Could he be sick?"

Naledi rubbed the horse's snout. She sniffed. She said, "He's not sick. He's drunk." The two of them tried everything. They made him drink coffee. They induced vomiting. They even gave him a cold shower. Nothing helped.

"There's not enough time," said Junior. "We have to pull him out."

"No," cried Jeremiah. "You're not pulling anybody out of this race. If the horse falls, we'll fall together. I don't care if you have to peel me off the track. I've been spineless my entire life. I'm not backing down now. Don't you understand? I've been afraid of everything—even my beloved wife. That's why I'm here. God knows every time she sat next to me, I cringed. I squeezed my legs so tight, I cracked my own nuts. Not anymore. I'm not going to let them keep dividing us between black and white, the thin and the morbidly obese, the rich and the middle-class. It's over. I've seen the promised land. It's a horseshoe-shaped circle paved with bricks. There's a sign hangin' above it. The sign says, 'Winner.' Now I don't know about the rest of you, but I'm walking into that circle if I have to crawl over a dead horse and die. Who's with me?" Everybody cheered.

The horses lined up. Crowds gathered. Bets were placed. "What am

I doing?" thought Jeremiah. His knees were knocking. The saddle kept shifting back and forth.

"Please, God," prayed Junior. "I know I don't deserve Your Mercy. For the sake of those who depend upon the company, I beg You. Let Clutch Bag win. Defy the odds, Lord. Show them Your Power."

"And they're off. Collegiate takes the early lead. It looks like the girth has come off Clutch Bag. I don't know how that jockey is holding on. Jalopy takes the inside, followed by Chesspiece as they make their way toward the first turn. Farmer's Market picks up speed while Bust by Anonymous takes the outside. Why the Long Face maneuvers past Hourglass with Alfalfa Molina in the mix.

"We're 23 and 2 in the first quarter mile. Va-Va-Va-Voom nudges past Chesspiece. Jalopy holds along the rail. Collegiate maintains his lead, followed by Jalopy on the inside, Bust by Anonymous and Alfalfa Molina. Why the Long Face is on the inside fighting Clutch Bag for fifth, two lengths ahead of Farmer's Market with Unkempt Woman on the outside, Va-Va-Va-Voom trailing by a length.

"50 seconds in the first half, a good pace here at the mile and a half classic as we turn into the back stretch. Bust by Anonymous out front, Alfalfa Molina right there as Collegiate and Jalopy fall back, replaced by Farmer's Market and Unkempt Woman. Why the Long Face coming up on the outside, followed by Clutch Bag whose jockey seems to be riding by the seat of his pants. Farmer's Market slips ahead. He's now in third. Why the Long Face pushes on. Bust by Anonymous is in first followed by Alfalfa Molina, a length and a half separates them from the pack.

"We're halfway through the far turn. A mile in one minute forty: still a long way to go. Why the Long Face with Farmer's Market: they're a length away from the lead. Nothing left for Unkempt Woman. Clutch Bag holding on. Five of them within two lengths of each other as we approach the final turn. Why the Long Face outstrips Farmer's Market on the inside. Alfalfa Molina drops back, with Bust by Anonymous holding pat.

"Why the Long Face is coming up on the inside. Clutch Bug behind. This is it. We're in the final stretch. Why the Long Face now ahead. Bust by Anonymous right there. Clutch Bag coming up along the rail: an amazing burst of energy. How is that jockey still alive?

Alfalfa makes a break. It's a four horse race. Bust by Anonymous—no, Alfalfa by a nose. Clutch Bag on the inside creeping forward. Why the Long Face—no—Alfalfa—Bust by Anonymous—Clutch Bag—Alfalfa—Bust by Anonymous—Why the Long Face—Clutch Bag wins the Belmont Stakes!"

Junior collapsed. He beat the ground with his fists. He couldn't believe his joy. Naledi shed a tear. Junior looked up at her. He climbed to his feet. "It's a miracle," he cried.

They embraced. Junior twirled Naledi around. He set her down. She cupped his face with her hands. She whispered, "Nicky, what would we have done if we had lost?"

Junior seized those hands. He gazed into the woman's eyes. He whispered, "Don't you know?" Naledi shook her head. Junior smiled. He jerked his head toward the sky. Naledi looked up. A blimp was passing over the roof of the grandstand.

"Your price is worth far more than rubies," said Junior, "or a company, or even the Belmont's million-dollar prize."

The blimp was scrolling a message. It said, "Naledi Mbete, will you marry me?" Naledi smiled. She looked into Junior's eyes.

"Yes!" she cried. They kissed. Naledi broke off long enough to whisper, "I will."

Gog

by John Hardrick

Much fiction surrounds the names Gog and Magog. According to my understanding, they were not giants or blood-thirsty monsters. They were not fallen angels. They were one man and one woman. They apparently loved each other, though they often quarreled. Whether or not they made up half their adventures is beside the point. They were definitely the first people to circumnavigate the world. The evidence for that, though circumstantial, is overwhelming.

Their origin story is known by a Huastec village woman in the Mexican province of Veracruz. It was told to her about sixty years ago by her great-grandmother, who herself learned the tale from a passing deserter from the French Foreign Legion who happened to take one of the village girls for his bride. The woman is far advanced in age. Her Spanish isn't good. She refused on quasi-religious grounds to be recorded on magnetic tape. I was forced to hire a translator from the capital—at great personal cost. This is what she said.

Three thousand years ago, the people of the Tyras River [i.e., the Dniester] witnessed the hand of God.

They observed a great flame descending toward the earth. They saw three separate balls of fire. The bravest among them did not run away. They did not avert their eyes. They watched it smash into the ground. A mighty force knocked them off their feet.

When the dust settled, the men gathered their courage. They found three rocks unlike any they had ever seen. Hauling them onto boats, they took them down the river to the Black Sea. They presented them to Gog, the lord of the hosts of the Matiani.

Gog touched the heavenly stones. The sages claimed they had come from the Bhag Indra himself. They were gifts of fire. To fire they ought to be returned. Gog took them to the holy furnace of Atar. In honor of the great Bhag, he sacrificed a small forest.

The fire burned brightly. The men operating the bellows had never felt such heat. Many of them collapsed. Beads of sweat formed on Gog's brow. They turned into cataracts. He threw the first rock into the pit. Something marvelous occurred.

The rock formed a bloom. The furnace of Atar had never seen such metal. Copper, lead, silver, even gold had dropped through its flues. This was new. It was a gift from the Holy Bhag.

The first bloom was the smallest. It was forged into a straight sword. Gog gave this to his son. It was meant for thrusting. It represented the Bhag Asvin, the horseman of the dawn.

The second bloom was larger. It was forged into a sickle sword. It was made for deflection and blocking. Gog gave this to his consort, called Magog. It represented the Bhag Mithra, the keeper of the light, whom Magog personified on earth.

The final bloom was tremendous. Forged into a curved sword, it was longer than the rest. It represented Voruna, the god of thunder and lightning. It was meant for slashing one's enemies from atop the highest horse. Like a hammer, it crushed their skulls. Like an axe, it split apart their bodies. It evened out their necks.

The enemies of Gog were known for their smooth necks. They cursed the land of Gog. Banding together, they pushed him against the Black Sea. Though his people stretched between the Tyras and the Tanais rivers, he was pushed against the sea.

Gog called on his ancestors. He prayed to Gomer, son of Japheth, son of Noah. His prayers went unanswered. His herds of antelope were driven away. The badger and the fox deserted him. His people fed themselves with fish.

"Why has Indra forsaken us?" they asked. "Why do the four corners conspire to drown us?"

Gog had no answer. He sought the wisdom of sages. They investigated the migrations of the celestial host through the halls of the mighty Bhag. They consulted centers of divination. They held councils. They argued. They returned to Gog with heavy faces.

"There is no doubt," they said. "The autumnal equal-night passes from the Scorpion's claws to Heavens' mistress [e.g. Virgo]. Southern peoples worship the claws as scales of justice. If Indra has ordered Asvin to abandon justice, there is no hope. Wealth will continue to erode at the hands of the Paralatai. Southern peoples will be tempted to invade. Many of them worship the woman. The highlands call her Ishtar; the lowlands, Inanna."

"Do they not worship Indra?" asked Gog.

"There is Anshar, father of An, who may be our Indra and Voruna. The disc of the sun itself they call Shamash. We hear that Sargon of Ashur, great king of the southern lands, represents himself atop the winged disc, known to us as Fravashi."

"No wonder Indra is offended," said Gog. "Sargon takes upon himself the mantle of the most high. He is possessed by the aka mainyu [i.e., to ancient Iranians, the spirit of evil]. We have no choice but to appease the Asha [i.e., righteousness personified]. Our people have been selected for this duty. They will follow the sea to the mountains. They will raid and plunder the lands of Sargon.

"We who have displeased the Bhag with our complacence will fight each other to the death. Our champion will carry our swords to the holy Hara Berezati [i.e., literally, the high watchtower, mountain abode of the gods]. He will offer them in sacrifice. This is the will of Gog."

Those who claimed descent from Gog assembled. The men from the west fought each other to the death. The men from the east did the same. The champion of the west faced the champion of the east. The champion of the west prevailed. He faced the son of Gog. The son of Gog was slain.

"Praise to the Holy Bhag," said Gog. "My son and I shall soon be buried with our forefathers." The champion of the west took the sword of the son of Gog. He prepared to face his great uncle in single combat. Gog took up his sword and the sword of his consort.

"You are the jewel of our race," he told the champion of the west. "May the Bhag Indra bless you. May the Bhag Mithra be with you. Take our people south. Conquer the towns of the two rivers [i.e., the Tigris and Euphrates]. Go to the holy mountain, the Hara Berezati. Offer up our swords to the holy host."

The man replied, "I shall, great father. I swear it by the Bhag Mithra." The champion of the west slew his king. He gathered the swords together. He lifted them. Turning to the people, he proclaimed, "I am Gog. Take the bodies of my family. Bury them in the banks of the Danu [i.e., the nearest river, probably the Dnieper]. Prepare for a long journey."

Gog walked up the river Danu. He was greatly troubled. "How am I to find the holy mountain?" he asked himself. "The Haoma [i.e. a caste of priests] say the stars revolve around it. The sun hides behind it at night. Water descending its slopes forms the great sea upon which the earth rests. What then should I take for a guide: that which drowns, that which burns, or those which, when one stares at them for long enough, gives one a sore neck?"

Gog stopped. He was being watched. He could see a bronze helmet peeking from among rocks in the distance. He thought, "A scout from the Paralatai. If he recognizes my metal, he will guess there is something wrong. His leaders will attack me while I am weak."

The helmet moved. A rider on horseback emerged from behind the rocks. The man was armed. A quiver was on his back. The rest of his weapons were hidden by the barrel of his horse. He approached obliquely. Gog thought he could see a spearhead—perhaps a scabbard.

Gog drew the straight sword of Asvin with one hand; the sickle sword of Mithra with the other. The great sword he left sheathed in his belt.

The horseman reached the river. He doubled back. He was carrying a bow in his hand. A spear was stuck in his saddle. A scabbard hung by his side. Gog prepared to cut the rider off. The horseman saw this. He reached back. He took an arrow from his quiver. He notched it into his bow. Gog thought, "May the Holy Bhag protect me." The bow was pulled back. It cracked. The arrow whistled. Gog slashed his swords together. The metal arrowhead glanced off.

The rider squinted. He put away his bow. He lifted his spear. He kicked his heels into his horse. He hurtled towards Gog. The spear leveled. Gog watched as the horseman's steed threw up a cloud of dirt behind him. They were close. They were right in front of him. Gog lobbed the straight sword into the path of the beast's eye. It saw the metal gleam. Its head jerked. The rider lost balance. Gog twanged the sickle sword against the spearhead. He grabbed a hold of the rider's arm. He pulled him off. He threw him. The rider rolled. His helmet flew. His scabbard dug into his side. He winced. He didn't have time to hurt. Gog was coming towards him. He climbed onto his feet. He drew his sword. Gog balked.

It wasn't a man. It was a woman with lizard's eyes. Her course, brown hair was cut short. Her lower lip was thick. Gog took another step. The woman jerked her small, round chin. She braced herself.

Gog laughed. He cried, "Lizard woman, you picked the wrong man to way-lay. I have slain my entire family. Who are you to parry with me?" He drew the sword of Gog, the Necksmoother of the Matiani. It swam like crystal in the morning light. The woman gulped. She tightened her grip. She tentatively pointed her sword forward. Gog beat Neck-smoother against it. The blade bent. The woman stared at it. After a moment, she gave Gog an icy stare. She stepped backwards. She put the tip of the sword onto the ground. She used her foot to bend it straight

Gog smiled. He said, "Don't tell me you still want to fight." The sword was pointed back at his throat. Necksmoother smashed into it. This time, the blade bent into a right angle.

The woman threw the sword away. She crouched low. She prepared to defend herself with her bare hands. Gog sheathed his sword. He grappled with the woman. He couldn't stop smiling—even as she bit his jaw. Gog cried out. He tried to laugh his way through the pain. He pulled the woman back by her hair. He whispered, "I like you."

The woman spit in his face. Gog had to make an effort to wipe himself on the woman's cheek. She hit him in the back, repeatedly. Gog's voice strained as he muttered, "I knew the lizard folk were ruled by their women. I didn't know you earned it." He threw her to the ground.

She scurried back. "Kill me," she yelled. Gog was surprised.

"Why would I want to kill you?"

"I will not be left to anybody's mercy."

Gog shook his head. "You are strange. What are you doing so far from the shadow of your own mountains?" The woman refused to talk. Gog stooped down. He said, "I'll tell you what. I don't care. I'm leaving this land. You're welcome to it." He straightened up. He turned around. He saw the woman's horse grazing by the water's edge. He walked towards it.

"Where are you going?" asked the woman.

"Away," said Gog. "To the land of the two rivers."

"To beg for your food?"

Gog turned. He said, "To conquer it."

The woman laughed. "How can you expect to conquer a land of kings? You cannot even rape a woman."

Gog thought about that. He snarled, "Do not anger me, woman."

"My iron is weak," she said. "Otherwise, I would have killed you." Gog nodded.

"Even in defeat," he said, "you are full of pride."

"Show me I am wrong. Cut the buckle of your belt in half with a single stroke." Gog wondered if it were possible.

"If I do," he said, "what shall I receive in return?"

"The satisfaction of being a man."

Gog considered that. He realized such satisfaction was something to be desired. He removed his belt. He placed the buckle onto a rock. He knelt in front of it on one knee. He addressed the buckle. He slowly lifted the blade. He addressed the buckle again. He slowly lifted the blade. He swung. The top bar snapped.

The woman laughed. "You're half done. Now the sword is too dull to do the rest."

Gog smirked. "What I might have done in one stroke," he explained, "I do in two for lack of a brace." He turned the buckle around. He addressed the uncut bar. He slowly lifted the sword. He addressed the bar again. He slowly lifted the sword. He swung. The bar broke—as did the woman—towards her horse. Gog ran behind her. She knew she had no time to mount. She reached into her saddle. She pulled out a dagger. Gog froze. The woman stepped backwards. She drew the dagger close to herself. Reaching the horse's neck, she jabbed the blade into its throat. The horse collapsed.

She asked, "How will you carry your swords now? Your buckle is broken. My horse lies dying. If you try to leave me behind, I will stab you in the back." Gog sympathized with her. She seemed like a decent woman. He asked her what she wanted.

She lowered her head. She aimed her eyes at Gog as if they were spears. In a deep voice, she said, "Make me your sword-bearer."

Gog glared. He wondered if she knew who he was. He asked.

"Of course," she said. "The legend of Necksmoother tears across the steppe like fire."

"If my people see you carrying my swords," said Gog, "they will take you for my consort."

"I am not an unworthy bride," said the woman. "I am the daughter of the queen of the Sauromatae."

"If that be true, why are we bargaining with daggers and dead horses instead of with gold?"

"It is none of your concern."

"That is where you are mistaken. I am on a holy quest. I cannot be tainted by villainy."

"I am no villain," cried the woman, "unless it be a crime to love. Have you not dispatched your whole family to the underworld? Let me ask me: is that how all your holy quests begin?"

"I will not debate the will of my forefathers," said Gog. "My predecessor ordered a tournament to the death. I am his champion. I am to lead my people against the lands of the south. Their king has defiled the order of the immutable truth. The Holy Bhag must be appeased. These swords were gifts from them. I am to take them to High Hara, the abode of the gods, to remind them that Gog is their servant."

The woman's eyes narrowed. She said, "The bridge of Judgment that spans the underworld: does it not lie in the shadow of High Hara?"

"So say those who drink the Haoma [i.e., in this case, the plant worshipped by early Iranians as a divinity, thought to bestow upon them immortality.]"

The woman put down her dagger. She looked into Gog's eyes. She said, "Take me with you." Gog squinted.

The woman ran to pick up the swords.

"Will you carry my sons?" asked Gog.

The woman cried, "I will." She picked up the weapons. She added, "As soon as I have stood on the bridge and peered into the underworld." She faced Gog with her legs astride. "For now, I am a warrior. We have a land to conquer."

Gog was impressed by this audacity. He accepted the woman as his consort. The people recognized her as Magog, living embodiment of the light of Mithra.

Gog and Magog led their people east. They skirted the shores of the Black Sea. They met distant clans of Matiani. Some joined. Others stayed behind.

Gog and Magog followed the river valleys into the southern mountains. They found two gigantic smoldering peaks [e.g. Mount Elbrus]. Gog sent scouts to investigate them. Finding no signs of divine habitation, Gog decided to wait. Magog told him the people were not prepared to risk a lengthy sojourn in the mountains. They resumed their journey.

Gog and Magog descended onto a great plain. They encountered a multitude of tribes. Each spoke a different tongue. "This," said Gog, "is the fruit of Nimrod, the first of the great kings. The Haoma claim he built a mighty tower to replace the Holy Bhag. Woe to he who attempts to pierce the firmament. What say you, Mithra?"

"Let us subjugate these people," she said. "One of them may know something of High Hara. It will be easier to gain their secrets from a position of authority."

Gog proceeded to conquer the people of the valley. There was little resistance. Taking their tribute, Gog said, "I am Gog, son of Gomer, son of Japheth, who disembarked from the boat of Noah. I seek the high watchtower behind which the sun hides at night, about which the stars revolve, and from which all waters flow. Who among you knows the way?" The people claimed ignorance.

"We know only the mountain from which your ancestor descended," they said. "It lies directly to the south. It is blocked by the armies of Rusas, whose father captured our citadel. Perhaps your watchtower lies to the southeast, for people there speak the way you do. The Hellenes of the sea would know more. They travel widely."

Gog went to the shore. He found a group calling themselves Hellenes [i.e., the Greeks]. They knew the valley as Kolkhis. They said it was ruled a long time ago by a king named Aeëtes, the son of Helios, himself the son of Oceanus. The latter ruled the underground river through which the former drove his solar chariot at night.

They claimed Aeëtes had a daughter named Medea. She had been taken to Hellas [i.e. Greece] by a man named Iason. Being deserted by him, she fled with their son to the mountains southeast of Kolkhis. There she founded a tribe. In her honor, they were called Medeans. As descendents of Helios, they would know the location of High Hara.

Gog gave the Hellenes thanks. He invited them to a feast. In his tent, they dined and drank with him. They marveled at his consort. Through her headdress of gold coins and chains, they caught sight of her eyes. They had never seen such a woman. "Those eyes," they whispered amongst themselves. "They are like the seeds of the amygdala [i.e. the almond tree]. Truly, she is a queen of unparalleled beauty."

Gog smiled. He said, "She is a warrior. Her people are ruled by their women."

The Greeks were awed. They said, "You truly are a great and brave man to have such a woman by your side."

They had a white heifer slain in her honor. They presented it to Gog. They told him their goddess was a fellow warrior. It would please her to watch Magog enjoy the gift.

Gog asked how their goddess might be indulged. They told him simply to have Magog preside over the creature's evisceration. They warned him only women were allowed to partake. A man could not be present.

"The women have already eaten," said Gog. The Greeks dismissed this.

"It is a gift," they said. "We ask only that your consort be granted authority over the meat." Gog agreed. He had the carcass placed in a tent. Magog retired with her handmaidens to perform the rite.

They went to slice the beast's belly. They realized it had already been done. It was sown back together. A knife emerged from the cow. It tore apart the stitches. A man burst out. The handmaidens gasped.

Magog was taken by the arm. The knife pointed at her throat. The women screamed. The knife dug into Magog's neck. She told the women to be quiet. Guards yelled from outside. They wanted to know if everything were alright. Magog assured them there was no call for alarm. Divinities, she said, had to be respected.

The handmaidens filed out of the tent in silence. Fear was written on their faces. The guards asked the last one about Magog. She said the queen consort wanted time alone with the goddess. She was not to be disturbed. Nobody saw the heifer escaping through the back. In the darkness, it was hard to see. Its hide had been scorched black.

In the morning, Gog realized his consort was gone. He rushed to the shore. He arrived in time to see the Greek ship leaving. He cursed it. He saw the Greeks on the deck. They taunted him. They shouted, "Athena has taken your queen. She is a prize worthy of the gods." The wind filled their sail. Gog dove into the water. The Greeks saw him swimming. They laughed.

Gog was outpaced. The Greek ship grew tiny on the horizon. The sea went dark. Gog became exhausted. He feared for his life. The waves threatened to bury him. All of a sudden, he found firm ground. It was solid, but slippery. Gog thought, "It's not just slippery. It's moving."

He glimpsed a body of scales bulging from the water. He couldn't believe his eyes. In a moment, the head of a gigantic serpent rose in front of him. Its maw was the size of a king's wagon.

Gog took one breath as the head snapped forward. In an instant, the world went dark. Gog felt himself being pushed down the beast's throat. It was a long way down. There was no air. Inside the stomach, the walls burned. Gog pushed against them. It took all his strength to unsheathe Necksmoother.

The sword cut the stomach to ribbons. The flesh began sticking to Gog's arms. He was finding it hard to move. He was running out of time. He thrashed himself about. His head hit a large ball. It was soft. His head bounced off it. It was the beast's air sac. Gog gripped the organ. Necksmoother jabbed around it. Water started trickling in. The skin was pierced. Gog jabbed some more. The water rushed in. The air sac squeezed past the scales.

Gog shot to the surface. He gasped for breath. He heaved himself onto his new raft. He watched his wounded prey slip quietly into the deep.

Gog passed out. When he awoke, he thought he was on dry land. The air-sac had stopped bobbing. A stink filled his nostrils. He looked around. The sea was weighed down with rotting fish.

Gog tested the carpet of corpses. It withstood his weight. He realized the hole he had cut into the serpent's side had given the beast an insatiable appetite. The wounds of Necksmoother would not be so quick to heal. With any luck, thought Gog, the fish would trap the Greek ship.

Gog walked. Fish stretched for miles. Like a fly in a gigantic spider's web, the ship appeared on the horizon. It was mired in fish meat.

Gog laughed. He could see the sailors trying to eat their way out. It was useless. Their vomit only added to the pile. By the time Gog reached the boat, they were rolling about on the deck like sausages.

Gog threw a fish into their midst. It hit one of them in the belly. The man grimaced. He accused the others. They cursed him. Each man drew his sword. They might have killed each other, if Magog had not emerged from the hold like a newborn Aphrodite, commanding them to stop.

"Do not be so rash," she said. "Each of you did his part to cause our present misfortune. One killed a heifer. The other stole a queen. One lifted anchor. The other unfurled the sail. If any seek vengeance, he need only sheathe his sword into his own gut."

As much as Gog admired his lady's wisdom, the compassion was ill-timed. Gog drew his hand down his face. He was going to have to kill them all himself. He climbed aboard.

The heads fell one by one. Magog watched in horror as they rolled past her. She saw their mouths still gaping. She cringed. She seemed unhappy.

Gog noticed the look. He said, "If you knew how close I came to death, you would not so quick to mourn these men."

"I rejoice," said Magog, "to be back in your arms. There is no need to reassure you with wild shouts. I knew you would come."

"There is something more than dignity holding you back. I would say it were the bloodshed, but you claim to be a warrior. Perhaps the gold I have showered upon you has finally softened your mettle."

"There is nothing to savor in the spilling of blood," said Magog. "I do not mourn these men their lost lives. I mourn my inability to prevent this slaughter. More than anything else, you should know I hate to be helpless."

Gog knew she spoke the truth. His consort was swayed, like many women, by complex emotions. Never before had he met one so well attuned to them. At the same time, Gog saw the error behind the eloquence.

"You may have been prepared to forgive these men," he said. "If you had begged me for their lives, I might have spared them. You neglect to consider not only did they transgress against us; through their abuse of their own god, they transgressed against the Asha, the world order. If they had taken you by force, I doubt their blood would be staining this deck."

Gog and Magog returned to Kolkhis. The people were amazed. "Truly," they murmured, "this man is a great hero. Did we not see him swim in vain after the Greek ship? Yet he has not only returned alive, he has brought with him his queen." Gog told them the story of the great serpent. They believed it.

Gog told his men to march southeast in search of the Medeans. The chiefs grumbled against him. "This land is kind to us," they said. "Let us stay here and settle. The people worship you as a hero."

They talked differently amongst themselves. Gog's informers told him, "They say, 'Who is he to command us? He killed his entire family. If they had wanted to challenge Sargon, they would have come themselves. They sacrificed each other because they knew it would be hopeless. All they needed was a fool who wouldn't realize it.

"Gog needs to know, if we continue in this manner, we will lose everything. Are we expected to push our herds over every hill until we reach High Hara? It is madness."

Gog sympathized with them. If the armies of Rusas were helpless against Sargon, what chance did he have? He allowed his chiefs to decide their own fates. Many chose, despite their qualms, to continue.

They marched southeast. They skirted the kingdom of Rusas. In the hills, they encountered a people named the Hayk. Their speech was almost intelligible. They said their king was named Bagadatti.

Gog smiled. "A man who worships the Bhag. We will find a friend in him." Gog's embassy returned with unexpected salutations. They told him the king would be happy to welcome a fellow son of Gomer. He would accept his brother's homage.

Gog shook his head. "I did not come to pay anybody homage. I have come as an equal." He returned his embassy with gifts of offal. Gog assembled his chiefs. He asked them if there were any who wished to submit to the king of the Hayk.

They laughed. "If we are to become vassals," they said, "we might as well serve Sargon."

Gog continued the journey. He encountered a large salt lake [e.g. Lake Urmia]. The settlements along its eastern shores had recently felt Sargon's wrath. "They breed horses here," said the men. "There is good pasture. If we stay here, we can raid the plains and roam the hills at our leisure."

Gog agreed. The urge to stop exploring was too strong to resist. He was worried his men would revolt if they weren't disbanded. Gog gave them a free hand. He said, "Those who wish to join Sargon may do so. Those who want to raid may raid. I only ask of you one thing. As Medea gave birth to the Medeans, call yourselves Gomerians, for it was I, a son of Gomer, who led you across the mountains."

Gog and Magog continued southeast in search of the Medeans. Encountering a tribe whose speech was intelligible, they inquired as to the location of High Hara. "We know this mountain," said the chiefs. "It lies to the east. Find the tribe of the Magi. Among our people, they are the ones who keep the Haoma."

The Magi were eager to hear Gog's story. He described to them the origin of the three swords. He explained his quest. They agreed that the holy disc of the wintering sun had escaped the Scorpion's claws. In heading towards the woman of the sky, it had placed all the descendents of Japheth in danger.

"We must strengthen our people," they said. "We must hasten to make ourselves worthy to face Ashur in battle. In the meanwhile, we encourage you to attempt to climb High Hara. Because of the danger involved, a direct appeal to the Bhag will be looked upon with favor. Seeing you in supplication, they will ignore your presumption in favor of your courage."

Gog was directed toward the mountains of the north-east. "Once you reach the plain, you will see it. The peak is sharp; the face, smooth. Beware of Azi Dahaka, the dragon that was chained there by Keresaspa. You will see his breath rising from the summit. Do not pass the chasms carelessly. He will snap at your heels."

Gog thanked them for their concern. He assured them he had already killed one serpent daughter of Gandaruba. "If Azi Dahaka has sons," said Gog, "I will arrange a meeting for them with Necksmoother."

Gog and Magog reached the valley. They beheld the sight of High Hara [e.g. Mount Damavand]. They gasped.

"Is it not beautiful?" asked Gog.

"It is majestic," said Mithra. "For some reason, I feel as though the twin peaks we passed on our way to Kolkhis were higher."

"Impossible. Your mind is being deceived by the surrounding hills. They make the mountain-top look shorter."

Mithra shook her head. "The twin peaks were also smoldering. We saw no dragons there."

Gog laughed. "I didn't realize you had gotten that close. If you were so curious, you wouldn't have wanted to leave."

"You admitted there was nothing there."

"I knew it could not have sheltered the morning sun."

"By what reason do you think a mountain shelters the sun? Does it not make sense to rest a chariot of fire next to the great sea?"

"The chariot rests as it is pushed along by the currents of the sea. The High Hara guards the threshold which the sun traverses."

"In the morning," asked Magog, "or in the evening? You say the sun hides behind it at night. In that case, we're heading the wrong way."

"Woman," said Gog. "Do not question my sense of direction. Do you not see the mountain that holds the firmament before your very eyes?"

"Where is the great river, I ask you. All I see is snow."

"Has it ever occurred to you that the great river might be inside the mountain?"

"The dragon is inside the mountain," said Magog. "Unless it's the kind that swallowed you and stopped the Greek boat."

"What is that supposed to mean?"

"It means you never once mentioned that I carved a hole in the boat and made it sink. If I hadn't paddled my way back to you on flotsam, you would have drowned."

"Is that the story you would have told the people of Kolkhis? My dear, you have no understanding of politics or public opinion."

"As in your brilliant decision to disband our army?"

"Don't start with me. Do you want me to leave you behind?"

"So you can take all the credit? I don't think so." Magog kicked her heels into her horse. She charged ahead. The next morning, before Gog had even finished his breakfast, Magog was over the first hill. By the time Gog reached her, she was climbing a steep ridge. They decided to camp there for the night.

It seemed to Gog like a good time to consummate their union. Magog disagreed. "I'm not ready to let you saddle me with children," she said. "There are other things I have to do first."

Gog didn't want to argue.

The next day, they entered a valley. A softly rising ridge seemed to lead all the way to the mountain. "It looks like a day's journey," said Gog.

His consort squinted. She noticed there were no trees along the ridge. They would have to find firewood to take with them. "Good thinking," said Gog. "Go find some."

Gog climbed down a rocky promontory. The ridge was only a few feet below. He leapt onto it. The ground was rough. It was dry. Gog realized a lack of water probably prevented growth. It didn't explain the lack of rocks. Before long Gog thought he had that puzzle figured out.

The earth had heaved below him. Gog concluded that earthquakes had knocked all the loose rocks off the ridge. Mithra returned with firewood. Gog told her to be careful. "I don't want to go climbing after you."

"Likewise," said Magog.

An hour later, there was another tremor. Before long, it happened again. "That was strange," said Magog. "The first quake went back and forth. That last one went up and down."

Gog chuckled. "I'm not surprised. This is the land of Yazata, the holy ones who labor for Bhag. Strange things are bound to happen."

Magog sneered. "Is Aredvi shooing away the aka mainyu? Is she unblocking the water of the great river?" Gog detected the slightest bit of skepticism in her voice.

He murmured to himself, "If only I could make your water flow. A glacier melts faster."

Magog jerked her head. "What did you say?"

"I said, 'With one really big quake, we'll fall below. It's a sure disaster. If you want to go back, I'll understand. I can go alone." Magog huffed. They kept going.

The earth refused to stay completely still. With great trepidation, Gog and Magog approached the foot of the mountain. As the sun began to set, Gog started a fire. His consort surveyed the day's progress.

"There's something funny about this ridge," she said. The ground was cracked like a dried-out river bed. She kicked at it. No matter how hard she tried, she couldn't make it crumble.

"I tried to tell you," said Gog. "This is the land of the Yazata." He started sniffing his nose. A smell was emanating from the charred ground. It reminded him of turtle soup. "Must be some kind of salt," he thought.

"Come look," said Mithra. "The end of the ridge resembles a giant tail. In the twilight, that part looks like a leg. Those rocks over there look like claws. Do you see it?"

Gog squinted. He studied the formation. He quickly realized what it was. Quite matter-of-factly, he said, "That is a leg."

The ground heaved. Magog shared a quick glance with her husband. The hillside lurched. The two stumbled. A deafening roar echoed through the valley. They realized they were on the back of a giant dragon. It was lifting itself. The hillside was getting steep. They were going to fall. Gog drew Necksmoother. He lifted it above his head. He thrust it into the quickly rising ridge. The earth bled. Gog turned to his consort. "Now!" he shouted.

Magog drew her sickle-sword. She failed twice to pierce the skin. Gog grabbed the handle. He lodged the blade into the beast. Magog's feet gave way. She grabbed hold. The dragon shook off the fire. Gog and Magog held for their lives.

"I thought you said the dragon was inside the mountain," said Gog.

"I thought you said it was chained."

"Give me the straight sword." Magog drew it from her belt. She held it out by the blade. Gog grabbed it. He pulled himself up. He thrust the straight sword into the skin above his head. "Stay here," he said.

Magog laughed dryly. "I don't have much of a choice."

Gog wrenched Necksmoother from the side of the dragon. He heaved himself up on the straight sword. He lodged the curved blade as high as he could. He repeated the procedure. The beast shook. It didn't help. The jabbing pain kept climbing up its back. It turned its head. It saw Gog. It snapped its teeth. They were twenty paces long. They didn't reach.

The dragon trained one of its nostrils on Gog. It was enough to make him flutter like a pennant. Wads of snot blasted into him. It made him heavy. His arms strained under the weight. The dragon blew harder. Gog held on. With each snort, the man grew stiffer. The dragon stopped trying. It was out of breath.

Gog raced up to the beast's ear. It was large enough for him to enter. He jumped inside. It was not the shelter he imagined. The beast shook its head. Gog crashed into the soft walls. If they had been hard, he might have been crushed to death. All he had to do was hold Necksmoother out in front of him. The sword pierced the flesh. Blood poured.

Gog had no strength left. He could barely hold his ground. Blood flooded around him. He thought of his beloved Mithra. She couldn't afford to wait. Gog threw himself into the torrent. He reached the dark recesses of the ear. His blade found a vital lobe. The beast's limbs fell numb. The entire creature, measuring twenty thousand paces [e.g. seven and a half miles], dropped to the ground.

Gog let himself be swept away. A massive waterfall poured from the ear into a giant lake of blood. Mithra saw her champion floating lifelessly. She jumped down from the beast's back. She bravely pulled Gog to shore. She revived him.

The blood took a long time to drain. It washed away everything in the valley. Only the trees pinned down by the corpse remained. Gog lit them on fire. He watched the flames encompass the creature. He estimated it weighed one and a half billion grains of wheat. It might have fed five hundred people for a year.

The fire flickered past the tip of the mountain. It melted all the snow. When the blaze died down, Gog and Magog ventured up the steep, bare slopes. They circled the mountain carefully. They sang loud songs of praise. They wanted to make sure the Holy Bhag knew they were coming.

Cresting the summit, Gog saw what seemed like a small valley. It was shrouded in fog. He was overjoyed. He was sure he would find the palace of the Bhag. He would stand on the bridge that spans the underworld. He would see his ancestors. Mithra would have no excuse. She would have to sleep with him.

Gog carved his way into the unknown. Mithra followed. Their breath was heavy; their steps, cautious. With an overwhelming sense of awe, Gog reached the end of the fog. His face fell. He was on the other side of the mountain. He had missed the palace. He turned around. He made several trips back and forth. He found nothing but a puddle of bubbling mud. He threw a rock into it. The rock went nowhere.

Gog and Magog watched the mud. They waited. The weather turned cold and windy. The fog cleared. Gog said, "I'm tired. Let's go."

Gog and Magog returned to the land of Gomer. "High Hara must be farther to the east," said Mithra. "The Magi must be mistaken." Gog didn't care. He tried to make love to his consort. She pushed him away.

Gog said, "When you're ready to be a real woman, come and find me."

"When you're ready to be a man," replied Magog, "I won't have to."

Gog spent his days fishing from the smallest island in the salt lake [e.g. Osman Island]. Shaped like a fist, it rose from the water to a height of ten paces. Magog would come by in her own boat. "Come down from there," she would cry. "You know there are no fish in this lake."

"If there is but one fish," said Gog. "I will catch it." Years passed. The man who sat on the smallest island in the salt lake caught no fish.

One day, a boat visited him. It was powered by two eunuchs. Its only passenger was a boy. He played a flute. He wouldn't stop playing it. Gog got so aggravated, he climbed down to his boat. By the time he gripped his oars, he could see the eunuchs were too far away to be caught. He climbed back up. The boat turned back. The sound of the flute grew loud again. Gog lost his patience again and again. Each time, the eunuchs had a head start. Eventually, Gog gave up.

The boy saw it. He ventured onto the island. He twirled his flute in his hand. He said, "Is it true you slew a dragon measuring twenty-thousand paces?"

"What difference does it make?" asked Gog.

"I don't believe you could. You can't even overtake a boat powered by eunuchs."

"Are you calling me weak?"

"That's what it sounds like."

"If you were a man," said Gog, "you would know better than to insult me. I have killed for far less than that."

"The way you killed the giant serpent?"

"You wouldn't know," said Gog. "You weren't there. You were still sucking your mother's reshteh [lit., very fine egg noodles]."

The boy laughed. "At least I know what those taste like." Gog swiped after the boy's ankles. The child dodged. He dove into the water. By the time the eunuchs pulled him out, Gog was gripping the oars of his boat. This time, he wouldn't give up.

The eunuchs rowed for their lives. "Faster," cried the boy. It was no use. Gog came alongside.

"This is what happens," he huffed, "when I get angry." Gog pulled in front by a length. He swerved into the eunuchs' path. The boats collided.

Gog boarded with sword in hand. The eunuchs guarded their necks with their shoulders. They raised their hands in supplication. With one fell swoop, Gog chopped off their fingertips. He lifted the boy by his tunic. He asked him why he should spare his life.

"Forgive me," sputtered the boy. "I had to test your patience and your strength. I am sent from the court of Sargon by his son. He wishes to arrange a meeting between Necksmoother and his father. He proposes five hundred men on each side in a fair fight. You would catch the king being carried in his chariot through the dense forests in the hills to the south. Sargon's son offers you me in return."

Gog laughed. "Why would I want you?"

"I was born to a woman in his harem who claims to be your sister."

"What kind of trick is this?"

"She told me you once painted her feet black while she slept. You convinced her you would have to amputate, unless she agreed to do your chores for you for a month in exchange for a cure." Gog fought the temptation to smile. The boy ventured to ask, "Is it true?"

"Never mind. About this business of a fair fight, why would Sargon's son trust me?"

"He doesn't. That's the point." Gog put the child down. The boy scurried back. Trying to catch his breath, he gulped. He said, "Please. Take me. If I go back, I'll be turned into a eunuch. I have a thing for women." Gog laughed.

"I know what that's like." He threw the boy into his boat.

The boy said, "Thank you."

"What's your name?" asked Gog.

The boy looked up. He was surprised. He stuttered, "My name is Enkidu." Gog jerked his head. The name was vaguely familiar. The boy said, "After Enkidu of legend, the wild-man from the story of Gilgamesh."

Gog nodded. He extended his hand. He said, "Welcome." The boy hesitated. Gog could see he was still afraid. He took him by the hand. He lifted him to his feet. "You're one of us now," he said. He vigorously patted the boy on the shoulders. "You're a Gomerian."

Gog formed an army. Many of his men were more handy with a lasso than with a bow or a spear. Gog had to reassure himself they would be enough. As they lay arrayed about the dense forest, he said, "Sargon's son is in a mighty hurry to rule. His father faces certain death."

Enkidu disagreed. "No matter what occurs, the Crown Prince will remain clean in the eyes of his gods. He has not led his father into a trap, but a challenge. Sargon must prove himself worthy of mounting the winged sun."

Gog sneered. "How thoughtful of him to provide a test. Would you be so obliging?"

"I wouldn't know. Your Lordship does not have a kingdom."

Gog laughed. "I have an army."

"If that's what it pleases Your Lordship to call it."

"It's too bad the women of Sargon's harem only taught you to use a sharpened tongue. If I weren't afraid you would cut off your toes with it, I might give you a real sword."

Enkidu replied, "A quick wit is the greatest of weapons."

"Men," said Gog, "do not snipe at each other like fishmongers' wives."

"I'll be sure to take your Lordship as an example," said Enkidu. Despite the indignant tone, he gave Gog an earnest look. He said, "As soon as my toes grow back."

Gog smiled. He drew the straight sword of Asvin, the horseman of the dawn. He held it out by the blade. He said, "A man can live without toes."

The army of Sargon broke through the trees. The people of Gomer attacked. Enkidu was horrified by their lack of experience. Though they were brave, they spread out too quickly. The force of the stampede was stemmed by the forest. Thick trunks provided cover. The king's men had a fighting chance.

Enkidu rushed to warn his uncle. Gog was nowhere to be seen. He had charged straight into the belly of the beast. "That's one way," thought the boy. Though he didn't have a whisker to call his own, he tried to rally the men.

Meanwhile, Gog carved a path towards Sargon's chariot. Necksmoother grew heavy with Mesopotamian blood. As the sun poked through the leaves, the king's porters saw the heaven-sent iron gleam and drip.

Sargon was dropped. The porters fled. The bodyguards' heads rolled to the ground. As pathetic as the situation was, the king seemed determined to defend himself. He braced his body. He lifted his sword. It was no match for the bloom of Atar. The king's head rolled.

Gog went home. He had lost much blood pursuing the king. He submitted himself to Mithra's care. She took off his clothes. She washed his body. She gathered cobwebs. She dipped them in honey. She placed the salve onto Gog's wounds. She wrapped them in cloth. Gog took her by the hand. He looked into her eyes. He said, "Thank you."

Mithra smiled gently. Gog returned the favor. He whispered, "You are as beautiful tonight as the day I first met you." Mithra blushed.

"I knew you would come," she said. She stroked Gog's forehead. "You are a brave man."

Gog grinned. He confessed it sickened him to kill the king of Ashur only so his son could take his place.

Mithra shook her head. "You have fulfilled an important part of your obligation," she said.

Gog sighed. He turned away. The words had been meant to relieve him. Instead, they had cut apart the hole in his heart. He bit his lip. He said, "I neglected my duty. I worked hard to climb that mountain. It was too much to see that I had failed, as if everything I had ever done had been in vain." He stared into Mithra's eyes. His voice deepened. The words seemed to come from the bottom of his soul. He said, "I don't want to turn from the things I believe. I want to follow them. I want to find them."

Mithra clenched his hand. "We will find them," she said. Tears welled in her eyes. "We will find them together."

Gog nodded. He looked away. It pained him to see Mithra cry. He said, "Enkidu has proven himself in battle. He should come with us."

Mithra wrenched her face into a smile. She managed to say, "Good."

The morning sun blazed through the open door. Mithra turned to face it. Sucking up her teary breath, she said, "High Hara is out there. It waits for us." She turned to face Gog. He gazed into her eyes. He held up their clenched hands. Together, they looked to the east with great hope.

The Cyclostoman League

by Debra Killian

The woman in the waiting room sat watching the secretary put files away. She couldn't help it. For an office worker on the moon, the secretary was extravagantly dressed. Sheer black stockings hugged her legs. A short, tan skirt stretched from one cheek to the other. Thin, white crape billowed over her shoulders like tissue paper.

The secretary approached the file cabinet in front of the woman. She used the heel of her shoe to open the bottom drawer. Like a child who sees change upon the counter, she hesitated. She would have to be quick. She put her heel on the floor. She leaned forward. She barely bent her legs.

The corduroy fabric bulged around her—it was right in front of the woman's face. A short ruffle was all that stood in the way of buried treasure.

Lunar culturalists call it 'the sardine effect,' thought the woman—or CHIC, the Condition of Highly Intrusive Cohabitation. The woman saw no reason not to take advantage of it. She leaned against the armrest of her chair. She bent her head. She peeked. The secretary was wearing seamless pantyhose—sheer to waist—nothing else.

The woman's heart skipped a beat. The secretary straightened herself. If she were being cruel, thought the woman, she would turn to see the ruddy, breathless reaction on her victim's face. She didn't. She went straight back to her desk. She sucked in her waist to squeeze past the edge. She kept her eyes low. She was making signals. She even bit her lower lip.

A door opened. It was on the far side of the long, narrow room. A man walked in. He was wearing the uniform of a bailiff. "Good morning, Bill," said the secretary.

The man murmured back the greeting. He walked briskly to the only other door in the room. He glanced at the woman. She was North Eurasian. She had short hair. She was wearing coveralls. The man stopped himself from huffing in scorn. He liked fashionable women. He said, "Is he ready?"

"Go ahead," said the secretary. The man disappeared through the door. The woman turned to look through the window. Oda Plaza kept rotating below her—behind her. "Whatever," she thought. The people, fifty yards away, seemed to be walking on a giant wall. Few offices had the luxury of terrestrial gravity. Apparently, thought the woman, Justice Jay Garibaldi deserved one of the best.

On the other side of the door, Bill said, "You wanted to see me."

The man standing at the other end of the long room said nothing. He was looking through the window. He was watching Earth spin like a bowling ball in slow motion. He finally said, "Thank you for coming." He turned to look at Bill. "I know you don't like to be disturbed." His voice was low and measured. The name on the desk read Justice Jay Garibaldi.

"I figured it was important." Bill assumed the stance of a proud servant.

Garibaldi turned back to the window. "It concerns the investigation. How is it coming?"

Bill knew his reflection was being watched. He tried not to betray any emotion. "I don't have any new leads. I brought the surveillance footage."

"Thank you." The judge glared into the darkness. Bill hated these pregnant pauses. They were unsettling. "Tell me," said Garibaldi. "Are you familiar with W. Vik Voss?"

Bill wasn't sure what to say. He replied, "I've read his books."

"Are they good?"

Bill cracked a smile. "It's not the real thing." Garibaldi kept silent. Bill was getting impatient. "Why do you ask?"

Garibaldi turned again. "I'm thinking of sending somebody."

Bill squinted. "To the far side?" The man slowly nodded. "You mean Voss? He's here on the moon?"

Garibaldi turned back to the window. "You wouldn't have noticed," he said. "The registry at immigration has the first name."

Bill said, "I sat next to Voss's ex-wife at the chemin de fer table in a casino at Cannes. She was there for the holo adaptation of one of his novels. I didn't happen to see it, but she was a fox."

"You mean the ex-wife."

"That's right. She said they were divorced."

Garibaldi walked to his desk. He pressed the intercom. He said, "You can show her in, Jessica." In a moment, the door opened. The woman entered. "Thank you for coming, Ms. Voss. The gentleman to your right is Bill Boseman. He's a bailiff with the investigative branch. He's read some of your work. He says he met your ex-wife in Cannes."

The woman smirked. "I take it she was gambling."

Bill Boseman was speechless. It didn't happen often. He recovered quickly. "I didn't know," he stuttered, "you were a woman."

Voss wasn't surprised. She sized up the man. She replied, "Neither did I."

"You must forgive Mr. Boseman," said Garibaldi. "He has a habit of being particularly uninformed."

"That," said the woman, "makes two of us."

The judge smiled. "What do you know, Ms. Voss, about Cyclostomans?"

Voss eyed Garibaldi suspiciously. She answered, "Only what I haven't forgotten from grade school."

"Namely?"

"Nothing you wouldn't know."

"Indulge me."

"They're aliens. They live on the dark side of the moon. They're descended from a jawless fish. The sexes are indistinguishable."

"Almost indistinguishable," corrected Garibaldi. "Are you familiar with their language?"

The woman snorted. "I don't speak slurpee."

"What about their customs?"

"I hear they procreate through their mouths."

"Are you a fan of Craterball?"

"What am I doing here?"

"I'll be blunt, Ms. Voss. Being unemployed on the moon is an expensive proposition. You haven't published in quite some time. You've recently gone through a divorce. You're not writing. Unless you're planning a book on prostitutes, I don't think you're researching."

The woman cocked her head. "What makes you an expert?"

Garibaldi gave her a cold stare. "The girls on the near-side are highly regulated, Ms. Voss."

"In that case, you should know how desperate they are. Every other slurpee is out there willing to blow a guy for a handshake."

"Never mind. I'm here to offer you work." The woman squinted in surprise. "Craterball," continued Garibaldi, "is the backbone of the lunar economy. Somebody on the far side is threatening it."

The judge motioned to Bill. The man produced a portable video player from his pocket. He handed it to Voss. "Press play," he said. She obliged.

"That is footage," explained the judge, "from a planted security camera on the nightstand of a human bookmaker who lived on the far side of the moon. You can see him in the left-hand corner. He's lying in bed."

The woman watched. The image was dark. A door opened. Vikki recognized the lights of a corridor module. They shone brightly into the room. The man in the bed stirred. A figure entered the doorway. "Please," said the man, "Admiral Pfflohkk." His voice was desperate. "I'll get you the money, Admiral. I'll get you the money." Something flashed. The man shook violently.

"That is a plasma gun," said Garibaldi. "We believe it was modified to deliver a fatal voltage."

The shaking stopped. The figure approached the bed. He wore a cap. In his hand, he did have a plasma gun. It seemed like he was checking the victim's pulse. He turned to leave. Vikki gasped. The man had no chin. He was Cyclostoman.

Bill took back the device. "This occurred two days ago," said Garibaldi, "in an eastern district of Pfflartfort. A week earlier, a Cyclostoman bookie was found dead in Blorpshire. We've traced the weapon to one stolen from a bailiff two years ago. Since then, our leads have dried up.

"My liaison with the Cyclostomans, a certain Captain Sheetrakk, claims somebody, perhaps this so-called Admiral Pfflohkk, is running an extortion racket. If this story were to break, the Cyclostoman League would face investigations. Our more zealous legislators would try to tamper with the leadership. The Federation would threaten to suspend the all-lunar series. The extent of the possible damage is vast. Imagine how many fewer customers your prostitutes would have."

"What does it have to do with me?" asked Voss.

"I need somebody like you to do a little independent research. Manpower is a luxury around here. I have a dozen or so informants on my payroll. Unfortunately, I don't trust most of them.

"There's a Craterball team based near the north pole—perhaps you've heard of them: the Bleeptown Blackguards. They're owned by a Cyclostoman named Zyplukk. He's not high on our list of priorities. I want you to hang around the team. Take pictures. Send them wirelessly back to us."

"That's it?" Voss sneered. "How much?"

Garibaldi's face was a study in impassivity. He replied, "I'll pay a standard fee for a daily report. Bill's in charge of the investigation. He'll evaluate your work. If he finds something useful, you'll receive a bonus. My secretary will give you the details."

"What about my costs?"

"Your flight and your accommodations are covered. You have a season pass to Blackguard games and a per diem line of debit. Anything else you'll have to negotiate upon your return."

"When would that be?"

Garibaldi paused. He studied the woman's peeved expression. He said, "I have no idea, Ms. Voss."

Vikki smirked. "I'll have to keep my receipts."

"Is that a yes?" The woman nodded. "Thank you. You'll be doing the entire lunar community a service." He motioned towards the door. "My secretary will take care of you."

Vikki turned to Bill. "How did she look?"

The man arched his eyebrow. He asked, "You mean, your ex-wife?" Vikki, thinking the issue obvious, made no attempt to confirm it. Boseman took the time to appreciate her features. He decided the woman wasn't so bad-looking. He answered, "Magnificent."

Vikki nodded. She bit her lip. She looked away. She said, softly, "Good. I haven't ruined her completely."

Jessica was helpful. She had a bright disposition. Voss wondered if she were a natural blond.

"Here are your tickets, Ms. Voss. Your flight leaves—"

Vikki gently gripped her hand. "Please," she said. "Call me Vikki."

Jessica smiled. She replied, "Vikki." She gazed into the woman's eyes. After a moment, she shook her head. "What was I saying?" Vikki let go. "Your flight leaves at 0800."

Vikki thought of her ex-wife. She thought of all the women she had bedded since becoming successful. The Moon was supposed to be full of eager, same-sexed girls. That's what the Lunar Ladylover's brochure had said.

Vikki rested her fingers on the woman's hand. "Listen. I need to spruce up my wardrobe. I can't expect to get anywhere like this. Would you be willing to help? You seem to know what you're doing."

Jessica smiled. She glanced at the door. "Jay asked me to take care of you. I guess we can leave now if you like."

The women left the gravity carousel. They hopped across Oda Plaza. Vikki leapt ahead. She made sure the .17 g force was having the appropriate effect on Jessica's body. She watched her bosom bouncing slowly. She said, "You're pretty good in those heels." Jessica smiled bashfully.

Vikki tried crop tops and halternecks. She found tight sweaters. Jessica suggested she buy a set of knee-breeches—one with buckles all the way down the sides, another with buttons.

"They're sexy," she said. "If you get cold, you can put on some thick stockings." She picked out some lightly tiered prairie skirts. "Beautiful. Wear the longer ones with high-heeled boots."

Vikki offered to buy Jessica a drink. "Absolutely not," she said. "It's courtesy Judge Jay Garibaldi."

The women laughed. They went to Vikki's favorite bar, The Naked Buttocks. Vikki sat her guest on one of the stools. She pulled her own seat close. She kept brushing her coveralls against the woman's pantyhose. Jessica said, "I hear you were married."

Vikki buried herself in her drink. Coming up for air, she said, "That's right. I was young."

"Were you in love?"

"I thought I was."

"What happened?"

Vikki imagined telling Jessica the truth. She was surprised to fall in love with her best friend. She never expected to marry her at the age of twenty-four. After eight years of wedded bliss, she had no idea she would have an affair with a man. Never did she expect her wife to find out.

Vikki replied, "We didn't see eye to eye." She considered it a measure of truth. If she had been honest with herself, she would have known her marriage was doomed. She recalled what she had written in one her books: "abandoning oneself to affection is never the same as deciding one is going to love a person for the rest of one's life."

Jessica wisely changed the subject. She pointed out that stairs on the moon were, on average, three times thicker than on Earth.

Vikki arched her eyebrow. "You're new here, aren't you?"

Jessica's face froze. Her lip dropped slightly. She said with a roguish smile, "Am I that obvious?"

Vikki grinned. "I knew the instant I saw you."

"How can you tell?"

Vikki looked down. Caressing Jessica's pantyhose, she said, "Your legs are shaved." Jessica smiled. She twirled her curly, blond hair.

Child's play, thought Vikki. "I need to try on these clothes," she said. "If there's something wrong, I won't have time to return them."

"Don't worry," replied Jessica. "I'll come with you. I'll make sure no seam is left unturned."

Jessica sat on the edge of Vikki's bed. Like all lunar mattresses, it was barely larger than a cot. "It'll have to do," she whispered. Vikki came out of the bathroom. She was wearing one of her new prairie skirts. Jessica said it looked great.

"Are you sure?" asked Vikki.

Jessica smiled. "Take it off." Vikki giggled. Jessica pulled her on top of herself. She wrapped her legs around her. She kissed her. She asked, "Are you ready to pack?"

Vikki grinned. "I thought you would never ask."

It took them a while to get to the jump-port. The place was crowded. Cyclostomans were playing synthesizers and steel pans. Vikki watched them bobbing their jawless heads like pigeons. She bit her lip. It was going to get worse.

Jessica wished her luck. Vikki wasn't sure how they should part. She wanted to peck Jessica quickly on the lips. She tried to get close. Her bags got in the way. She put the bags down. She stepped forward. It was too late for a quick peck.

The women gazed into each other's eyes. Vikki smiled. She looked down. She could feel Jessica staring at her. There was no turning back. Vikki collected Jessica's fingers in her hand. She looked up.

Jessica got close. Vikki put her hands on the woman's hips. They kissed three times. They embraced. Vikki nuzzled her face into Jessica's soft, blond hair. She broke off. She picked up her bags. She walked away. She passed the line for passengers. She told herself not to turn around. She did. She smiled. Jessica waved. Vikki looked away. She had come to the moon to avoid these things.

The passport officer checked Vikki's papers for longer than necessary. He beckoned for a guard. A bewildered Vikki was escorted into a room. Inside stood Jay Garibaldi.

"I'm sorry to bother you, Ms. Voss. I believe my secretary showed you how to operate the PDA." Vikki nodded. "May I see it?" Vikki pulled it from her purse. "It's very important this not fall into a stranger's hands." Garibaldi pointed to a red button. "This device uses a special silver-oxide battery. If you should ever need to destroy it, hold down this button for five seconds. The battery will overheat. It will catch fire. It might even explode. Be aware of that."

Vikki shook her head. "Why? Is this all necessary?"

Garibaldi's face betrayed no emotion. "There's always a chance you'll find yourself in danger. I want you to be prepared." He wished her a safe trip.

Vikki boarded the jump-ship. The sling released. The missile shot into the sky. Earth glimmered in the distance. The intercom ringed. "Attention ladies and gentleman, agnathids and agnathas. This is your captain. We have completed a successful jump. Rockets are functioning properly. Please expect to reach Pfflartfort in eight hours. Thank you."

The ship arrived on time. As Vikki exited the terminal, she noticed a man standing next to two uniformed Cyclostomans. He was holding up a sign. It said, Vic Voss. Vikki approached. The man looked confused. Vikki pointed to the sign. "Are you waiting for me?"

The man asked if she were Vic Voss. Vikki nodded. The man looked her over. He said, "You're a woman."

"Last time I checked."

"I'm here to take you to Captain Sheetrakk, that is, if you don't mind." Vikki agreed. The man took her to an electric car. It was smaller than the ones driven on the near side. The two Cyclostomans fit easily into the front. Vikki and the man had a hard time squeezing into the back.

"I apologize," said the man. "I didn't realize you would have so many bags."

The concourse was crowded. Cyclostomans were everywhere. It took a while to get to the vehicular elevator. Vikki was glad she didn't have to rub shoulders with so many aliens.

The car stopped in front of a modest module. It didn't seem like the actual police station. Vikki wondered if it were some kind of annex. The rooms were small. The man seated Vikki at a desk in one of the offices. An unusually large Cyclostoman entered.

It said, "Shleeplaptip-bzz-kk-sh-kk." The slurping sounds were supposed to be words.

The man translated. "She says she welcomes you." The Cyclostoman sat at the opposite end of the desk. Its jawless mouth flexed like a wet vagina—the only difference being, this thing was full of teeth.

The man continued. "She's not sure what you'll find. She doesn't mind if you look. The man you know as Garibaldi is not to be trusted. She presumes you were sent here to find a so-called Admiral Pfflohkk. She assures you this person does not exist. No self-respecting Cyclostoman

119

would call herself an Admiral. We don't have a fleet. Anyway, don't get into trouble. She understands you're headed to Bleeptown. It's not her favorite place. Don't make her go there. That is all."

Vikki stared at the alien. She asked, "Are you Admiral Pfflohkk?" The creature puckered its mouth. It started sucking in air with a loud, continuous squeak. After a moment, the sound sputtered into a series of quick smacks. Vikki realized it was laughing.

"Blup-shlee-kk."

"No," said the man. "Certainly not."

Vikki left. The translator took her bags. He walked her out. He mentioned he was heading to Bleeptown. "Would you like me to take you?"

Vikki pursed her lips. "How convenient. Don't tell me you live next door."

"Don't you recognize me?"

"Should I?"

The man smiled. "The Cyclostoman League isn't that unpopular. I play center court for the Blackguards."

Vikki wasn't impressed. "I don't watch sports."

"That's alright. I don't read books." He offered her his hand. "I'm Flynn Champa."

Vikki shook the hand—once, firmly. "Viktoria Voss."

"What about the 'W?'"

"What about it?"

"What does it stand for?"

"I'll tell you when I trust you."

Flynn laughed. "I'm not keeping tabs on you."

"What are you doing?"

"You're not familiar with the far side. Take a look. Do you see many humans?" The man had a point. The courtyard was full of aliens.

Vikki felt sick. "How can you stand it?"

Flynn chuckled. "Let's say I'm glad you're here. I suppose I have Admiral Pfflohkk to thank for that."

"So much for my cover. I'm supposed to be researching your team."

"Don't worry. Nobody here cares much for intrigue."

"You seem to know a lot for a man who plays Craterball."

"Don't underestimate the game."

"Are you the team's only human?"

"There's one other: a guy named Joel. He's from West Africa. He's our power forward."

"Does he speak slurpee?"

"Not as well as I do. I'd be careful with that word, by the way."

"How did you know the Captain was a girl?"

"I wouldn't call her that. She's old."

Vikki shook her head. "They all look like back-country cretins to me."

Flynn laughed. "It's the whiskers." He pointed discreetly. "That's a man. That's a woman. That's a man. I'm not sure about that one."

"How can you tell?"

Flynn winked. "I can smell it."

The rocket sled zoomed towards Bleeptown. Despite the roar, Flynn tried to familiarize Vikki with Craterball. He shouted, "It was originally played outside in space suits. When the colony was young, technicians spent their free time throwing moon rocks into holes. The game evolved. People used two craters—one for each team. The ellipse described by them would form the field."

"How big would the field be?"

"Not as big as old-timers would have you believe. They like to talk about fields thousands of meters long, hundreds of people on each side. It's hard to reconcile that with the records. By the time the colony had so many people, the game was being played indoors. We had a professional league within two generations. Now we broadcast to millions."

"And you can afford to take the rocket sled."

Flynn nodded. When the ride was over, he took Vikki to the stadium. She was impressed. A network of magnetic rails was capable of seating people against the roof.

"You should come later," said Flynn. "We have a huge game against the Pfflartfort Fantails. You'll see what it's like when it's full."

Vikki smiled. "I think I will. I want to see this thing in action."

Flynn chuckled. "The harder they come, the easier they fall. We've already made you a fan."

"I wouldn't bet on it."

Flynn sidled up against her. "I'll tell you what: for every game you don't attend, I'll read one of your books."

Vikki laughed. "You'll make me write new ones."

Flynn smiled. "You'll be at a loss for words."

The man was right. As soon as Vikki was settled into her apartment, she came to watch. The excitement was contagious. Cyclostomans strapped on magnetic harnesses. Their jawless mouths puckered with glee the instant they zipped up the sides of the domed roof.

Partisan fans concentrated around their team's crater. The creativity of their coordinated taunts was mildly amusing. Vikki considered the metaphoric potential. Two rival villages coming together, through an elaborate dance involving large stones, they would settle their long-standing dispute: who is the better village?

Shamans in the form of mascots and cheerleaders tried to entrance the people. Loud music blared. Lights flashed. The warriors emerged. Large video screens detailed their physical attributes. The show, thought Vikki, was as primitive as it was modern.

The announcer cried, "At six foot two, one hundred and eighty pounds, denizens of Bleeptown, stand and recognize number forty-two, your power forward, Joel." The crowd on one side cheered. The West African trotted loosely onto the court. Vikki huffed. This was one of the reasons she didn't enjoy watching professional sports. Athletes were always treated like prize-winning chattel.

Vikki watched the first quarter come to an end. She left her seat. She ventured into one of the restaurants in the gallery. She found an open stool at the edge of the balcony. A menu lay on the counter. It was full of food for Cyclostomans: hot dogs, french fries, cucumbers pickled in brine. They liked things cylindrical. Vikki decided on the blue moon cheese squeeze. Her waitress said something in slurpee.

Vikki apologized. She explained she didn't understand. The waitress left. A wave of embarrassment flooded Vikki's heart. She regretted not having paid attention in grade school. Cyclostomans were incapable of speaking human languages. It was a matter of courtesy to attempt to understand what they were saying.

The waitress came back. She held up a card of phrases. She pointed to the one that said, "Would you like that slick or double slick?"

Vicki said, "Double slick is fine. Thank you."

The closest portable radio was on. It was broadcasting in slurpee. Vikki switched the dial.

A commentator said, "If Flynn Champa wants to lead this team back to the championship, here's the bottom line. He needs to work on that forward pass."

"You're right, Tim. Joel is always on the mark. I rarely see him out of position."

"When it comes to fumbles like that," interrupted another one, "I blame Champa. A lot of guys stick with the 'Stoman league 'cause they don't like pressure. It's bad enough when three balls are in play. If he sees the passing guards converge, he can't think about the risks. He needs to go for broke."

The game resumed. Vikki watched the players leap and flip. Their pecs bounced beneath their shirts. Vikki grew aroused. She realized the beauty lay not in the outcome, but in the execution. She tried to focus on the way all the players were moving in regards to each other. In the fourth quarter, a primal instinct took over. Vikki wanted the Blackguards to win.

She cheered. Joel's thrust up the middle has provided an excellent feint. The passing guard tossed back to Champa. From the center court, he threw it high and long. The game was tied. There were seconds left.

The voice on the radio zipped, "Joel kicks off the side of the small hill. He leaps into the air. The ball bounces off the far wall. Joel reaches back. He scoops up the ball. He tosses it into his other hand. He stuffs it into the crater. The buzzer sounds. The Blackguards triumph eleven balls to ten! It's victory for Bleeptown!"

Vikki went back to her apartment with a vicarious feeling of accomplishment. She decided the assignment wouldn't be so bad after all. Craterball would get her writing again. Reaching her door, Vikki swiped her keycard. The lock beeped. The light turned green. Vikki pushed the door open.

Her apartment was ransacked. Everything was on the floor: her clothes, her notepads, her electronic newspapers—even her toys. Vikki gasped. The PDA was gone. She stormed back to the stadium. Barging into the administrative office, she told the frightened, bewildered

Cyclostomans that if any of them were responsible for burglarizing her apartment, she would go ape-shit . She was going to call the bailiffs.

"They'll sweep the air vents," she cried. "If they so much as find a whisker, you'll all be arrested in the middle of a game." The aliens tried to calm her down. She demanded to know where she could find Flynn Champa. Somebody drew her a picture. It was a stick figure waist-deep in a pool of water. The alien said, "Shlup-pa."

The baths were on the other side of the stadium. It was the only place to bathe in Bleeptown. Vikki marched to the lobby in a matter of minutes. Placing her shoes and her stockings into a locker, she hastened down the tiled corridor. She passed vaulted chambers one by one. Pools of water stretched to the walls. It was odd to see Cyclostomans naked. There was nothing between their legs.

Vikki stopped. At the back of an otherwise empty pool, Flynn was seated against the wall. A Cyclostoman had its mouth wrapped around his modesty. Vikki strode up to the edge of the water. Flynn saw her. He blanched. He pushed the Cyclostoman off of him.

Vikki said, "What makes you think you can get away with it? I want it back."

Flynn knit his eyebrows. "I'm sorry. I don't know what you're talking about."

"My PDA. You ransacked my room." Flynn seemed dumbfounded. He started searching for words. "Don't tell me you were playing in front of millions of viewers. You had one of your slurpees find it."

Flynn tried to shush her. "Please don't use that word."

"You were the only one who knew about it. You saw it when I wrote down your phone number."

"Anybody could have broken into your room. That module is owned by Zyplukk. He leaves the keycards everywhere."

Vikki stormed off. Flynn climbed out. He begged her to stop. Naked and dripping wet, he followed Vikki down the corridor. "How do you know I had anything to do with it? Maybe a random crook stole your PDA." He watched Vikki put on her shoes. She took her stockings in her hand. Without so much as giving Flynn a dirty look, she left.

Vikki bounced down Bleeptown's main concourse. She wondered

what to do. She couldn't contact Garibaldi. Jessica had told her ten thousand times, "Never lose sight of the PDA."

Vikki was too upset to wonder why Cyclostomans were scurrying around like shrews. She hardly noticed. When she reached her apartment, she found a note stuck to the door.

It said, "I know where it is. Come to the radioactive pool. Dress sexy." The word 'sexy' was underlined—twice.

Vikki chose not to change. Her cream-colored halter top and knee-breeches would have to do. She returned to the bathhouse. It was totally deserted. The sign for the radioactive pool glared at her from across the corridor.

Vikki walked briskly. Her heels clicked against the tiles. The sound echoed throughout the dark building. Vikki realized it was sunset. By the time she passed the last partition, she could barely make out the sign of the black trefoil in front of her.

She turned. Her heels snapped on the tiles. A figure, half-submerged, leaned against the far wall.

The faint light of dusk streamed through the lune-shaped window above him. The figure pushed off the wall. It was a man. His body glistened in the lingering rays.

It was Joel. His pectorals rippled with each stroke of his arm. He waded across the pool. His chest heaved slowly. His mouth opened. He murmured, "Nau di son de set, wuman." His voice rumbled, thought Vikki, like the shifting boulders beneath a lion's foot as its crosses the muddy wallow in search of prey.

"Dis fiftin de dem long," he said. "Na yu don rich Jol fo di wota fo ivnin. If yu kom fo di wata nko? Hau den? Hmm?"

"Where is it?" asked Vikki.

The man smiled. "Di tin we de meik di pikcha? Luk." He nodded towards the side. Vikki turned her head. A small Cyclostoman emerged from the shadows. A PDA was in its hand. Vikki looked back at the man crouching at her feet. She huffed contemptuously. She turned to take possession. The creature was gone.

Joel fell backwards. His laugh echoed across the pool. "E go kwik. E veks. Di tin we de meik di pikcha na wahala. Bad fo di biznes. E de no kom bak."

"How do I get it?"

"No krai, wuman. E go put di tin fo mai haus. Wen wi don tek bat, wi go go. Kom fo di wota. Kom."

Vikki whispered, "Alright." She leaned down. Gracefully, she unbuckled her knee breeches from the bottom up. She undid the last clasp. The fabric dropped. Joel smiled. With one quick motion, Vikki removed her halter top. She pulled her panties down, wiggling out of them until they dropped. Naked but for her shoes, she beckoned Joel forward.

The man waddled up like a dog. Vikki removed her feet from the pile of fabric around her ankles. She performed a battement en avant, fully extending her foot. Joel was mesmerized. He gingerly removed one shoe. The procedure was then repeated.

Joel placed the shoes carefully onto the tiles. He proffered his hand. Vikki took it. She waded into the water.

She asked, "What kind of radiation is this?"

Joel chuckled. "Di kaind we di meik di man gro big."

"I think you've had enough already."

Joel laughed. "A no go tank di water for dat. A go tank yu."

"Why don't you go tank me back home?"

Joel smiled. "Wi go go wen di taim don kom."

"Where is everybody?"

Joel grinned. "Di 'Stoman dem no go fo di dak bat. Fo di fiftin de dem no go."

"They must get smelly."

"Wuman, stop di toktok. Yu go mek mi won kresman." He tried to kiss her on the lips. Vikki successfully evaded him. She climbed out. She walked to the neighboring bath. Joel followed. Vikki could tell she was going to have to play along. As soon as "di taim don kom," she went back with him to his apartment.

Vikki lost track of time. At some point she found herself lying drowsily next to Joel's naked body. "Hee-hee." Vikki jerked her head. It sounded like the faint call of a chickadee. "Hee-hee." It was getting louder. Escaped birds were known to live in lunar corridors. "Hee-hee." Vikki hoped it wouldn't bother her for long.

"Chick-a-dee-dee-dee." The sound came directly from the other side of the wall.

Somebody knocked. Joel roused himself. Vikki felt a sudden rush of terror. She thought of the video. She remembered the man being killed in his bed. What if this were Admiral Pfflohkk? she thought. What if she were about to die? Vikki rubbed her eyes. She wanted to see death coming.

"Hee-hee." Joel opened the door. Somebody handed something to him. A few slurps were exchanged. Joel stepped back. Vikki caught sight of the Cyclostoman from the baths. The door closed. Joel put something on top of the dresser. He climbed back into bed. He noticed Vikki awake. He kissed her. He rubbed her breast. His hand drifted down.

"Hee-hee." The sound of the chickadee grew faint.

Vikki woke. Joel was gone. A candle burned on the dresser. The PDA was next to it. Vikki got up. There was something on top. It was a keycard. Vikki picked it up. She toyed with it. She wondered what it meant. Was it for this room? she thought. She turned to put it in her breeches. It slipped to the floor.

Vikki took the candle. She jerked it down fast. The flame went out. In the darkness, Vikki patted her hand along the edge of the dresser. She reached beneath it. She found something. It was a toy pony. Odd, she thought. She put it on top. There had to be matches. She picked up the PDA. She turned it on. The glare wasn't strong. Vikki stepped back. She took a photo. The flash revealed everything.

Vikki found the card. She slipped it into her pocket. Putting on her breeches, she tried to turn on the light. It wouldn't work. She opened the door. The lamps in the corridor were dim. She realized power was on reserve. She checked her PDA. The clock said three hundred thirty hours of night left. She shook her head. This would never happen on the near side. Power stations on the peaks of eternal light guaranteed electricity.

Vikki groped her way through the corridor. This is unconscionable, she thought. How are people expected to live in semi-darkness—when a man like Garibaldi has terrestrial gravity?

Vikki found herself at the food court. It was empty. The windows let in the glow of starlight. The vending machines were on. Vikki ventured towards them. There was a man at one of the tables. He was alone. Vikki squinted. It was Champa. He was eating soft noodles.

Vikki went to him. She apologized for her outburst at the bathhouse.

Champa waved it off. He offered Vikki a seat. She asked why he wasn't with the team. Flynn chuckled. He gestured towards the lights.

"This," he said, "is not common. One of the power stations failed a few hours ago—in time for nightfall."

"Where is everybody?"

"The Cyclostomans maintain the power grid. Didn't you know? They'll be back as soon as they fix it."

Vikki sat down. "I guess I don't know very much." She bit her lip. "It makes me feel kind of stupid."

"Don't worry. There's only one thing you need to know. There are batteries for the vending machines in case they go out. They're right by the fire extinguisher."

"Do all the Cyclostomans work?"

"Every last one."

"It doesn't seem fair."

"It depends on who you are."

"It shouldn't matter. The fact of being human doesn't excuse anybody from helping."

Flynn put down his chopsticks. He gave Vikki a hard look. He said, "Do you know who these people are? Do you know why they're here?" Vikki averted her eyes. "Nobody likes to talk about this. Every Cyclostoman you will ever meet is descended from a frozen embryo. They were going to be destroyed on their home planet. Somebody didn't think that was right. Their government decided to send the embryos to us as a gift."

"How did they know they would survive?"

"Cyclostomans don't gestate in their mothers. They knew that as long as the embryos survived the trip, all we would have to do is incubate them, raise them, make them understand who they are—you can appreciate the difficulties."

"I had no idea," said Vikki. "They don't talk about that in school."

"The government doesn't want you to know about those details. It was a mess. The Cyclostomans never recovered. Every last one has a complex. You'll see. They have different ways of dealing with it. Sheetrakk doesn't trust humans. Zyplukk's wildest wet dream is to transfer the team to the near side, even if we're at the bottom of

C-League. If he didn't like banging his nurses so much, he'd get a fake jaw."

"Do they do that?"

Flynn chuckled. "I forget how little most humans know. Cyclostomans do crazy things. Getting a fake jaw is one of them. It's not popular. Their mouths are their genitals. The surgery leaves them irreversibly sterile and impotent. It's a big taboo."

"Are they able to speak human language?"

"Eventually. Their ability to speak their native tongue is impaired. They lose a few liquid sacs. It's painful. It takes a lot of discipline to make it worthwhile."

"I'm surprised anybody would try."

"The first ones didn't have a choice. Our government forced experimental surgery on them. It's one of the reasons there's so much distrust. At least it made them fight for their rights. Cyclostomans enjoy huge responsibilities now. They don't just work on the power grid, they manage it. The near side relies on them for power. Why do you think we're in the dark instead of them? The Cyclostomans are afraid to let humans suffer. They'd be risking intervention. The truth is they could hold the near side for ransom."

Vikki realized something. Her eyes bulged. She remembered seeing the Cyclostomans scurrying around. One of them had been prepared. It had taken advantage of it. Joel was there. He and the Cyclostoman had orchestrated it. Why? To steal a PDA and give it back? Vikki darted her eyes at Flynn. He was squinting at her. She quickly excused herself.

"Are you sure you have to go?" asked Flynn. "It gets lonely like this." Vikki apologized. She turned away. She tried not to walk too fast. It was too late, she thought. Flynn knew something was up. He was part of it. He could have written the note. Vikki asked herself, Why? What was the meaning of this ridiculous game?

Vikki groped her way through the corridor. Her hands were shaking. She stopped. She took a moment to breathe. She calmed herself. There is no great conspiracy, she thought. All she had to do was confront Flynn. He would tell her the truth. He would explain the note. It would be nothing. She had the PDA. What was there to fear?

Vikki went back to the food court. Flynn was gone. Vikki stopped herself from calling him. She didn't want to confront him over the phone. It would be ineffective. Vikki toyed with the keycard in her pocket. Joel was dumb enough to leave it with her. He would pay the price. Vikki thought, "We'll see how he likes having his things ransacked."

She went back to Joel's place. The door opened. The dim light from the corridor shone on the dresser. The candle was there. The matches were in the corner. Vikki glanced at the mattress on the floor. Joel was back in bed.

"Damn it," she thought. She would have to wait until he left. She closed the door. She thought, at least I'll have some fun. She stumbled to the dresser. She picked up the matches. She lit the candle. She brought it with her. She didn't want to trip over the mattress. It would make her look unsexy.

Vikki reached the foot of the bed. She put down the candle. She lifted the blanket. She climbed in.

"Did you miss me?" she whispered. She caressed Joel's chest. It was wet. Vikki pressed down. Liquid oozed.

She turned to take the candle. There was blood on her fingers. Vikki jumped to her elbows. She turned to the body. Her heart raced. She couldn't see anything. She grabbed the candle. She brought it close. Joel was stabbed. There was a knife sticking out of his chest.

Vikki gasped. The candle dropped. It fell onto the blanket. Threads started to burn. Vikki picked it up. She lifted it in front of her like a talisman. Wax dripped onto her hand.

Vikki winced. She brought her hand to her mouth. She could taste blood on her lips. It was everywhere. It was on her hands—on her pants—on her top. Vikki shook. She crawled backwards. She hit a chest of drawers. She huffed. The candle went out.

What was she going to do? Vikki breathed heavily. She wanted to talk to Jessica. Her voice would calm her down. Garibaldi would help. Vikki stuffed her hand into her pocket. She wrenched out the PDA. She started to dial the number. She thought, "What will I say—that I was sleeping with a man?" She hung up. It would be safer to send text: there would be no questions. She could take a picture. Good idea, she thought. The flash illuminated the room.

Something caught Vikki's eye—something in the window. She

checked the picture. She zoomed in. It was a reflection. "Of what?" she asked herself. She realized it was the figure of a man.

Vikki thought she heard something move. She jerked her head. She was going to scream.

Hands clamped her mouth. "Quiet," snapped Flynn. Vikki froze. The man growled, "I came right after you left. This is what I found."

Vikki panted through her nose. She gulped. Flynn eased off. Vikki took the hand. Moving it away from her mouth, she held it. She whispered, "I didn't do it."

Flynn squinted. He said, "I didn't say you did. I want to know what you're doing here—who are you working for?"

Vikki sniffed. "You know what I'm doing."

"Why is my friend dead? Who were you going to call?"

"Garibaldi. Sheetrakk mentioned him. You remember. He's a judge on the near side. I only met him yesterday. You have to believe me" Vikki was on the verge of tears. "Let me report it. Please. I don't want to get into trouble."

Flynn got up. "Do what you have to do." He walked towards the door. "I'm going to want answers."

"Wait." Vikki dug into her pocket. She offered Flynn the key to her apartment. "Meet me at my place."

Flynn shook his head. "I don't trust you."

"Do you want me to tell them you were here?"

Flynn thought about it. He took the card. He left. Vikki sent Garibaldi a text. She turned off the phone. She closed her eyes. She waited.

Within the hour, a team of investigators was crowding the apartment. A generator fueled a pair of floodlamps. Boseman took Vikki's statement in the corridor. He kept holding back a smile.

"I'm not sure you're being entirely forthright, Ms. Voss."

"I told you. Somebody ransacked my room. I didn't feel safe."

The man cast a sidelong glance at the corpse. Without turning his head, he shifted his eyes slowly back to Vikki.

"I'm somewhat bothered by your clothes," he murmured. "They seem excessively soiled. Is there an explanation for that?"

"I was sleeping in the room," said Vikki. "It was dark." The bailiff nodded.

"Could you give me a more detailed description of this Cyclostoman?"

"I didn't see it that well. It was dark around here."

"I understand. Don't worry. I'm told power will be restored shortly. You said it had a chickadee." Vikki nodded. "Are you sure about that?"

"Do you want me to mimic the call?"

"There's no reason to get excited. I'm not questioning your statement, Ms. Voss. I'm only trying to make sure you're not forgetting anything. If you have nothing to add, I suppose you're free to go. We'll be in touch."

Vikki went back to her place. Flynn pounced. "What's going on?"

"You tell me. Did you write the note?"

"What note?"

"Dress sexy?"

"I have no idea what you're talking about."

"Who left it?"

"How should I know?"

"There was a Cyclostoman hanging around. It took my PDA. It's involved."

"In what?"

"In the murder of your friend."

"Impossible."

"I have video of a man being killed in Pfflartfort. A Cyclostoman shows up on the camera. It might be the same one." Flynn scoffed. "I'll show you." Vikki played the file. Flynn shook his head.

"I've never seen this. I don't know anything about it."

"It's been kept quiet."

"I don't know who that Cyclostoman is. It's not the one you have in mind."

"How can you be sure?"

"First of all, if the killer had the evidence, why wasn't it destroyed? More importantly, the Cyclostoman here is an agnathid, a Cyclostoman male. The one you're talking about is an agnatha. She's a bookmaker from a prominent family. She's rich, polite, and well-connected. She wouldn't have anything to do with this."

"She could have orchestrated the outage."

"To what end?"

"Your friend is dead. Flynn, this Cyclostoman is involved. At the very least, we ought to talk to her. I want to know what is going on—why she stole the PDA."

"That makes two of us."

"Where does she live?"

"Pfflartfort."

"Let's go."

Vikki marched out. Flynn followed. They tried the rocket sled. It was unavailable. They went to the train station. It was empty. Nobody was leaving until power was restored. They waited.

Fifteen minutes passed. Cyclostomans trickled onto the platform. Within an hour, a large crowd had gathered. A train lumbered onto the track. Vikki and Flynn tried to get aboard. They were squeezed in by Cyclostomans from every direction. Vikki noticed a passenger in a space suit. "Thanks a lot," she thought to herself. "This car is packed as it is."

The train made all local stops. People got off. More passengers got on. The man in the space suit lingered. Vikki stared at him discreetly. She thought to herself, technicians sometimes take trains from one stop to the next. She had never seen one go this far. She mentioned it to Flynn.

"Are you sure it's the same one?"

"I'm positive."

Flynn shook his head. "It doesn't mean anything. Sometimes it's the fastest way to transport a suit."

Vikki nodded. She tried to forget it. The man stayed with them until Pfflartfort. Vikki watched him out of the corner of her eye. Flynn took her hand. He led her through the crowded station. Vikki kept looking over her shoulder. The man in the suit fell behind. Vikki decided he wasn't following. A few minutes later, they reached an apartment.

Flynn rang the bell. A Cyclostoman spoke on the intercom. Flynn talked in slurpee. The door buzzed open. Vikki entered. She marveled at the luxury. A spacious atrium led towards a magnificent garden. Sporangia loomed overhead on gigantic stalks. The capsules were as large as a power forward's shoe. A Cyclostoman approached. Vikki recognized it from the baths.

Flynn spoke to it. His slurpee was better than Vikki expected. The Cyclostoman grew distressed. It started speaking fast. It gestured for Flynn to wait. As it left, Flynn turned.

"She says she's harboring a woman and her daughter. They're on the run from the woman's husband. She thought you were sent to find them. She panicked. They were staying in Joel's room. The blackout was supposed to give her an opportunity to stow them on one of the access towers at the north pole. She wants me to go there now and move them. I told her it's silly. It's better to leave them where they are."

The creature came back. It was holding a map. It pointed to one of the power facilities. Flynn refused to look at it. The creature circled it with a pen. It tried shoving the map into Flynn's hands. He wouldn't take it. He told Vikki it was time to go. He headed towards the door.

Vikki took out the PDA. She played the video for the Cyclostoman. She asked it if the murderer looked familiar. The creature shook its head. Flynn moaned, "She doesn't know anything. Come on."

Vikki followed Flynn back to the station. They boarded a train for Bleeptown.

"I'm sorry," said Flynn. "I shouldn't have told Joel about you. I must have mentioned taking you to see Sheetrakk. Joel was involved with a lot of different people in a variety of ways. I'm sure I don't have to explain to you what I mean. You experienced it. I know I did."

Vikki sat catatonically. She watched the tunnel lights cast shadows along the wall of the car. Something about them bothered her. She took out the PDA. She played the video. She stared at the image of the man stirring in bed, the door opening, the lights shining from the corridor. They were casting a shadow. Vikki looked at it. She had seen it before. Where? she thought. It was familiar. It was bulbous.

Vikki reached up. She pulled the emergency stop. The passengers lurched. The train screeched to a halt.

"We have to go," she cried. She leapt towards the door. Flynn jumped after her. "That woman is in danger," she yelled. "We led the killer right to her." Vikki tore through the cars. She reached the end. She jumped into the tunnel. Flynn had no choice. He followed.

They reached the apartment. They found the door drilled open. Atrium furniture was knocked over. The Cyclostoman was on the ground. Vikki turned her onto her back. She made sure she was still breathing. "The map!" she cried. "Where is it?"

Flynn looked around. He couldn't find it.

"If that map is gone," said Vikki, "that woman and that child aren't safe."

"I'll call Sheetrakk."

"No!" Vikki gave Flynn a grave look. "If that woman is charged with kidnapping, I'll never forgive myself. We have to go ourselves."

"To the north pole? How?"

"The rocket sled."

"We can't rent rovers in Bleeptown. We would have to drive from here."

Vikki started towards the door. "We'll call the medics on the way. Come on."

Flynn shook his head. "It's not that easy. The pole is at least six hours away. They rent rovers for joyrides. They use oxygen purge systems. They'll last an hour and a half."

"Don't tell me you can't get primary life support. People go on expeditions."

"It costs money. You have to make a reservation. You're supposed to take a guide."

"I'll pay."

"You are crazy."

"I'm not asking for help. I'll go on my own."

Flynn followed Vikki to the rover park. He knew they wouldn't let her go by herself. He purchased a deluxe PLSS+ speed rover package for two. He paid the extra insurance for going alone. He bribed the sales clerk to get them on the road as soon as he could.

They drove north. As they neared the peaks of eternal light, Vikki spotted a vehicle. It was approaching an access tower. "That's the one," said Vikki. "Step on it."

Flynn clenched the wheel. "If we go any faster, we'll fly off the moon." The other rover stopped a few yards from the entrance. The driver got out. He started leaping towards the door.

"He's going to beat us," said Vikki. "He'll lock us out."

"Not if I can help it." Flynn leaned over. He grabbed a rock.

"What are you doing?"

Flynn got up. "They say I need to practice this shot."

"We're too far."

"Hold the wheel." Vikki leaned over. She tried to keep the car steady.

Flynn took aim. The man was now less than a hundred yards away. Flynn whispered, "This is for you, Joel." He launched the rock. It flew.

Vikki watched it barrel towards the station. The man was closing in on the door. His back was turned. Vikki squinted. The rock was heading towards him. It gleamed in the headlamps. It was on target. It hit the man's shoulder. "Yes," cried Vikki. The man grabbed his arm. He twisted around. He bounced to the ground.

Flynn parked the rover next to the other one. Vikki leapt into the pressure lock. She turned around. She gasped. The man was up. He was pulling Flynn by the arm. He threw him. Flynn staggered to regain his balance. The man picked up the rock that had knocked into him. He smashed it into Flynn's visor. The plastic cracked. Flynn fell to the ground. The man turned.

Vikki shut the door. She pressed the button to pressurize the chamber. The inner door opened. The man stepped to the window. He banged on it. The sheen of his visor gleamed. He pressed the button to depressurize. The inner seal began to close. Vikki stepped into its path. She couldn't block it forever. She would have to jam the door. Vikki unscrewed her helmet. She backed over the threshold. As the seal slid shut, Vikki positioned the helmet in its way. It stuck. It was holding. The motor strained. Vikki let go. The helmet budged. Vikki grimaced. It was too late. The helmet popped out. Horror took hold of Vikki's face. The seal was reestablishing itself. It would take moments for the air to clear.

Vikki turned. The emergency door was a few meters away. She could hear the chamber repressurizing. She sprinted. The inner door opened. Vikki leapt. Plasma fired into her back. The shock pulsed throughout her suit. She fell to the ground.

The intruder dropped to his knees. He clutched his arm. His suit was torn. It had depressurized. The man doubled over. He hit his helmet against the floor. He fell to one side. He rolled around in pain.

Vikki collected herself. The suit had absorbed most of the voltage.

She crawled past the threshold. She kicked the emergency door shut. There was no way to lock it. There was nothing to make a barricade. As soon as her pursuer recovered, he would simply screw it open.

Vikki stumbled around. There was no way out. There was a window. She banged into it. She was disoriented. A space suit appeared in front of her. It shocked her. It was Flynn. He was alive. He patted his chest. He waved his arm flat near his waist. He was running out of air. Vikki looked back. The door was opening. Flynn knocked on the window. He pointed up.

Vikki looked. There was a shaft. "Of course," she thought. This was an access tower. A ladder led to the next level. Vikki jumped. She climbed with her hands as fast as she could. She heard a noise. "Hee-hee." It echoed throughout the shaft. "Chick-a-dee-dee."

Vikki kept climbing. The shaft was high—ten stories at least. She looked down. The man was on the ground. He was pointing his gun at her. He put it down. She was out of range. "Hee-hee."

Vikki reached the top. She scampered over the edge. She looked down. The man was climbing with his one good arm. It would take him time. Vikki looked around. The module was empty. At the other end, there was another shaft. "Hee-hee." There was no way of knowing how far Vikki would have to go. Flynn was running out of air.

"I'll call for help," she thought. She cupped her mouth. She realized she had a weapon. Her PDA was in her pocket. Vikki tried to remove her glove. It wouldn't budge. She twisted her wrist as hard as she could. The glove loosened.

Vikki screwed it off. She pulled her arm into the body of her suit. She found the PDA. She squeezed it through her collar. She took it with her gloved hand. She pressed the red button. Vikki counted. It was supposed to take five seconds. She looked down. The man was half-way up. Vikki reached ten. Something was wrong. "Hee-hee."

She realized her glove was too thick. She was pressing more than one button. She tried to push the red one with her tongue. It was too difficult. She tried using her teeth. She couldn't reach. She pushed her arm back into the sleeve. It got stuck. She put the PDA in her mouth. She tried to squeeze her hand between her neck and the collar. It was impossible. She put her free hand between her legs. She tried to twist off the glove. It wouldn't move. "Hee-hee."

The man was getting close. Vikki tried again to push her arm through the sleeve. It was stuck again. She pushed harder. It refused to budge. Vikki clenched her teeth. She pushed as hard as she could. She thought her arm was going to break. Tears welled in her eyes. "I can't," she thought. She looked down. The man was less than ten yards away. She had to do it.

Vikki pushed. Nothing. She pushed again. Nothing. She pushed one last time. Nothing. Vikki gave up. She sighed. Her arm budged. She pushed it again. It moved. "Come on," she thought. She squeezed it through. She grabbed the PDA. She held down the red button. She counted, "One one-thousand. Two one-thousand. Three one-thousand." She held it over the shaft.

Vikki looked down. The man was five yards away. The PDA was getting hot. It was burning her hand. She couldn't hold it much longer. She winced. "Ow!" It dropped. It tumbled towards the man. Flames flashed from the battery.

The man saw the fiery device falling onto him. He tried to shield himself with his hurt arm. He groaned. The PDA burst. A crack echoed. Dust filled the shaft. It cleared. Vikki saw the man plunging down. He hit bottom.

Vikki slid down the ladder. She glanced at the man's visor. It was broken. The face was bloody. There was no time to look at it. Vikki ran to the air lock. Her helmet was stuck against the inner door. Vikki peered through the window. Flynn was outside. He was careening back and forth.

Vikki pulled on the helmet. She tried to kick it out. It twisted. She pulled it again. It slipped out. Vikki fell to her back. The door closed. Nothing happened.

She looked outside. Flynn was nowhere. Vikki realized he had collapsed. She would have to open the door for him. She tried to put on the helmet. It wouldn't lock. The door had bent it out of shape. Vikki panicked. She couldn't go outside without her helmet. She would pass out. She could break the seal. Air from the access tower would protect her.

Vikki looked around. A fire extinguisher hung next to a length of hose. Vikki unraveled the rubber. She weaved it through the crank wheel of the emergency door. She would have to hold it open. The man, she thought.

She dragged the body into the frame. She propped it against the door. She looked at the face.

It was Bill Boseman.

Vikki tied the loose end of the hose around her waist. She gave herself enough slack to reach the outer door. She took the fire extinguisher. She stepped in front of the inner seal. She hurled the canister into the window. She grimaced. It hadn't even left a scratch.

Vikki thought of the plasma gun. It was modified. The laser might be strong enough to burn a crack into the glass. She hopped over Boseman's body. The gun was on the floor. Vikki brought it back to the seal. She aimed it at the window. She fired. The glass cracked.

Vikki picked up the extinguisher. She slammed it into the window. The crack got bigger. She did it again. It was working. She rammed the canister again and again. The window broke.

Vikki knocked out the shards. She hoped the locking computer would be fooled. She stepped towards the outer door. She braced herself. There was only one way to find out. She pulled.

Air blasted past her. Flynn's body lurched. Vikki reached for it. She grabbed the arm. The current pressed her against the door. There was too much slack. Boseman's body was buckling.

Vikki planted her foot. She kicked. Flynn's body fluttered. There was too much force. Vikki grimaced. Her back gave way. She slammed against the door. She wouldn't let go. She braced herself. She planted her foot again. She kicked. She roared. She pulled.

Flynn's arm made it past the threshold. Vikki grabbed his collar. She heaved on it. Flynn's shoulder made it. She let go of the arm to grab the back. The arm smacked her in the face. Vikki roared. She got the torso inside. It was working. She grabbed the waist. Piece by piece, Vikki pulled in Flynn's limp body from outside. It collected behind her. As soon as the soles of his boots had crossed the threshold, Vikki shut the door. She collapsed against it. She panted.

Flynn was unconscious. Vikki wondered if he were breathing. She unscrewed his helmet. She put her face over his mouth. There was nothing. Vikki squeezed his nose. She formed a seal around his mouth with her lips. She breathed. She broke away. There was nothing. She did it again. Nothing. One more time. Vikki slapped the man in the face. She slapped him again and again. She slapped him as hard as she could.

He flinched. He wheezed. He opened his eyes. He wheezed again. He grabbed Vikki's hand. He tried to smile. He coughed. He cleared his throat. He said, "Do you think I can ask you a personal question?"

Vikki sighed in relief. She said, "What?"

Flynn grinned. He coughed some more. He said, "The 'W'—what does it stand for? Wonderful?"

Vikki smiled. She could barely hold up her head. "Wiebke," she replied. "It stands for Wiebke." She passed out.

An hour later, a jump-ship landed next to the tower. A man in a space suit climbed out. He opened the outer seal. He saw the broken window. He returned to the ship. He took out a large tank of air. He repressurized the module. He succeeded in opening the emergency door.

Vikki was on the other side. She was pointing a gun at him. "Take it off," she said.

The man obeyed. The helmet came off his head. Vikki was not surprised. It was Garibaldi.

"I came as soon as I lost your signal."

"You've been tracking me."

Garibaldi motioned towards the body. "Is he dead?" Vikki nodded. "It's better that way."

"Start talking."

"The woman and the child: are they safe?"

"You should be more concerned with this gun."

"I apologize, Ms. Voss. This was bad luck."

Vikki laughed. She gave Garibaldi an icy stare. She said, "It seems a bit more sinister than that."

Garibaldi nodded. He said, "Bill was a decent man. He was a friend of mine. He started gambling. When he said he met your ex-wife in a casino, I wasn't surprised."

"Tell me something I don't know."

"He was extorting bookmakers on the far side. It was his accomplice you saw on the video."

"What about the Cyclostoman from Pfflartfort?"

"She laundered money."

"How?"

"Through a fixed lottery. Boseman's wife played it."

"She was part of it?"

"I don't know how much she knew. I didn't have time to depose her. When people started getting killed, I shared my suspicions with her. She panicked. I had to relocate her. I made it look like she had run off with a Craterball jock. My attentions turned to Bill. I had to keep up the pretense that I didn't know what was going on."

"I was some kind of decoy?" asked Vikki.

"It doesn't matter. Bill and I had remote access to your PDA. He saw something in one of the photos you took: a toy his daughter left behind. If not for that, none of this would have happened."

Vikki shook her head. "If you knew so much about the money laundering, why didn't you bring him in for lottery fraud? You could have stopped him from killing an innocent man."

"I made a mistake. I apologize."

"I want to know why."

"It's complicated." Vikki cocked her head. Garibaldi sighed. "I was helping a friend."

"Who?"

"I had an established relationship with the Cyclostoman from Pfflartfort. It got in the way of my judgment."

"How?"

"You don't need to know." Vikki squinted. She wagged the gun. Garibaldi stared into Vikki's eyes. "We have something in common, Ms. Voss. Through our personal failings, we both alienated women who trusted us. The Cyclostoman you met used to be my wife."

Vikki squinted. She realized what Garibaldi was saying. Her eyes widened. A feeling of awe welled in the pit of her stomach. She whispered, "You're not human." Garibaldi clenched his jaw. Vikki shook her head. "Why?"

"For the good of my people—I will never regret it. As for this unfortunate affair, we should put it behind us. I trust I can depend on your silence, Ms. Voss. It would serve both our interests." Vikki made no attempt to argue. "If you will allow me, I will dispose of this body. You're welcome to return with me to the near side."

Vikki shook her head. "I'll stay here for a while."

"Are you sure? There is a risk to your health with no weight room."

"There's an ergometer on the tenth floor. There's a kitchen and supplies. I'll be fine."

"You will forgive me for repeating my question. Are the woman and the child safe?"

"A friend of mine drove them to Pfflartfort."

"Mr. Champa?"

"That's right."

"You'll be wanting to keep that gun?"

"If you don't mind."

"I do. It's material evidence."

"What should I do with it?"

"My wife will come to pick it up. Do you happen to know where Mr. Champa deposited the witnesses?"

"I have no idea."

"Are you sure about staying?"

"It's bright. I want to try to clear my head."

"I understand. A team will be sent to fix the airlock. Don't let them know you're here." Garibaldi moved to put on his helmet. He stopped himself. "One more thing, Ms. Voss. There's somebody back home who's worried about you. What should I tell her?"

Vikki smiled. "Tell her I'm fine." The man nodded. He put on his helmet. He dragged Boseman's body to the jump-ship.

Vikki watched the rockets blow. A cloud of dust mushroomed around them. Moon rocks scattered. The ship climbed. The flames cut out. The thrusters sputtered into action. Up in the airless sky, the small, white box slipped through the peaks of eternal light. The sun glistened off its surface. Vikki followed it for as long as she could—until the darkness of the lunar night swallowed it.

Into the Desert

by Robert Crossland

Tristan Kalvis was typically American. He grew up in Buffalo. His grandfather was Lithuanian. His mother's family was mostly Welsh. She claimed to be, on occasion, one-thirteenth Seneca—"or," she would say, "was it one-fifteenth?"

Tristan inherited this dubiously unconscious disregard for common sense. He joined the Navy after four years of studying Russian literature and four years of what he liked to call "minding his own business."

He became a public affairs officer. He earned a master's degree in communication. After a few years at the Pentagon, he was stationed in Bishkek, the capital of Kyrgyzstan. Nobody outside the service understood why the Navy would send him to a landlocked nation. Bishkek was as far from the ocean as physically possible.

Every fourth of July, Memorial Day, and/or Labor Day barbeque, Tristan would explain the BGM-109 Tactical Tomahawk Subsonic Land

Attack Missile has an estimated operational range of two thousand five hundred and three kilometers, allowing it, hypothetically, if fired in that direction, to reach the embassy, putting it well within the boundary of the Navy's sphere of operations.

Tristan was knowledgeable about the Navy. He was well organized. He rarely got orders wrong. The Chief of Mission liked hamburgers without ketchup. The Defense Attaché drank coffee strong. The woman from the US-AID office refused to tolerate the Security Assistance Supervisor's steak sandwich leaking grease all over her boxed salad. "Take it back," she would say. "I don't care what you do with it. Feed it to the poor if you like."

When the embassy hosted functions for locals, the mayor would complain his beshbarmak had too much coriander. The Foreign Minister preferred shashlyki without eggplant. The woman from the US-AID office would insist that all foods containing horsemeat be kept on a separate table. "I don't care if it's in their culture," she explained. "If there's going to be a boiled sheep's head, I don't want to see it."

"What would you like to drink?" Tristan would ask her. "Kumis or camel's milk?"

The woman would shake her head. "What's the kumis?"

"Fermented mare's milk."

"I'll have the water."

"Are you sure? It's from the tap."

One day, the embassy hosted a concert. A family of Kyrgyz musicians performed. Tristan took a liking to one of the daughters. He asked her if he could get her a drink. She didn't seem to understand. He asked, "Govorish po russki?"

She replied, "Da."

Tristan said, "Kumis or camel's milk?" The girl laughed.

"I'll have a Coke."

Tristan started dating her. He would drive her around on his motorcycle. He was mortified to learn her father was already planning their wedding. His girlfriend laughed.

She said, "He doesn't want me to end up like my sister."

"What happened to her?" asked Tristan.

"She ran away." The girl pulled a picture of her sister from her pocket. "I show this to everybody in case they see her." Tristan admired the photo. "Her name is Adi."

"She's not as beautiful as you," said Tristan, "but close. I hope that's not why she left."

The girl giggled. "She fought with our father. He's very old-fashioned. Adi always had a different opinion. When she started working for Avon, it was the last straw. He didn't like the idea of her selling make-up."

"What did I do to get on his good side?"

"It's the way you ride your motorcycle. He thinks you were sent by our tribe's totem."

"What kind of creature is it?"

The girl thought about it. "What do you call it?" she asked. She twitched her nose. Tristan chuckled.

"The small one or the big one?"

"The big one."

"It's called a hare."

"You should be proud," said the girl, "They're very fast."

"They eat their own shit."

"What?"

"Never mind. Do you know what they say about a guy with long legs?" The girl shook her head. Tristan smiled. He stroked the length of his thigh with the edge of his hand. He said, "Long pants."

An official from the State Department came to see Tristan one day. The secretary told him, "Kalvis? the lieutenant?" was "out to lunch." She rolled her eyes.

The visitor smiled. He had seen this attitude before. Wherever Tristan went, he left behind a trail of scorned women. They always refused to disguise their spite. He explained he was an old friend.

"I see." The woman went back to her nails.

"I'm sorry. When do you expect him?"

"How should I know? Ask his girlfriend."

The man nodded. He mentioned he was a classmate. The woman gave him a frosty smile. "In college," said the man, "he was known as Mr. 'Whoa.'"

"That's funny," replied the woman. "I didn't know he was Chinese."

She thought it was clever. She repeated it to Tristan when he came back. He had a good idea who was waiting for him.

"George," he said, entering the conference room. "What are you doing?"

"I've come to see you."

"I bet." The two of them embraced. "Are you still in D.C.?" George nodded.

"I'm I-N-R."

"What's that?"

"The Bureau of Intelligence and Research."

"Shouldn't that be B-I-R?"

"They don't want us telling people we work for beer."

"What are you? Some kind of spy?"

"It's classified."

Tristan found a couple of glasses and a bottle of whiskey. "Don't worry. I have some sodium pentathol here."

"You don't have to ask twice. I need your help."

Tristan poured the glasses. He nodded. "We'll find you a girl."

"That's not what I'm talking about."

"Always the procrastinator."

"We're going to China."

"Chinese girls are nice."

"We'll be posing as tourists."

"Not a bad line."

"We'll be collecting information."

"Know thy enemy." Tristan handed him a glass. They clinked.

George watched Tristan bring the cup to his lips. He said, "It's business." Tristan took a sip. He swallowed it. He cocked his head. He squinted. George sighed. He knew his friend would be skeptical. He turned around.

Never do that, thought Tristan. He must have told George a hundred times, "It makes you look weak."

"Our commander-in-chief," said George, "is interested in promoting his influence in this region. I've been told to make contact with subversives in Xinjiang." George paused. He wondered if he had pronounced the word correctly.

Tristan prepared to take another sip. He said, "The kind our last boss put on the terrorist watch list?" George turned back. He shrugged feebly. Tristan continued, "I assume we won't be helping the Chinese destroy them."

"We're looking for leverage against Beijing."

"Leverage or bargaining chips?"

"The more distracted they are in the west, the less of a threat they pose in the east."

"Until they offer you something."

"The Uyghur have something to gain by cooperating with us."

"They have everything to lose."

"I'm not going there to sell them out. I'm not going to arm them either. I've been asked to assess the situation. Your Russian is good. Your Chinese isn't bad. I hear you've even picked up some Turkish— and I don't mean just the language."

"You don't know what's going on, George—and I don't just mean my personal life. The Chinese are engaged in a full-scale crackdown."

"That's why I need you. If you don't come, I have to go alone. Look at me. Do I look like a tourist to you?" Tristan grinned. "Have I ever been anything but the opposite of relaxed?"

"Don't worry. You won't go by yourself. I'll get us a car. We'll drive through Kazakhstan. We'll be in Yining before you know it."

"We have people in Yining," explained George. Tristan squinted again. This time, his eyes got very narrow. "We'll be taking the bus to Kashgar. We'll be making a tour of the southern rim."

Tristan's mouth slightly dropped. He started slowly shaking his head. "There aren't any groups down there."

"That's the problem."

Tristan huffed. He clenched his teeth. He said, "George, you sure as hell know how to ruin my day."

The road to the southern border carved a four-hundred-mile-long serpentine trail through the mountains. Tristan calculated, with a maximum of three bathroom breaks, the trip would take at least twenty-four hours. "A bird," he explained, "cruising at an average speed of fifteen miles an hour with one eighty-minute-long break for lunch would beat us there in half the time."

George was not convinced. He insisted on taking the bus. It was essential to maintaining cover.

Tristan begged. "At least cut the trip in two. You don't want to sleep on the road. You want to sleep in a bed." The thought appealed to George's sense of hygiene. He was willing to consider it.

They boarded the bus. Sitting in the fifth row, swarmed by a crowd of faded wool suits, ducking constantly to avoid the corners of empty bamboo trunks, only to be broadsided by the next faux leather bag, Tristan watched with growing exasperation the line of two-bit traders endlessly parade past him.

At the last moment, blond hair stepped onto the bus. The long bangs hid the owner's face. Shrouded by the partition, they carefully climbed the next step behind another smarmy salesman. The length of the hair revealed itself. It flowed past the creature's shoulders. Tristan clenched his fists. It had to be a woman. It didn't matter if she were ugly. As long as she weren't on the wrong bus, he wouldn't have to kill himself.

The creature paid the driver. It turned. It tossed its head. It was a woman—a gorgeous one. She was looking for a spot. Tristan sprang to his feet. He offered her his. The woman demurred. Tristan insisted. She waved her hand. Tristan took it. He pushed her into the seat. He turned. He politely asked the man on the other side of the aisle if he could move towards the window. The man refused. Tristan offered him money. The man shook his head. He offered him more. It worked.

The woman's name was Polina. She was Russian—an archeology student. She was heading for a dig.

"Amazing," said Tristan. "An entire city swallowed by sand. What kind of people lived there?"

"Di Griks callt dem Tocharians," said Polina. "Tu di Chaynees, dey wur Moon peepul."

"Moon people." Tristan thought about it. He said, "That sounds—" He searched for the right word. He looked into Polina's eyes. He smiled. He said, "Sexy." Polina chortled.

"Dey wur callt Moon peepul bicos dey wur whait. Dey hat di ret hare ant green ice."

"Green ice?"

"Laik you." She pointed to his eyes.

"I see. We must be related." The woman shook her head.

"Dey went east ant sout arount di mountains tu Eendia. Dey wur pusht bai di Turkeys peepul."

Tristan nodded. He tried to hide his smile. "Are you getting this George? They had red hair and green eyes. The Turkeys peepul pushed them to India."

"Let the woman talk."

"Bai di taim di Chaynees met dem, dey wur already over di mountains of di east. Di wans who stayt beehaint wur—how do you say dis? Submeetink."

"After the king's skull was turned into a drinking cup."

"Correct. Dey hat to deal weet bof di Chaynees who wur wantink tu control di tradink ant di Turkeys peepul who di Chaynees wur tryink tu keep behint de wall."

"I'm assuming the Chinese were victorious."

"Eet deetn't happen overnait. Dey kept puttink soljurs in di nort of di desert ofer ant ofer. In di sout, eet was four hundret years before dey put di soljurs in di eastern-most seeti—not to mention di west. Dees soljurs wur not lastink lonk. Een Chayna eet was chaos. Een di west, deeferent Turkeys peepul come, layk Gokturks ant Uyghurs. Always eet was Turkeys peepul comink, pushink di Chaynees ant takink ofer di whait peepul."

"We didn't stand a chance."

The woman shrugged. "Eef you look at di Uyghur peepul now, sumtaims you see dey haf di blont hair. We wur doink sumtink."

"I'd much rather be doing that kind of work. Wouldn't you agree, George?"

"I'm afraid I'm not very big on archeology." Tristan laughed.

"Excuse him. He's not very handy with a tool. George, we should check this place out. They found a hundred buildings petrified by sand. They call it, 'the Pompeii of the desert.'"

"It's not on our way."

"We should make a deviation."

"I don't think so."

George was incorrigible. When they reached the layover, he hid in his room. "I'm not going to ask her to have a one-night stand," he said.

"Technically," said Tristan, "it's not a one-night stand if you're hoping for more. It's what's called a test."

"I hate tests."

"What kind of a spy are you? You're embarrassing me."

The next day, they reached the border. The bus driver collected bribes from the traders. Inside the small, poorly lit station, the guards were generous enough to offer certain medical certificates. They claimed the Chinese officials would ask for them.

Polina offered her passport. The guard looked it over. "Apollinariya Baranova."

"Polina," said Polina. "For short."

"Do you have AIDS, Ms. Polina?" The woman shook her head. Tristan breathed a sigh of relief.

"Would you like to buy a certificate attesting to this fact?"

"Alright."

"That will be one hundred som."

Tristan turned to George. "The AIDS certificate is only three dollars. Are you going to get one?" George squinted. He sneered. He shook his head. Tristan's face fell. He caressed George's shoulder. "I'm sorry," he whispered. "I didn't know."

At the bus station, Tristan was forced to part ways with his new friend. He watched her walk into the gentle Kashgar afternoon, hips swinging in her light, flower-print skirt—in Tristan's mind—to the doleful tune of Korobushka, playing slowly at first in his head, quickening pace with each progressively tantalizing step, until the remains of his hope were crushed. "Game over," he thought to himself. He turned to George. He cried. "How could you? You let her slip through our fingers."

"We have more important things to worry about." George gestured towards a man lurking in the shadows. "We're being followed."

Tristan took a look. He couldn't believe it. He gave George a pathetic shake of his head. He waved at the stranger. George watched incredulously as Tristan walked up to the man. He rubbed his face in anxiety. Tristan laughed. He was patting the man on the back. The stranger smiled. Tristan came back.

"What the hell are you doing?" George asked.

"This man," said Tristan, "wants to help. He's ready to offer you a sixteen-year-old girl for the entire day and night for only two hundred yuan. That's thirty dollars."

"Forget it."

"I tried to bargain. The man is shrewd. For another hundred, he'll throw in the girl's mother."

"Come on."

George tried to contact one of the people on his list. The address led him down a squalid alley. Tristan feared for his shoes. George sighed. The man wasn't home. The landlady said she didn't know if he would ever be back. "If you find him," she told Tristan, "tell him he owes me three months of rent."

George suggested they wait at the hotel for a few days.

Tristan disagreed. "Give this lady your mobile phone number. She'll have the guy call as soon as he gets home."

George held up the phone in his hand. "This," he explained, "is a satellite phone. If he calls this phone, he will be charged three hundred yuan per minute. We might as well hang Christmas lights on his neck that spell out 'subversive.'"

"There's no need to get angry. Don't you have somebody else on the list?"

"Not in Kashgar."

"Let's get on another bus. We'll hit this guy on the way back."

George wondered what made Tristan so eager to get moving. He would have expected him to love wasting time at the hotel. He decided not to jinx it by asking him. On the way to Hotan, the bus driver put on a Turkic movie. Tristan watched. The plot was hard to follow. There was an old man. He was mourning. There were soldiers pushing people around. A young woman danced with what may have been her husband. The husband may have been the old man's son. It seemed the son was killed at some point by soldiers.

The driver put in another movie. This was a costume drama. A large group gathered. The men watched women dance. An old man spoke. He looked like a chief. The dubbing was atrocious. The chief stared at one of the dancers. She was beautiful. The camera took in the crowd. All the men looked like lechers. There was more dancing.

Tristan counted, on one hand, the men who didn't have large moustaches. On the other, he counted the men who weren't wearing turbans. He challenged George to find more than he could. George brushed him off. He tried to go back to sleep.

Hotan was full of Uyghur. They kept their distance. Tristan shook his head. "It seems the People's Armed Police got here before us." George couldn't find a single person on his list. "Don't worry," said Tristan. He slapped George on the back. "We'll get them on the way home."

They boarded another bus. Tristan watched the barren landscape unfold. It was comforting to know there was no lack of rock and sand. He looked to the south. The Kunlun mountains stood like craggy knuckles. They stretched endlessly eastward. Every year, thought Tristan, the sun would melt snow from their peaks. The water would trickle into the valley. It would seep its way unseen across the desert. It would reach the main river. It would be hemmed in by the Tian Shan mountains. It would swing back into the desert. In time, it would end up on the snowy peaks once again.

"Is it a tragedy or a comedy?" he asked. George roused himself. He was resting against a migrant woman's shoulder.

"What's that?"

"The desert we call the universe," said Tristan. "Is it preparing us for something big?"

"I thought you were watching a movie."

"I was thinking about the hydrosphere."

"I'm sorry. I slept through earth science."

"Water keeps moving," mused Tristan. "It doesn't really go anywhere."

"Tell that to the locals. Weren't you listening to Polina? The desert's been growing for two thousand years. The Communists made it worse. There are sand storms in Beijing now. They say they're building a Green Wall of China. Good luck. It'll take them a hundred years to dig the holes."

"Look at the desert highway," said Tristan. "They lined five hundred kilometers with shrubs. It didn't take them that long."

George laughed. "As long as there's oil in the desert, they'll keep those bushes alive. The poor people can starve."

The bus entered a small town. Tristan saw a building with big, square buttresses and top-hinged shutters. The sign read, "Lucky Jewel Guesthouse."

"This is it," he whispered.

He squeezed by the passengers. He told the driver to stop at the upcoming traffic circle. He roused George. "Come on," he said. "Let's beat the crowd."

Tristan gathered their bags. George wondered why nobody else was moving. The bus slowed to a stop. Tristan and George stepped off. The driver pressed the gas.

"What's going on?" said George. "I don't have any contacts here."

"Exactly." Tristan gestured grandly. A square column stood in the middle of the intersection. Chairman Mao's portrait graced every side. White Han characters spelled out the first of many Mao quotations found in The Little Red Book. It was from his opening address to the first National People's Congress. It said, "The force at the core leading our cause forward is the Chinese Communist Party. The theoretical basis guiding our thinking is Marxism-Leninism." They were words the people here had to live by.

George threw his bag to the ground. "You told the driver to stop."

Tristan smiled. "This is a small community. We should visit the sites, get to know some people. We'll talk about Beijing, a free Tibet, organic food. With any luck, we'll bump into a few revolutionaries."

"This is not smart."

"I told you. There's a crackdown. You're not going to find anybody in the cities. This town has one public security bureau. I don't think they have guns."

"What are we going to see around here?"

"There's a monument to Chairman Mao right in front of you. Turn around. There's a post office, a mobile phone center—even an Avon store. Would you like some cosmetics?"

"Do I look like I need some? Point me in the direction of the nearest four-star hotel."

Tristan obliged. He found the best room in town: a deluxe suite listed at six hundred fifty yuan. Tristan negotiated down to five hundred. He talked the hostess into putting extra soap and towels in the room. He said, "It's for my friend. He's a little particular." The woman smirked.

She said, "That's what they all say."

"It's not like that," explained Tristan. "We went to school together."

"I'm happy for you."

Tristan asked about the local bazaar. The hostess told him he was in luck. Tomorrow was Sunday. The crowds would spill onto the main road. It couldn't be missed. Tristan thanked her.

The next morning, Tristan left George sound asleep. He walked onto the main road. Beyond the monument to Chairman Mao, men crowded around a cow on its side. Tristan joined them. The cow's legs were tied. One man was carrying a huge knife. He crouched next to the beast's neck. With the edge of his blade, he felt for the end of the jaw.

A girl came to watch. She had blond hair. Tristan smiled. The man sliced through the beast's neck. Blood sprayed. The girl jumped back. She couldn't have been more than eight. Tristan thought her pretty. The blood started gushing from the gaping hole. The cow grunted. The men had to hold her down.

Blood pooled along the poorly-graded street. It mixed with dirt and dew. It spread close to Tristan's shoes. He stepped back. Somebody showed up with a hose. Tristan inquired about live camels. The man gestured beyond the donkey carts.

By mid-morning, George was out of bed. The hostess told him where to go. He was surprised to find the bazaar bustling with people. He bought himself some pomegranate juice.

Tristan spotted him. He shouted, "We're going for a trip." George sipped from his cup. Tristan came up to him. He said, "I bought a pair of camels. I found a guy with a truck. He'll take us north to the village. From there, we're going into the desert."

"What," asked George, "is in the desert?"

Tristan smiled. "Weren't you listening to Polina? There's an archeological site."

George took another sip. "This is why we're here? To visit your Russian girlfriend?"

"She digs you, man—no pun intended."

The guy with the truck was Chinese. Tristan asked him to take the scenic route along the river bed. The man shook his head. He couldn't afford it. "Too bumpy," he explained. "You will give the camels tits." The man smiled. He was missing most of his teeth.

Tristan agreed to settle for the desert highway. As they drove down it, they could see sand stretching to infinity. The fifty-yard-deep walls of shrub on either side seemed comically insufficient. The driver wouldn't shut up about them. "Nobody think we can do it," he said. "Everybody in West say, 'You crazy.' Chinese man do it. We give proof to world of great superiority of China technology innovation. We develop over three hundred technique to build road. Three hundred. You see.

"Go to America. Tell them how beautiful road is in China. They will not believe. It is. I ask you: two things man build and see from space? One, Great Wall of China. Two, Great Highway in Tarim Basin, also in China—but more important: my province, Xinjiang. Long live Xinjiang. Long live China."

They passed a house with a red roof. Three minutes later, they passed another one. The driver explained they were pumping stations. People signed up to live and work in them for six months. Officially, his cousins lived in three of them. Unofficially, one lived in Shanghai; another in Beijing. The third ran a brothel in Quiemo. They each earned eighty dollars a month. They split it equally with him. He smiled. "Big money."

They passed a gas station. A few minutes later, they stopped. The road was blocked. A six-wheeled cab-over-engine truck pulling an even longer trailer was overturned. There was no way around. The dunes were too thick on either side. A policeman from the local security bureau told them a bulldozer was on its way.

A man drove by on a motorcycle. George watched him weave and dart through the sand. He leapt over the dunes. George groaned. "What are we doing with camels?" he asked. "We need two of those."

"True," said Tristan. "It's a shame they don't sell that model in the U.S.. The brakes are good. It's got steel rims, a solid engine guard; the front forks have stiffer springs than previous models. It's sleek. The speedometer shows the correct speed. In and of itself, that makes it one of the best dual-purpose bikes on the market."

"What makes you such an expert?"

"The Marine Corps purchased them a while back. They were refitted to run on aviation fuel. The manufacturer promised a civilian version. I've been waiting for it for years. It's got twice the fuel economy."

George huffed. "Don't tell me you've gone green."

"The original gas tank cut into the frame. To get to the fuel reserve, you would have to tip the entire bike on its side. Your mother got tired of falling off."

George humphed. The bulldozer showed up. It pushed the overturned trailer out of the way. The truck squeezed by. A few kilometers down the road, they turned west. Thick, stunted poplars dotted the horizon. By the time they reached the village, the ground was rife with seaberry and dogbane.

The driver quoted a proverb. Tristan turned to George. "I think he made it up himself. He says, 'Let your friends feast on the first. Make your enemies toast you with the other.'"

"Why is that?" asked George. "Is dogbane poisonous?"

"It's used to treat high blood pressure," said Tristan.

They stopped in front of a concrete building. It was the only concrete in sight. The other side of the road hosted two wattle and daub huts. They were restaurants. One had a special on bread; the other, soup. George huffed. "They look like muddy shoe-boxes."

"When you were a child," said Tristan, "did you ever bring home bugs from the yard? This is what it was like for them."

Tristan took down the camels. The driver told him the best way to arrange a return trip was to send a villager to the bazaar. Tristan thanked him.

George watched the truck turn around. Its suspension bobbed. Metal clashed. Dust leapt into the air. The hulking frame disappeared behind its own trail of smoke. The weary moan of the drive train cut into George's soul.

"Come on," said Tristan. "The site's more than twenty-five miles away. We need to get moving."

They crossed to the far side of the nearest field. They shadowed the road north. George wondered why they hadn't just kept driving.

Tristan explained, "I wanted you to practice your camel-riding before taking you into the desert. You're not used to mounting an animal with two humps."

George scoffed. "It's better when they don't smell like stale pee."

"Let's hope the next one doesn't."

"Do you honestly think this will help?"

"Women love it when you show interest in their work."

"I'm talking about coming all the way out here to practice my riding."

"I didn't want you to fall in front of the villagers. You want to impress them. If I had taken you straight into the desert, you might have been thrown onto the sand. I might not have heard you. The last thing you would have seen before dying of exposure would have been a camel's toe. Is that what you want? To almost make it?"

"You're right," said George. "I'm not a ladies' man. I'm comfortable in groups. I split bills. I sweat. I iron my socks."

The camels groaned. It took Tristan and George an hour to reach the edge of the desert. Mottled grey bricks began gleaming in the distance. Tristan spotted two thirty-foot towers. They were flanking a half-domed portal. The doors were aqua blue. "This is it," he said. "Polina mentioned the mosque. It's supposed to be a popular pilgrimage destination. She called it 'the Mecca of the East.'"

"Looks lonely."

"We should stay here for the night."

"You said we could make it in a day."

"We started late. This will give you a chance to wash your feet."

The imam charged three dollars for a room. George thought it was overpriced. He pulled back the sheet on his bed. "This isn't a bed," he said. "It's a door on a stack of bricks. The hinges are attached."

"I'm sorry," said Tristan. "Did you notice the goat skull outside? It was on the ground. Whatever complaints it had, it now keeps to itself."

"What is your point?"

"Respect your surroundings."

George didn't listen. In the morning, Tristan woke to the sounds of shouting. Somebody was upset. George was standing by the window.

"What's going on?" asked Tristan.

"How should I know? I don't get anything. You say this is some kind of holy site. I went walking this morning. I saw old rags hanging from dead trees. It was disgusting."

Fear tinged with shame welled in Tristan's stomach. He said, "George, what did you do?"

"Nothing any decent bloke wouldn't have done. I picked up the garbage. I threw it into the furnace."

157

Tristan held his head in his hands. "Those rags," he said. He looked up. "They were offerings for the dead." George stared blankly. "You desecrated one of the holiest sites in East Turkestan."

"That explains the shouting."

Tristan and George ran to their camels. The imam appeared in the portal. He was shaking his fist. George and Tristan rode west. At the end of the wall, they turned north. They reached the end of the complex. Ridges of sand rose in every direction. A tunnel carved its way toward the desert. Another tunnel led back to the mosque. The imam emerged at its mouth. He was still shaking his fist. Tristan kicked his heels into his camel.

George winced. "I don't think we can make it," he cried. It was too late to stop Tristan. He neared the tunnel to the desert. He ducked. His head squeezed through. George kicked his heels. He closed his eyes. He ducked. He heard hooves clattering against paving stone. On the other side, he felt the warmth of the sun. He was alive. He opened his eyes. A gigantic ridge of sand stretched in front of him. Tristan was climbing it.

George followed. On the other side, he found another ridge. On the other side of that one, another, and so forth. After a while, Tristan stopped. He looked puzzled. He said, "Where are we?"

George squinted. "Don't tell me you don't know. You said all we had to do was follow the river."

"In case you haven't noticed," said Tristan. "The river is underground."

"Weren't you checking the compass?"

"Not from the beginning. If we're off by even the slightest bit, we're doomed. Polina could be over the next dune and we wouldn't know it."

"Why don't we head towards the road?"

Tristan shook his head. "The road turned east when we went west. It could be fifty miles from here."

"Should we retrace our steps?"

"Call."

"What would I say?"

"It doesn't matter."

"It could cost me my job."

"You don't have to call the office."

"Don't be gullible. You think they don't have a tap on me?"

"Do you want to be embarrassed or dead?" George took out the phone. He decided to call his sister. "Tell her," said Tristan, "we were being chased by a gun-toting imam."

"Cathy? How are you? I'm good. I'm lost. I'm in the field. I was wondering if you could help. Exactly. Thank you. I'm in the desert—the Taklamakan—in western China. I know. I was supposed to meet somebody. He didn't show up. I can hold." George pulled back the phone. "She's bringing up the satellite."

"Excellent."

George looked up the longitude and the latitude on his phone. He sent the information via text. Tristan heard Cathy say, "Hello?"

"I'm here," said George. "Did you get the coordinates. Good. I'll tell you later. Remember when I got lost around the Capital? There was a Second Street on both sides. Sort of like that—except with sand."

Tristan looked to the sky. "Can she see us?" He waved.

"It's not a live feed, moron. Sorry, Cathy—not you. What's that? Thanks. Love you, too. Give my best to Mother. Good-bye."

"What did she say?"

"The road is south-southeast. It's not far. If we don't waste time, we can make it to one of the pumping stations." Tristan laughed. "What's so funny?"

"You make one phone call, George. You hear one familiar voice. Now you're bursting with confidence."

"There's nothing wrong with that."

"It's what got us into this mess."

"Am I the one who stopped the bus?"

"I told you coming to China was foolish. You didn't want to listen."

"It was worth a try."

"You assumed poor, oppressed people would want to see you. You have all the money and all the toys."

"I came to help."

"Without understanding, help is a hindrance."

"Why did you lead us into the desert?"

"Why did you desecrate a holy shrine?"

Arguing was useless. It was too hot. Tristan turned south-southeast. George followed. The camels marched on. At some point, Tristan spotted timber. It was reinforcing a hole in the side of a dune. "A dugout," he cried. "We should take cover."

Tristan reached the hole. Dismounting his camel, he climbed in. He felt a draft. It was wonderful. The chamber was dark. Tristan ventured deeper. He stretched his hands. He felt a wall. It was brick. It was cold. Tristan smiled. "It's a building," he said. "It's been buried by sand."

"I can't see anything," said George. He was standing in the hole.

"Do you feel a draft? There must be a window." Tristan ran his hand along the brick. He found a curtain. He opened it. "A back door," he cried. Tristan crawled through. The passage was short and tight. On the other side, a large dune blocked the view. A crawlspace led to the left. Tristan decided to climb the sand.

George came up through the passage. "What do you see?" he asked.

Tristan reached the top. He smiled. Turning to George, he said, "The highway—it's not far." He glanced at the dimples his feet had left in the sand. There were identical marks in the crawlspace. They led around the dugout. Tristan stared at them. He whispered, "Uh-oh."

George noticed them. He looked at Tristan. They said, "The camels." They rushed back into the building. They stumbled over each other in the dark. They reached the entrance. They poked their heads out in time to see a man driving their camels over the top of the nearest dune. He disappeared.

"My phone," said George. "My passport. My diplomatic badge."

"The water," said Tristan. He pulled George inside. "We can't afford to stay," he said. "That man is probably part of some smuggling network. They don't like strangers."

"It's too hot to go out there without water," said George.

"It's not far to the road," said Tristan. "If one of us collapses, the other might be able to get help." He crawled through the back door. George followed. Tristan climbed the dune. George climbed after him. Tristan reached the top. He saw the highway to the east. He went south. George was confused. He reached the top. He saw trucks driving on the highway.

"I hate to ask this again," he said. "Why aren't we being driven? Couldn't somebody just pick us up?"

"If by being picked up you mean getting kidnapped," said Tristan. "Who knows who's out there? I'll take my chances in the heat. I'll reach civilization on my own two legs."

George conceded the point. After what seemed like an eternity, they reached a pumping station. Tristan knocked on the door. He knocked again. "Just our luck," said George. "Our driver's cousin lives here."

They walked through the rows of shrubs. George spotted a functioning dripline. He fell to his face getting to it. Tristan watched him kneel, cupping his hands like a schoolboy. He was counting the drips. Tristan wanted to say something. He decided it was too hot to bother.

George grinned. He had enough for a decent swig. With exquisite care, he brought the water to his lips. He threw back his head. He slurped. He gagged. He spat. He retched. He wiped his chin. He looked at Tristan. He said, "It's salty." Tristan nodded.

They kept going. The gas station appeared on the horizon. George staggered towards it. "Is it a mirage?" he asked.

Tristan was barely able to shake his head. He whispered, "I don't think so."

"I mean the convenience store."

"No," said Tristan. "It was there before."

Step by step, the station grew bigger. It looked real. George and Tristan got closer. They saw people. They were walking. Some of them were pumping gas. A few of them exchanged words with each other. George and Tristan headed towards the store. They reached the door. They both grabbed the handle. It was real. They pulled. Nothing happened. They were pulling in opposite directions. Tristan tried to push George away. George refused to let go. He tried to push Tristan. They both fell to their knees. They tried pulling again. It was useless. It was too hard for them to cooperate. A customer had to open the door for them. George and Tristan crawled inside.

They headed towards the refrigerators. George muttered, "Water." Tristan groaned, "I don't think these people understand English."

"What," asked George, "is the Chinese word for water?"

"It's shoe-eh."

"Shoe, eh?"

"As in, Feng Shoe-eh."

"You mean, Feng-Shway?"

"No, Shoe-eh."

"Shhweh?"

"That's the word for tax."

"What's shway?"

"Nothing."

"Get outta here."

They reached the refrigerators. It took an enormous amount of concentration to open the door. They each grabbed a plastic jug of water. As soon as liquid touched their lips, their heads were seemingly pulled from the sand. Each gulp brought them a step closer to steady ground. Half the water ended up on the floor. It didn't matter. They wanted to bathe in its coolness. The jugs were empty within seconds. They took fresh ones. Tristan turned to the speechless clerk. "Don't worry," he said. "We'll clean it up."

They never got the chance. Four masked men burst into the station. One of them smacked George in the head. Tristan held up his hands. It didn't help. He was knocked out.

When Tristan regained consciousness, he couldn't see. He was blindfolded. His hands were tied. He was in the back seat of a car. Tristan concentrated on the road. It had to be the desert highway. He was sure of it. No other road could be so smooth. His driver had made a point of mentioning it. The sun was to Tristan's right. It was sunset—no question about it. They were heading south. They turned west. They were heading towards town. Tristan heard vehicles. It was the traffic circle. They turned right. They were entering an Uyghur neighborhood.

The car stopped. Somebody got out. A gate opened. The vehicle rolled into what Tristan assumed was a courtyard. The door next to him opened. Somebody pulled him out. He was led unceremoniously up a few steps, and through a door, and into a room—there was commotion. Tristan was dropped onto a carpet. Somebody fell next to him.

"George?"

"Yes."

"Are you alright?"

Somebody yelled. Tristan assumed he meant, "Quiet!" He took the advice. Minutes turned into hours. Somebody approached. He knelt in front of Tristan. He took off the blindfold. Tristan blinked. It was a boy. He crawled over to George. Tristan took in his surroundings. He was on the floor of what seemed like somebody's living room. The walls were decorated with rugs. George gasped. He had a black eye.

Tristan asked, "Is it painful?" George smirked. A man came into the room. He was holding up a digital video camera. He pointed it at George. He watched him on his flipped out viewscreen. He zoomed in. He zoomed out. He shook his head. He yelled out a few harsh words. He told the boy something. He left. The boy put back the blindfolds.

"Don't sweat it," said Tristan. "These guys look like amateurs."

"That's what troubles me," said George.

Somebody came back. The boy took off George's blindfold.

"What's going on?" asked Tristan.

"It's a woman. She's got some make-up with her."

"Let me see."

"Damn it. If you need to know, she's pretty. For a terrorist, she's very pretty."

The woman shushed him. She whispered a few words. Tristan cocked his head. He recognized the language. It was Kyrgyz. His girlfriend often used the same phrase to plead with him when they went shopping, "A moment, please."

Tristan chuckled. He said in Russian, "Make-up. Your father would never approve."

The woman stopped whatever she was doing. Tristan imagined her staring at him. She said, "Why would you say that?"

Tristan smiled. "I know it for a fact."

"How?"

"Your sister told me."

"I don't have a sister."

"She'd be disappointed to hear you say that."

"If you know me so well, what color are my eyes?"

"Brown—just like your sister's."

"Lots of girls have brown eyes."

"They don't all share the same totem."

"How would I know? I worship Allah."

"I understand," said Tristan. "I didn't go for it myself—until your father told me I was sent by it. He wants to make me his son-in-law."

"Why's that?"

"Your sister—I'm sorry, I forgot you don't have one—his daughter says it's the way I ride my motorcycle. I can tell you it's not from twitching my nose."

George watched the woman shake her head in disbelief. He wondered what the two of them were saying. The woman whispered, "Who are you?"

"I would love to introduce myself," said Tristan. "As long as it's eye to eye."

The woman removed Tristan's blindfold. Tristan paused a moment before opening his eyes. He smiled. Adi's photo hardly did her justice. She was gorgeous. "Are you sure you don't have a sister?" he asked. "She says you play the jigatch very well." The woman puffed in disbelief. "She says you should never have given it up." She shook her head. "My name is Tristan. Tristan Kalvis. This is my associate, George Hausmann." Tristan said in English, "Say hello, George."

"Excuse me," said George. "What the hell is going on?"

"This," said Tristan, "is Adi." The woman was shocked to hear her name.

George looked her over. He mumbled, "How do you do?"

Tristan said, "I've been dating her sister."

George jerked his head. He knit his eyebrows. Turning to Adi, he asked, quite seriously, "Is that why we're here?"

Tristan laughed. He asked Adi if he and George were going to be killed. Adi gathered her wits. She stammered, "I don't know. I don't think they've decided. They were discussing it. They want to hold you for ransom."

"Your father doesn't have that kind of money," said Tristan. "He's dead set on having me for a son-in-law." Adi couldn't believe what was happening. Tristan asked, "Were you going to post us on the web?" Adi could barely bring herself to shrug.

"I'm not a kidnapper," she said. "They just wanted me to cover the eye."

"Were you threatened?"

"Can you tell him I'm sorry?"

Tristan turned to George. He said, "She wants you to know she's sorry."

"Thanks," said George. "Now tell me what the hell is going on."

Tristan turned to Adi. He said, "We work for the president of the United States. If we become friends, we can help each other. What do you say?"

Adi turned away. She brought her hand to her temple. She shook her head. She bit her lip. She turned back to Tristan. She said, "I guess my sister could have done worse. What should I do?"

"What can you do?" asked Tristan. "Who's in charge?"

"Nobody. They're boys. They're not bad. I told them how dumb they are. They saw you at the market. One of them had the bright idea to kidnap you. They weren't going to do it. They knew it was stupid. It's only because they say you half-dead on the highway. They decided to wait for you at the station. I guess they talked themselves into it." She shook her head. "Do you know what they're doing now? They're watching television. They're trying to decide which news channel should get the videotape of you being held hostage. They don't have a gun to wave at you. They knocked you out with a stuffed shoe."

"Will they let us go?"

"Of course." Adi left the room.

George turned to Tristan. "Well?"

"I told them we could help."

"What do you mean?"

"You're in the market for revolutionaries. This is our chance to make some."

"We're prisoners."

"Not if we can make a deal."

"I don't want you to give them any promises."

Tristan laughed. "Do you hear the cavalry coming? One way or another, we're going to cooperate."

"Name, rank, and serial number—that's it."

"Don't be a douche."

Adi came back. She untied them. She invited them to the kitchen. "Would you like something to drink? How about tea?"

"I'd love some. George, would you like some tea?"

"If it's got sugar in it—I have a headache."

They passed a room. There was a crowd of boys arguing around a television set.

"George," said Tristan. "Do you mind watching TV for a while? I have something I'd like to discuss with this young, beautiful woman. I promise I won't be long." George squinted. He didn't want to go in. Tristan beckoned. "Remember: play nicely. If you have any problems, I'll be in the next room." George was too confused to argue.

Tristan turned to Adi. "Why do these boys trust you? What's your secret?"

Adi laughed. "I'm their spiritual sister, I guess. They think I know everything."

"Why?"

Adi shrugged. "They must see something in me."

"It can't be just your beauty. They don't care that you're foreign?"

"They're young. They used to hang around the Avon store. My manager made me deal with them."

"By joining their gang?"

"They've been harmless until now."

"What are you hiding?"

"You wouldn't understand."

"Try me."

"Are you familiar with the Fragrant Concubine?" Tristan shook his head. "She was an Uighur woman, famed for both her beauty and her natural scent. She was unfortunately discovered by the Chinese emperor. The Chinese like to say she was given to him as a gift. The Uyghur tend to disagree."

Tristan smiled sheepishly. "I think I know where this is going."

"The Chinese say the Emperor went to great lengths to please her. He had her entire village re-created with a functioning mosque and a bazaar. Jujube trees were imported. They bore golden fruit. The Uyghur say the concubine didn't care for it. She kept daggers up her sleeves, prepared to strike the emperor at any moment. The Chinese say she eventually fell in love. She bore him children. Whatever the case was, the Uyghur are convinced the Empress Dowager had her eunuchs strangle her to death."

"I can't wait for the animated version."

"I was getting to that. Scientists reconstructed her face from what were supposedly her bones. It was all over the news. The boys in there think I look like her."

Tristan smiled. He leaned in close. He inhaled. He whispered, "You don't smell so bad either." Adi giggled.

It wasn't long before Tristan took George aside. He said, "I have a plan. Twenty-four hours a day, tankers drive down the desert highway. They're full of oil. If we help these people steal some of it, they can sell it to Kyrgyz caravans. Adi's tribe crosses the border every week. We can make arrangements with the refinery in Jalal-Abad. They will buy it. We could fund ourselves an insurgency. Congress would never have to get its hands dirty. Everybody wins—except the Chinese."

George shook his head. "Even if we could somehow bribe somebody at the fields, the executives would get involved. It's not worth the risk."

"They wouldn't even know what's missing."

"How is that possible?"

"We'd be skimming it off the top."

"Of what?"

"Of the trucks."

"When?"

Tristan's mouth curled into a mischievous grin. He said, "While they're on the road." The audacity of the plan dawned on George. Tristan said, "What's three or four barrels from every tanker? To the Chinese in Korla, it's a mistake, a faulty meter, a bad reading. To these people, it could be a fortune."

"It's insane."

"Haven't you seen a fighter jet refuel in mid-flight?"

"Washington would never agree."

"Don't give them a choice. By the time they sit down to talk about it, we'll have a warehouse of oil. There's a fuel equipment supplier in Urumqi. I'll try to get as much as I can on credit."

"Whose? Your Chinese driver's?"

"His brother-in-law runs a repair shop."

"This is ridiculous."

"I'll need some cash to prop him up."

"I can't use company funds without-"

"I'm not talking about a war chest. Take it from your personal account if you have to."

"My what?"

"This is all for your sake, George. You are going to be the toast of the entire Washington intelligence community."

"You can't talk me into this."

"The security assistance officer in Bishkek has contacts with the refinery. He'll know what to do. Adi's father can make arrangements with the tribesmen. Trust me. He's very persuasive."

"Tristan, this is going nowhere."

"George," said Tristan. He rocked him by the shoulder. "You will be known as the father of East Turkestan. All you have to do is write a check."

George sighed. "What's this driver's name?"

Tristan smiled. He said, "Cash."

George left for Bishkek. Tristan made the trip to Urumqi. He ordered supplies. He had the tankers shadowed. He trained his crew.

"Remember," he told them. "Replace the chained cap. Don't drop the old one. We don't want to leave any cause for suspicion."

Tailgating at speeds of over two hundred kilometers an hour, the men practiced climbing onto the hood of their truck. They grew skilled at cutting chains, unplugging valves, attaching hoses—all the while, their faces whipped by blowing sand.

At home, they bragged. They described how their hair snapped like ten thousand snakes frightened by the wrath of Allah. Tristan and Adi beamed like proud parents.

The day came to attempt their first heist. Tristan couldn't be there. He had to give himself an alibi. He made arrangements for "Cash" to wait for his call at the hotel lobby. He left Adi's car along the desert highway with a flat. He hitched a ride to the gas station with a stranger. Before heading to the telephone, Tristan stopped by the restroom. Of the two stalls, one was taken. The other was soiled. Tristan wiped the seat as well as he could. He turned. He dropped his pants. He sat. The man next door was wearing expensive shoes. They looked familiar. Tristan chuckled. He said, "Nice shoes."

"Tristan?"

"George?"

"What the hell are you doing?"

"What are you doing?"

"They stopped me at the border. They're holding me as a witness."

"To what?"

"To our own kidnapping. The investigator brought guards from a special armed police unit. They have sub-machine guns."

"How many of them are there?"

"Two. He's got a guy from the local PSB as well. You were wrong about them. They have guns. This one has a nine millimeter."

"Are they looking for me?"

"Don't worry. I saw the sketch. They got your nose all wrong."

"So you didn't make it to Jalal-Abad."

"I barely made it to this restroom."

"It doesn't matter. Today's only the first heist."

"You're kidding. Where?"

"North of here."

"When?"

"Soon."

"You've got to stop it."

"Impossible."

"We're heading up the road in a humvee. This guy drives like a maniac. If we pass your team while they're on the back of a tanker, we're done." George was right. He added, "You have to do something."

"Hold on."

"Forget about wiping."

Tristan burst from the stall. He climbed through the bathroom window. He peeked around the corner. Two armed men were milling in front of the entrance to the store. There was a humvee parked next to them.

"What am I going to do?" thought Tristan. He looked around. There was a man tanking a sedan. He was too close to the humvee—there was no time to find keys. A guy in a truck—too far away—too ready to drive off. A car pulled in—behind him, a young man on a motorcycle. Tristan recognized him. It was the man from the accident.

Tristan took another look around the corner. George was coming out of the station. A man in a tight uniform was next to him. He was escorting George to the humvee.

There was no time. The motorcycle couldn't outrun the humvee. The only way Tristan could get ahead of it was to leave now. For the first time in his life, he was grateful the gas tank cut into the frame. With a little bit of luck, there would be enough fuel to get somewhere.

Tristan shot towards the bike. The man had stopped twenty yards away. He had killed the engine. He was taking off his helmet. Tristan reached him in two seconds. He yanked him off. "Sorry," he said. He climbed on. He kicked the starter. The engine fired.

Tristan sped down the road. He heard shouting behind him. He saw the humvee in his rear-view mirror. It was taking off in pursuit.

"Now what," thought Tristan. There was a truck in the distance. Tristan thought about hijacking it. If he could somehow flip it over— he shook his head. That was ludicrous.

Tristan sped up. He got close to the truck. There was a tarp over its bed. He came alongside. He peeked underneath the canvas. There was something green. It was a watermelon. The truck was full of them. If he dumped them, thought Tristan, the humvee might crash. At the very least, it would slow it down.

Tristan dropped behind the tailgate. It was being held up by bolts. He sped up to one side. He stretched out his hand. He grabbed a hold of the bolt on that end. He pulled it as hard as he could. It refused to budge. It was capped with a nut.

Tristan kicked the bike into neutral. He grabbed the bolt with one hand; the nut with the other. He twisted. He could see the humvee getting closer. "Come on," he whispered. He kept turning his hand as fast as it would go.

The nut flew off. Tristan pulled out the bolt. He grabbed his handlebars. He dropped back. He kicked the bike into gear. He came up along the other side. He grabbed the bolt. The nut—it was stuck. It wouldn't turn. The humvee was closing in. Tristan grunted. The nut— it budged. It turned. Tristan twisted it. The humvee was on top of him. Tristan's hand couldn't go any faster. The humvee was right behind him. He could hear the window rolling down. The nut—it came loose. Tristan pulled the bolt. He leaned away. He pushed the throttle. The tailgate crashed. Melons flew. They bounced off each other. They exploded onto the humvee's windshield.

Tristan saw it in his mirror. He zoomed to the front of the truck.

He cut in front of it. The driver tapped the brakes. He saw Tristan speeding off. He hit the gas. Watermelons poured. The driver noticed it in his mirror. He panicked. He floored the brakes. The humvee almost crashed.

Tristan kept going. He realized he was running out of fuel. On the road, he would be helpless. In the desert, he might stand a chance. If he were lucky, he could reach the mosque. Adi was there praying for the success of the mission. She could help.

Tristan stopped. He pushed the idling motorcycle towards the west. The humvee was four hundred yards away. It was moving out from behind the truck. It was gaining speed. The armed police wanted more. Tristan hoped they were foolish enough to follow. He leaned down. The petcock valve was already in the reserve position.

Tristan straightened up. It was going to be close. The humvee was barreling towards him. He squeezed the clutch. He placed his foot on the gear pedal. He pushed all the way down. He twisted the throttle. He curved his lips into a slight smile. Whoever was behind that wheel, he was trying to run him over. Tristan remembered his time at the Pentagon. He had written a press release once about a drunk-driving marine. His humvee had left skid marks for twenty yards at that speed. If this man wanted to avoid a collision, he would have to hit the brakes now. He didn't. Tristan released the clutch. His tire screeched. Like a mad march hare, he leapt towards the dunes. The humvee careened to a halt. It paused only for a moment. It turned west. It burst into the sand.

Tristan weaved through the shrubs. The humvee tore through them. In the barren desert, it was no contest. Tristan jumped cleanly over every ridge. The humvee plowed them over. After a few minutes, Tristan no longer saw the vehicle—only the plume of sand it sent spiraling into the air. With each jump, the poplars in the distance grew bigger.

All of a sudden, the motorcycle jerked. Tristan felt an onset of dread. The engine was going to stall. He checked behind him. It was clear. The bike was slowing down. He had no choice. He stopped. The engine stalled. "Damn it," he cried. He got off. He leaned the bike to its side. Fuel from the cut-off compartment sloshed toward the petcock valve. He lifted up the frame. He got on. The humvee crashed past the dune behind him. He kicked the starter. Nothing. He tried again. His heart dropped into his pants. One more time—the engine sparked. The tires kicked up sand.

Somebody fired. The mirror cracked. They were shooting at him. Tristan leaned to the left. Tsiga-tsiga-tsiga! Wisps of sand shot into the air. They were firing sub-machine guns. Tristan went over a ridge. The mosque's towers gleamed in the distance. He was close.

Tsiga-tsiga-tsiga! Tristan zoomed around a dune. There were trees. He headed towards the thickest patch. The humvee swerved behind him. It trampled over shrubs. Tsiga-tsiga-tsiga! Bullets dashed into the sand. Tristan felt one zip by his ear. "This is it," he thought. He reached the trees. He started weaving between the narrow trunks. Passing bullets sheared off their bark. The humvee had to move to the side. This was Tristan's chance. He made a bee-line for the back of the mosque. Tsiga-tsiga-tsiga! He flew over a dune. One last ridge, he thought. Tsiga-tsiga-tsiga!

He was right. Tristan leapt over the ridge. The tunnel was below him. He came down the slope. He drove into the ruins. He stopped in front of the other tunnel. He dropped the motorcycle. He ran into the courtyard There was a set of open gates on the other side. It led to another yard. He heard the humvee roll up to the outside tunnel. He heard car doors slamming. He was at the door of the mosque. He stopped. He leaned down. He untied his shoes. He took them off. He placed them neatly in the corner. Adi opened the door.

"Thank God," she cried. "What's going on?"

"Armed police. They have George." Tristan went inside.

"What's he doing here?"

"Never mind." Tristan ran to one of the windows. "There's four of them. One is from the local PSB." Tristan saw the imam shuffling around. "Ask him if there's another way out. I could slip past the shrine. Maybe find one of those dugouts." Tristan groaned. "This is insane. They'll put up roadblocks. I'm toast."

"You'll have to stop them here," said Adi.

"With what?"

Adi held her tongue. Tristan realized the imam was behind him. He turned around. The man was holding out an AK-47.

Tristan was speechless. The man nudged the weapon towards him. Tristan took it. He said, "Thank you." He found a way to climb to the roof. He crawled towards the edge. In the shade of a poplar tree, he watched his enemy fan out in the courtyard.

The investigator was in the middle. He was holding up an automatic pistol. He was flanked on either side by the submachine-gun-wielding guards. He stepped forward. George and the man from the PSB were out of sight.

The imam entered through the gate.

Tristan thought, "What is he doing?"

The investigator shouted, "Stop. We're looking for a terrorist. We know he's here in your mosque. Bring him out to us." The imam said he knew of no terrorists. "I know you're lying. You're harboring a criminal. If you don't cooperate with us, you'll end up in prison."

Tristan spotted Adi in the opposite corner of the courtyard. She was on top of the wall. "How did she get there?" thought Tristan. There was a rock in her hand. She was going to try to throw it at the guard closest to her.

Tristan aimed his gun at the man. He wasn't that close. If Adi missed, he would turn around and shoot her. "What about the other one?" he thought. "He could see the rock in the corner of his eye." He switched aim. He second-guessed himself. He switched back. There was no time. Adi was swinging her arm. "Damn it," thought Tristan. She threw. Tristan switched aim again. He fired. His target fell. The officer turned. Tristan aimed at him. He ran out of sight. Somebody else fired. It was Adi's guard. Tristan looked. Adi had not only missed, she had fallen into the yard. The guard was running towards her. Tristan aimed. He fired. He shot him.

Somebody yelled, "What's going on?" It was the man from the PSB.

"The roof," cried the officer. Tristan fired as close as he could to the man. Adi got up off the ground. She was in pain. Her leg hurt. She limped towards the gates. Tristan fired again. He watched Adi disappear into the other yard. He fired one last time. He crawled backwards. He jumped to the ground. He ran around to the ruins. In a low growl, he said "Ey-hey, an-may. Air-way are oo-yay?" There was no answer. He said a bit louder, "I ed-say, air-way are oo-yay?" Nothing. He shouted, "Ey, Orge-gay. Say something."

George said in a loud voice, "I think he's back there." Somebody shushed him.

A head popped out from the tunnel. It was the man from the PSB. Tristan recognized him from the accident on the desert highway. He looked frightened.

Tristan said in Chinese, "Help us. We'll pay." The man spotted Tristan. "We're from America. We work for the president. We'll make you the richest man in town. You'll get away with it. Trust me. Lower your gun." The officer looked back into the tunnel.

Tristan heard George say, "Don't look at me. I don't speak a word of Chinese."

The officer pulled George out by his arm. Holding him close, he lowered his gun. Tristan crept forward. He asked George if he were alright.

"It's my pants I'm worried about. They'll never be clean again."

Tristan lowered his AK-47. He asked in Chinese, "Where's the other one?" The officer waved his gun towards the tunnel. Tristan stepped to the edge. He craned his head around the corner. There was nobody.

Tristan turned his back on the man. Creeping towards the other end, he wondered if he had made a mistake. "Stop!" cried the officer. "Put down your gun." Tristan paused. He was in greed's hands now. "I said put down your gun." He did it. "I've got him!"

The investigator popped into view. He stepped into the tunnel. He pulled Adi in with him. "Take care of this one," he said. He pushed Adi towards the officer. He told Tristan to put his hands on his head. He obeyed. He was told to get down. Thinking about it, he took too long. The investigator knocked him to his knees with the butt of his pistol.

Tristan felt a foot on his back. He was kicked to his hands. He was bopped on the skull for good measure. Tristan winced. He wondered what was taking so long. A shot rang out. The investigator collapsed. Blood squirted from the back of his head.

Tristan looked around. Adi held the policeman's pistol—her arms stretched out, a look of unmitigated shock plastered on her face. Everybody held his breath. After a moment, the policeman took back the gun.

Tristan murmured, "Nice shot."

They threw the bodies into the back of the humvee. They drove the car into the desert. Tristan plowed it into the side of a dune. He cut the fuel lines. He placed the spare tire around the investigator's head—"just to be sure," he said. He lit the fuel on fire. Everything burned. Once the flames had died down, everybody helped cover the smoldering wreck with sand.

Adi had brought with her a dead branch. She stuck it into the top of the mound. She tore a piece of cloth from her dress. With a somber look, she tied it to the stake.

George felt compelled to do the same. He tried to tear off a bit of his shirt. The cloth refused to rip. He tried several times. Adi offered to help. George insisted he could do it. He attempted to use his teeth. It hurt his mouth. George took off the shirt. He put a foot on one sleeve. He tugged it as hard as he could. "I can't believe it," he said. He looked at the policeman. "It was made in China." Eventually, it tore.

George tied the sleeve to the branch with an awkward solemnity. He looked ridiculous with one sleeve.

Tristan reached into his pants. He tore off a square of fabric from his boxer shorts. He pinned it onto the branch.

The policeman didn't want to stick out. Ripping the manufacturer's tag from his tie, he wrapped it around the branch and knotted it.

Back at the mosque, Tristan had George call the hotel. Cash was still waiting in the lobby. "Finally," he said. "It's time and a half for making me wait."

The policeman was getting agitated. He wanted the money. George told him there would be no problem getting it. Tristan was reminded about the motorcycle. He assured the officer he would return it. The policeman frowned. "I have no idea what's going on here," he said. "I don't want to know. Just get me my money."

The truck arrived. Tristan wanted to put the motorcycle in the back. The bed was full of adult toys. "Sorry," said Cash. "You told me you only needed a tow."

"Never mind," said Tristan. "Do you have a siphon?" Cash glanced at the policeman. Their eyes met. The policeman squinted. Cash looked back at Tristan. He shook his head.

Tristan sighed. "I'll find one." He searched the bed. He found a doubled-ended toy with a hollow center. It was long enough. Tristan shoved it into the tank. He looked around. Everybody was staring.

"If you think I'm going to do this in front of you," he said, "you're wrong. Get in the truck." The men slinked off into the cab. Tristan turned to Adi. "Can you find me a bucket?" She ran off. Tristan looked down. He said to himself, "What I do for democracy."

Adi came back with a bucket. "You can stay," said Tristan. He noticed Cash staring at him in the mirror. "Hey," he said. "Move that thing." Cash obliged. "Don't forget to pick me up from the station."

Tristan knelt down. He tentatively took hold of the toy. Adi pushed him back. She wrapped her lips around the tip. She sucked. She gagged. She pulled away. Gas flowed.

Adi ran off to wash her mouth. When she came back, the truck was gone. Tristan was sitting on the motorcycle.

He asked, "Will you be alright?"

Adi nodded. "I'll take the bus."

"That's not what I mean."

Adi glanced away. She said, "I'll be fine."

Tristan gave her a hard look. Adi stared back at him. Her eyes, he thought, are big and brown. They're beautiful.

Tristan started the engine. "Your father misses you," he said.

Adi gulped. "I know."

"You should think about going home."

Adi shook her head. "My sister and I would only fight."

Tristan smiled half-heartedly. He said, "You have nothing to fight about."

Adi turned away. After a moment, she looked back. She nodded. "We do."

Tristan cocked his head. He asked, "Like what?"

Adi paused. She whispered, "You."

The sun glared. The wind picked up. Adi stood. Tristan sat. The engine panted.

Tristan looked down. He started turning the bike backwards. Halfway through the turn, he stopped. He caught Adi's eyes. She held them.

Tristan kicked the motorcycle into gear. He revved the engine. Adi looked to the ground. Tristan revved it again. Adi looked up. They shared one last look. Tristan released the clutch. He sped down the road. He wondered how their boys had done.

The Alley of the Daisy Queen

by Christopher Hight

Last night, I dreamt I was in Paris.

I was in the back seat of a broad car. It was American. Cold leather warmed beneath me.

A headrest blocked my view. I turned towards the window. It was dark outside. I realized I didn't have a head. There was nothing in the glass—not even the faintest reflection. I moved my hand towards my eyes. I couldn't see it. I tried to feel my heart. My hand sank into my chest. I had no chest. I panicked. I clutched the seat. I felt the leather on either side. Slowly, I brought my hands together. My buttocks were gone. What the hell was I sitting on?

The smoothness of the leather reassured me. I stroked it. I thought of my leg: the poison ivy I once brushed pulling overgrown grape vines from the trees: the week-long rash I suffered, whose blisters having burst, whose pus having wept dry, left that spot intoxicatingly numb, sprinkled with delightfully silky bumps, a token of pain patiently endured, an itch fitfully ignored, a small triumph of will, now faded into memory, temporarily rescued from the abyss of oblivion.

I looked through the window. The shadow of trees—immense, floating, rustling things—terrified me. The feeling grew. It stretched towards me like a tube of darkness. It burst through the window. It skewered me. In vain, I grasped at the door. I was pulled into the middle of the seat.

Something darted. I turned my head. I jumped. I breathed a sigh of relief. It was the road, bathed in headlights. Somebody was driving. There was a passenger. I stretched my arms. I gripped the corners of the bucket seats. I tried to pull myself. I barely moved. My arms were powerless. I sat back.

The light emitting diodes of the console spelled out the time. It was the middle of the night. The dashboard, awash in a dim glow, seemingly floated—a stage lit with miniature footlights. It was polyvinyl chloride. It was dark—like burgundy. Hard, smooth, horizontal, finite, it complemented the straight and endless road. It was: the cross of the crucifixion. I blinked. Was that right? Was the dashboard the beam? the road, the pole plunging headlong into earth? Whither did it will me go?

I decided, no matter what occurred—should the windows rattle, should the latches snap, should metal bend, should the doors twist off their hinges, I would not be afraid.

The passenger turned. I recognized him. It was my friend, Nikky. He stared at me with wide eyes. It was a challenge. I sank into my seat. The eyes stayed fixed above, as if I had only been blocking their view. The driver turned. It was the man Nikky introduced to me as Gheorghe, the Romanian who married his cousin. They stared for a moment. Together, they faced forward.

"Last time I was here," said Nikky, "the road was empty. The Reine was on her last legs."

Gheorghe glanced over at him. "How many?"

Nikky huffed. "I could count the transvestites on one hand."

"How many real girls?"

"Not enough. A parade of would-be johns pushed me all the way through."

"What time was it?"

"Midnight."

"What time of year?"

"April. The weather was nice. It was strange. I was surprised there weren't more."

"The forest gets cold. They were huddling in the bushes."

"I doubt it. If anybody had seen anything, they would have stopped. It was a steady stream of traffic."

"They were tourists."

"That's what it felt like: a safari."

"Last year?"

"Maybe."

"Cops were around."

"They weren't raiding then, were they?"

"How would I know?"

"You don't come here often?"

"Why would I?"

"You don't like man-girls?"

"It makes me wonder about you."

"I heard from somebody who talked to somebody who knew somebody who used to work here that most of their patrons aren't gay. What do you think of that?"

"I think it's stupid. Why would it be true?"

"Maybe homosexuals think transvestites are queer or something."

"If you want one of these people, why wouldn't you be gay for wanting them?"

"How should I know? I don't touch 'em for nothin'."

"You're straight."

"They're disgusting. They're from the poorest families in Martinique or French Guiana or something."

"If that's true, why would anybody want them?"

"It's the best AJ in town: good price, no questions, no problems. These boys like their work. You can tell. Billy pops out. If he's a happy camper, it gives a proper john a good feeling. It shows it's not just about money."

"They make you use a condom."

"Of course. That's for your own good. If you don't like it, you'll need to find a real junky. They can't afford to come here—to the forest? You'd have to go to Nation Place. You wouldn't like it. They're all about money—not like these girls."

"They are not what I call girls."

"It's your schlong in somebody else's donut hole. That's what counts. I'm telling you. These girls are the best. AJ, BJ—you think it doesn't mean something to a guy who has to pay? Whoa. Here we are. Look at this. What a crowd. There's a lot of people here. Did you see that? Oh, boy!"

"It is crowded."

"These girls aren't bad."

"Look over there."

"Where? Nice. I give her a seven. The other one is ugly. I'll give her a two."

"Is that guy holding a snake?"

"You can call it that. This place has a lot of action. You have to watch out. I thought a girl back there was gonna be hot. She turned around. Her face was a mess. Just pass this guy."

"If he wants to stop, he should pull over."

"He's afraid of getting swamped. It's a buyer's market out here."

"I've never seen so much ass."

"This is incredible. Did you see that?"

"Not bad."

"That was a dude."

"You're joking."

"No."

"I don't believe you."

"Turn around. Never mind. There's too many people. You can't see anything. That girl back there was hot."

"Whatever."

"I can tell. It's hard—under these circumstances. You don't have time to see every angle. A man's gotta be careful. That one I saw back there isn't gonna last long. By the time we circle around, she'll be gone."

"This rubbernecking is insane."

"Nice butt. What the hell does she want? Don't bend over! Crap.

Let's go. Don't honk: I don't want to see that shit next to the window. Drive!"

"That was close."

"Unbelievable. Look at these babes. Is that a man?"

"I'm going to say, yes."

"What about the other one?

"The one flashing us? The one in white?"

"Look at those titties."

"You think she's a man?"

"She used to be. Did you see the one with the screwed up surgery? What was she doing?"

"Some guys like that."

"Good point. It's a freak show every way around. I'm waiting for the transmidgets to pop out."

"This guy found somebody."

"She's doesn't look too bad. I want to see the customer. I wanna make sure he deserves it."

"Is he gay?"

"He's the straightest man in the world."

"He wants ass."

"His wife doesn't treat him well."

"It's hard for guys who want a girl for anal."

"You need to know where to look."

"Where do you go?"

"Where do I go?"

"You know—where do you go?"

"You want to know where to go?"

"I don't want to know where to go. I want to know where it is—so I know."

"Where to go?"

"I don't want to go."

"What's wrong with the girl you have?"

"Nothing."

"You realize she's my cousin. She doesn't put out?"

"What?"

"She won't let you in the ass?"

"No."

"I thought so."

"I'm not saying that."

"You want it in the ass—from her."

"I don't."

"She won't give it."

"You don't understand. I could never bring it up."

"You want me to ask?"

"No."

"I'll tell you where. In my opinion, the best place is a swinger bar. Paris has great ones. You need to be lucky. Sometimes you find an orgy. Sometimes there's a bunch of women in their sixties—which I don't mind, if they're hot."

"How much is it?"

"The Euro screwed everything up. It used to be two hundred francs for the first drink—that included free condoms. You could pay six hundred for an open bar. It depended on the day. It was always cheaper if you were a couple. Some clubs only allow couples—I don't mean you and me."

"What was your favorite?"

"Le Big Smack. That joint is famous. It's been around for a while. It's near the Pantheon. They have a restaurant—not bad—it's expensive. The club is cheap. I don't think it opens until late. They're trying to keep a reputation. They don't want it ever to be empty."

"What's it like? Do people watch?"

"Not necessarily, but most of the time."

"I don't think I could take it."

"It's not for everybody. I wonder where else to send you. Don't go to one of those American bars: they'll rip your pants off. They make you buy champagne. You end up shitting money for nothing."

"What about the street?"

"The Champs is your best bet. It's hard to find—how should I put it? Palatable meat? The young girls get picked off fast. They're eager to please. The rest have warts. There are girls who actually drive around. They pick you up. They're expensive. I wonder who pimps them. I bet it's the guys on Avenue Foch. Ever been there?"

"No."

"It's alright. It's like the Bois de Vincennes only better. Instead of vans, they're parked in beamers. They're the most expensive girls in Paris. They're clean—most of the time. You get to go to an apartment. It's fun: millionaire alley. We should drive by. Where are we anyway? You turned off the road. We're in the middle of nowhere."

"Aren't you going to give Marco a call?"

"Good idea. We can't be sure where that asshole is. Whoa!"

"What?"

"Did you see that?"

"What?"

"A girl—in a white cloak."

"Where?"

"I saw her—on the edge of the light."

"What did she look like?"

"Beautiful."

"Yeah?"

"She was wearing a—whatchamacallit—a habit—like a nun."

"She was dressed like a nun?"

"A veil and a—what's it? A wimple: she was wearing a wimple."

"You think she's a nun?"

"I don't think so."

"Why not?"

"I saw flesh."

"What do you mean?"

"I saw her hip."

"How?"

"It slipped out. It was gorgeous."

"How does that happen?"

"I'm not sure. It was sexy. She must be a hooker."

"Dressed like a nun?"

"I have to go."

"What do I do?"

"Stop. Don't stay here. When I get out, keep going. Turn around up the road. On your way back, catch her in your high beams."

Gheorghe brought the car to a halt. Nikky peered at a switch. He made sure the interior light wouldn't come on when he opened the door. He slipped outside. He gently pressed the latch shut. Gheorghe drove off. The frame of the car sliced through me like a plate of wires.

I looked around. Darkness surrounded us. Headlights—presumably from the Allée de la Reine Marguerite, site of the Bois de Bolougne's nighttime bazaar—glowed feebly through the thick stands of trees.

Nikky was close. I could feel him holding his breath, listening for footfalls.

The car swung around. Nikky stepped into the bushes. Headlights approached. Something gleamed in the moon. It was a woman. She was wearing a white cloak. The figure stopped. The car rushed towards her. The brights came on. The cloak flashed. My head jerked. My eyes balked.

The woman stood with her head arched back, shielding herself from the light with her hands, her cloak pushed past her arms, her breasts exposed. Gheorghe passed. The dim glow of the tail lamps momentarily brightened the woman's feet. She wasn't wearing shoes.

Gheorghe kept going. I could hear Nikky's breath grow deep. I wondered what he was thinking.

The wisp of white moved. She quickened pace. Was she scared? Nikki stepped on a branch. I heard it crack. My heart leapt. I glanced at the figure. She wouldn't stop. Had she not heard? She knew how dangerous it was. Her ears had to be perked. I gasped. I thought maybe the sound was drowned out by the thumping of her heart.

She was alone—in the Bois de Boulogne—at night—why? Walking with purpose—where was she going? For what? If a prostitute, why here? Was she lost? Her first night on the job? Ridiculous. On a midnight stroll, why the wimple? A nun? Heaven forbid.

She was a whitetail deer about to be caught once again in our headlights. Had she any idea we were stalking her—an innocent woman in the woods—what could she know? It was my dream; her nightmare. What was she to me? An image? A figure of a brave and beautiful woman? Vulnerability personified?

I was frightened. I wanted no harm to come to her. Nikky troubled me. He was so unpredictable. What would he do? Would he hurt her? Would he make her do something she didn't want to do? This was my dream. I was helpless. I had no hands to hold back my friend—no body but that which was made of air.

I prayed.

Nikky could not harm this creature: this woman floating in shadow:

this blur of something horribly sacred—a strange beast of different fabrics, white and black—a veil was it? on top of a disembodied head? a bright strip of white fluttering behind? a bird with a shimmering tail? What kind: a dove? A penguin? A canvasback pochard in flight—about to be shot?

The car was back; the woman, in front, turning, slowing, seeing the headlights beginning to bathe her brilliantly—an attractive girl—a witch for all we knew hiding behind a mask of maidenhood—stood entranced, a pale face with a round shape—a clean, sharp jaw—a beautiful, blunted chin. What being could possibly harm her? The moon hid, shamed to see a mortal daughter of Eve walk with such authority. It was a proud mien on a worried—at the same time, not unprepared woman—an uncompromising beauty—who betrayed little fear upon her unwelted brow.

The headlights dimmed. Were they paying her homage? Were they apologizing for blinding her? The engine stalled. The car came to a creaking halt. Nikky whispered to himself, "Now, now, Gheorghe. Let's not be so obvious."

A breeze puffed the woman's veil. An under-veil of white peeked out. The crown held them in place. The creases of a carefully wrapped linen wimple budged. The woman imperceptibly cocked her head. Imperceptibly, she squinted. She started holding her arms back as if preparing to run. My eyes fell to her pleated guimpe. It hung from her shoulders broad, firm, clear-finished—a serge from the fiber of a noble sheep. The chevron weave pointed down.

Her breasts were bared. She wasn't wearing a tunic. Only the flimsy fabric of a friar's scapular covered the length of her body beneath her cloak. With her arms stretched back, two nodules of beautiful fat bulged from beyond her hems, settling under their own weight like egg white beaten to a soft peak, waiting to be folded into batter. The satin of her scapular suddenly sashayed across her nipples. It fell against the side of one breast. It squeezed itself into her cleavage. Pluck, I begged quietly to myself, the obnoxious apron out.

The woman was turning. I could see her leg—her hip—how gracefully the satin yielded. I watched her muscles flex in slow time.

Sartorius led the way, twisting around the quadriceps, gripping the crest of the pelvic girdle, whence many muscles start their path—like gluteus maximus, rectus femoris, the three vasti: lateralis, medialis, intermedius—great ships whose massive hulls sartorius escorts down man's thigh—cuddling, wrapping himself over and around them—until he falls spiraling down the inner side, inserting himself at the tibia, the shimmering place behind which robust and shapely gastrocnemius makes his dwelling: the propeller, whom the ancients framed with gleaming buskins.

The woman's gastrocnemius bulged. With the humble soleus, it pulled her heel: oh splendid tuber! growth that takes the brunt of our standing, balancing our attempts at uprightness, seed from which blossoms man, which the serpent bites, protect yourself from harm; may we lift you as you walk: that you might crush the serpent. May all our heels be protected. May they not be spoiled by weight. May they glide across earth fearing no evil, no serpents, no stones to bash them. May they be as beautiful as that woman's heel, flying as it was across the road of my dream, casting small, delicate shadows.

She was running on the balls of her feet, bouncing away from our mysterious motorcar. She went not knowing where she was headed. Nikky positioned himself in the way. The woman crashed into his arms. There was no time to be afraid. I could feel the gust of her breath. It swept me off my feet. Nikky held tight.

"Are you alright?" he asked. The woman stared. She was overcome with shock. Nikky squeezed her.

He repeated, "Are you alright?"

The woman swallowed. She whispered, "Yes." The voice unfurled and disappeared like a curl of smoke.

"Don't be afraid," said Nikky. "That's just my ride. My friend was looking for me." The woman held her tongue. "You shouldn't be walking out here: it's dangerous." Silence. "Criminals are known to drive around. They prey on lonely people." Silence. "I'm not one of them. I'm not supposed to be here. I'm passing through. You shouldn't be alone—do you have a phone?"

The woman opened her mouth. She hesitated to speak. She finally said, "I'm not alone."

"I know. You're not alone anymore. I'm here. You could've scared yourself half to death running like that. You're not even wearing shoes. Imagine if you had cut your foot."

Nikky looked into her eyes. She stared back. She murmured, "You? What are you doing?"

"Me?" Nikky realized he was still holding tight. He let go. "I'm sorry. You're asking me why I'm here. I was walking. I left my wallet during the day. I didn't notice until after dark. I knew exactly where it was. I had my friend drop me off. I have it now. Would you like to see?" Nikky smiled sheepishly. "I apologize. It wouldn't prove anything. What are you doing—if you don't mind me asking?"

The woman considered the question. She replied, "I was told to come."

Nikky nodded. "By whom?"

A moment passed. The woman suddenly turned.

"Wait!" She stopped. Nikky observed her. "You're very beautiful."

"I have to go."

"Don't!" She stopped again. Silence. Nikky squinted. "Where are you going?"

She thought about it. She said, "I'm." She looked off into the distance. She stared vacantly. She didn't seem to find an answer. She turned back. She whispered, "I don't know."

Nikky smiled. "You said you were told to come."

She ran.

"Wait!" cried Nikky. "Let me help." He caught up. He darted in front of her. He stopped her by the shoulders. "Who?" he asked. "Who told you to come?" Her eyes filled with—not terror—something like ambivalence. Nikky pressed the question. "What's his name?"

She tried to pass. Nikki pushed back.

"How did you get here?"

"Let me go."

"Answer."

"I walked."

"From where?" The woman stopped tussling. She dropped her head.

"I'm sorry," said Nikky. "I ask silly questions. Would you like a ride?"

The woman looked up. She glanced at the car. "No."

"I'll pay."

"For what?"

Nikky smiled. "For the ride."

"What do you mean?"

"I'll pay you for the privilege of giving you a ride."

The woman shook her head. "Why?"

"How much?" She kept shaking it. "I have a thousand Euro." Nikky pulled a pair of bills from his pocket. They fluttered in the breeze. The head stopped shaking. The bills were each worth five hundred Euro.

The woman whispered, "A thousand?"

Nikky nodded.

She shook her head again. "I don't know."

"I'll give you half. You can walk away with it if you like." Nikky held out the money.

The woman stared at it. She pursed her lips. She asked, "For how long?"

Nikky smiled. "It's up to you. I can take you wherever you want."

"I don't understand."

"What's the problem? Do you want me to swear I won't hurt you? You're not going to be safer out here. All I want to do is talk."

"Why?"

"You're incorrigible. Come on." Nikky offered the woman his arm. After a moment, she took it. They walked together to the car.

Nikky opened the door. He stood behind it. The woman held onto the frame. She bent down. Her breasts sagged in the moonlight. Nikky licked his lips. "Gheorghe," he uttered. "We have a new passenger." Gheorghe turned around. He watched the woman slide towards the window. Nikky followed her in. "We're going for a ride."

Gheorghe smiled. "Hello!"

The woman swallowed. "How do you do?"

"My name is Gheorghe. I'm from Romania." The woman pulled her cloak tightly across her body. Gheorghe glanced at Nikky. He looked back at the woman. He said, "I will be your driver."

The woman nodded. "Thank you."

Nikky closed the door. "Welcome to the back seat of my car. I hope you find it comfortable." He turned on the interior light. "Where would you like to go?" Silence. "How about the Reine? Driver, take us to the Alley of the Daisy Queen—the scenic route." Gheorghe turned on the engine. He put the car in gear. They drove.

"What's your name?"

The woman bit her lip. She opened her mouth. She closed it. She thought about it. She opened it again. She said, "Barbara."

Nikky offered her his hand. "I'm Nikky. That's short for Nikita." She didn't take it. Nikky put it down. "Where are you from?" Silence. "I'm sorry. I don't mean to pry. I'm a man of bad habits." He eyed Barbara's cloak. She pulled it tighter. "Not like yours."

He watched her chest rise and fall. She jerked her head. Nikky calmly caught her glance. He relished the moment. The woman looked to the floor. She said, "You're wrong. Flesh is a bad habit."

Nikky stretched his eyebrows. "I agree," he said. "It gets so wrinkly." Barbara looked out the window. She was surprised to see people. They were on the Reine.

Nikky mused, "Most religious think vestments are a block that separates them from regular folks. In our case, I like to think it's brought us closer together." He put a hand on Barbara's leg.

Her head darted towards Gheorghe. "Stop," she cried. Gheorghe obliged.

Nikky looked out the window. They were surrounded by half-naked freaks. He grimaced. He whined, "Don't stop."

The door opened. Nikky saw Barbara jump out. He swore to himself. He crawled after her. He jogged behind her through the thick swarm of flesh. He yelled, "What's going on? I haven't paid you."

Barbara glanced over her shoulder. She cried, "I don't need it."

"Where are you going?"

"Home."

"Let me take you."

"No."

"Why not?"

"You can't."

"Who do you work for?"

"You don't know Him."

"What's his name?"

"It doesn't matter."

"I'll protect you."

The woman stopped. She turned. She cupped her hands. She begged, "Please. I don't need your help."

Nikky stuffed the bills into her palms. He wrapped his own hands around hers. He whispered, "I don't believe you."

Barbara squirmed. A phone rang. The sound came from Nikky's pocket.

"Your phone," whispered Barbara. She looked pleadingly into Nikky's eyes. "It's ringing."

Nikky wanted to ignore it. Barbara started wrenching her hands. He had no choice. He let go. He watched the woman squeeze past the shoulders of spotlighted freaks.

Nikky took out the phone. The display spelled out the name, D-Boy: Marco. Nikky flipped it open. "Yo?"

"Kita!" cried the voice on the other end. "What's goin' on? You lookin' for a buzz?"

"I've been trying to reach you."

"Playa, playa! You know what they say. Allow me to call you."

"I'm on the Reine."

"North or south?"

Nikky looked around. "I'm not sure."

"You don't know? Are you high? I told you to wait for me."

"I was chasing somebody."

"Don't tell me you got your pocket picked."

"Relax. It was a woman."

"A woman picked your pocket?"

"I wish."

"What do you mean?"

"I couldn't get any kind of action."

"Are you having an outbreak?"

"It's not like that."

"Are you sure it was a woman?"

"Her tits were falling out of her crop top. She's dressed like a nun."

"Sounds kinky."

"She's got a veil and almost everything."

"I want to see her."

"That's the problem. She ran off."

"Why?"

"I have no idea. She refused money."

"What kind of hooker does that?"

"That's what I want to know. Do me a favor. Look around. She's wearing a white cloak."

"I don't have time."

"Do you want my business?"

Marco tried. It was useless. There was no sign of a white cloak—no veil, no guimpe, no scapular. It was like she was a ghost.

Nikky sulked in the back seat. He blamed Gheorghe. "Why did you stop?"

Gheorghe shrugged. "She told me to."

"Do you always do what you're told?"

"I'm married."

Marco blamed Nikky. "You should never have offered her cash. How are you going to pay for the dope?"

"You don't take checks?"

Marco shook his head.

Nikky reassured him. "I'm good for it." He sucked on a pipe. He blew out smoke. The windows were getting cloudy. "I was desperate. What was I going to do? Rape her? I had to give her something. A thousand is all I had."

"Listen to him," scoffed Marco. "They don't make thousand Euro bills. You gave her at least two."

Nikky shrugged. "I can't help being rich."

"Rich people," explained Marco, "know not to pay a hooker before she's screwed. Otherwise, you're the one getting the shaft."

"Words of wisdom," replied Nikky, "from the drug dealer who just smoked me up for free. You should go into pimping."

"My father wouldn't like it. He's an MP."

"What's that—a micropenis?"

"A member of parliament."

"I know what it is. I'm wondering why selling dope is better."

"It promotes foreign trade."

"Flesh isn't imported?"

"If I went into pimping, people would accuse my father of nepotism."

"You're saying he runs a whorehouse."

"He is the chairman of his party."

Nikky laughed. "Keep your eyes open. Tell me if you see her." He took a deep drag from the pipe. He held it. He held it some more. He kept holding it. Marco checked his watch. Nikky exhaled. "This is good," he said. "I think I'm done." He offered the pipe to Marco.

"No, thanks." He waved. "I'm off."

"If you happen to see a hooker," mentioned Nikky.

"I know," said Marco. "I'll call."

Nikky watched him leave. He passed the pipe up front. Gheorghe packed the charred opium. He fired a lighter. He puffed.

Nikky stared at the freaks through the window. His eyelids grew heavy.

Gheorghe said, "I was wondering." He looked back. Nikky was dozing off. "Wake up." Gheorghe put down the pipe. He reached through the bucket seats. He slapped Nikky on the knee.

Nikky jerked. "Huh?" Gheorghe slapped him again. "Whaddaya wan...?"

"I was wondering. I have this problem. I need cash. Are you listening? I need to borrow some money." There was no response. Gheorghe waited. He shouted.

Nikky moaned. Without opening his eyes, he murmured, "What is it?"

Gheorghe climbed through the seats. He cupped Nikky's face. "I need cash—tonight. I can pay you back—later." Nikky opened his eyes. Immediately, he closed them. "If I don't get the money to these crooks tonight, they're going to stick a lupara up my ass."

Gheorghe's hands were the only thing holding up Nikky's head. He pried apart his friend's eyelids. "If I take you to an ATM, can you get me the money? Just nod." He let go. The head collapsed onto Nikky's shoulder. Gheorghe lifted it up. He let go again. Again the head collapsed.

"Is that a yes? What's your pin number?"

"Huh?"

"Your pin number? What is it?"

"Up your momma's butt."

"This is no time for games."

"Go," said Nikky. "Outside." He tried to point through the window. He couldn't lift his arm. His lips curled into a smile. "Earn it."

Gheorghe laughed nervously. "This is no joke. If I don't pay them, they're going to kill me."

Nikky furrowed his brow. Like a little boy, he asked, "Why?"

"Don't worry about it."

"Okay." Nikky passed out.

Gheorghe sighed. He thought drugs would loosen up his wife's cousin, not knock him out.

He jumped into the front seat. He cursed himself. He started the engine. He drove down the Reine. He turned left. The road was one way. He passed a road to the right. It was also one way—the wrong way. Gheorghe reached a carrefour. Instead of staying on the same road, he bore to the right. He reached a fork. The road to the right was one way—the wrong way. Gheorghe had to go left. He reached a lake. He almost drove into it.

Gheorghe looked to either side. This road was also one way. He had to go south. Gheorghe passed tennis courts. There was a road to the right—one way. Gheorghe took it. He reached the Reine. He whispered to himself, "What the hell?" He was confused. He kept going. A road appeared to the right. He took it. He found himself back at the Reine. He was going in circles.

Gheorghe took a moment to think. It was difficult with the opium. He drove further down the Reine. He took a left. He reached an intersecting road. He took the right. He stopped. He realized he was too far south. He backed up. He took the left. He passed a suspiciously familiar-looking avenue. He kept going. He reached the end. The road was one way. He had to go north. He thought he saw tennis courts. He reached the end. The road was one way. He had to go right. He reached a lake. Again he almost drove into it. "Damn it," he cried. "There must be a way out."

Gheorghe retraced his steps back to the Reine. He passed it. He kept going. This time, he didn't take the right. He reached a carrefour. "Here we are," he said. He turned right. He was on the Allée de Longchamp. He would pass the Reine. He could take a right—the first or the second. He would reach the Porte Dauphine. Avenue Foch could take him all the way to the Arc de Triomphe. Traffic turning onto the Reine blocked his way.

Gheorghe took a short cut. He turned abruptly onto the Route du Point du Jour à Bagatelle. He reached the cul-de-sac. Long green lawns glimmered through the trees. He veered onto the Route de la Longue Queue. He would shadow the Reine north. He could reach the Boulevard. Avenue Charles de Gaulle would be a stone's throw away.

There she was. She was on the right side of the road, waiting to cross. Gheorghe slowed. He stopped in front of her. He looked into the back. Nikky was still unconscious.

The passenger-side window rolled. Gheorghe asked, "Would you like a ride?" Silence. He turned on the interior light. "Remember me?" Barbara nodded. "Don't worry. He's asleep."

Barbara peered into the back. Nikky's supine body seemed to prove Gheorghe right. She thought about it. "Thank you," she whispered. She came to the door. She opened it. She pulled her cloak tight. She climbed in. She grabbed the door. It swung closed.

Gheorghe pushed a switch. The doors locked. He grabbed the woman's arm. He cried, "My friend gave you money. I need it. Give it to me." The woman reached for the lock. Gheorghe stopped her. He grabbed her with his other hand. She wrenched herself free. She managed to unlock the door. Gheorghe caught hold. Barbara bit the hand. It let go. The door opened. Barbara leapt out.

Gheorghe pulled the handle on his own door. It wouldn't open. It was locked. Gheorghe unlocked it. He opened it. He tried to jump out. His seat belt held him back. He unbuckled it. He got out. He saw Barbara disappear into the forest. She had run around the car. Her instinct was to continue heading in the same direction. If she had only gone the way she had come, she might have been spared. The Reine was a hundred yards to the east through a dark stand of trees.

To the west, the forest was not half as thick. Within minutes, Barbara was on the edge of a long stretch of lawn. Moonlight colored everything an eerie shade of grey. In the distance, the pastel walls of the Château de Bagatelle gleamed. It was hopelessly far away. It didn't matter. Barbara ran.

Gheorghe reached the edge. He was not a slim man. It took him a few moments to catch up. He grabbed Barbara's cloak. He pulled her back. He wrapped himself around her. He clamped her mouth shut.

"I want the money," he seethed. "That's it. You didn't earn it. You got it for nothing. Hand it over."

The woman's breath teemed from her nose. She tried to say something. Gheorghe eased off his hand. The woman whimpered, "I don't have it."

"You lie."

"I gave it away."

"Tell me where it is."

"I don't know."

"Damn it."

Gheorghe ran his hand over her entire body. If there were pockets in the cloak, there was nothing in them. The woman bucked. Gheorghe realized what he was touching. His hand was on her naked hip. He clamped the woman's mouth even tighter.

Gheorghe reached inside. There was nothing. He pushed his fingers as deeply as they would go. They made a squelching sound. He pulled them out. They were wet. He brought them carefully to his nose. He sniffed them. It smelled good.

The woman kicked. She tried to break free. Gheorghe wouldn't let go. He got the fingers back inside. It was so warm. He thought, "Yes." He took the fingers out. He tugged the woman's wimple. He stuffed a bit of it into her mouth. He held it. He yanked on the veil. The crown came tumbling off. He placed the end of the black fabric on the woman's mouth. He wrapped the whole thing around. The other end was still pinned to the crown. The under-veil got into his face.

Gheorghe tore it off. He needed both hands. He forced the woman to her knees. He straddled her with his legs. He wrapped the white fabric around the black one. He tied it. He smiled. The woman's cries were muffled.

Gheorghe pushed her forward. She grabbed at the gag. Gheorghe forced her arms back. He thought about what to do. He wrapped the cloak around her arms. He would have to tie it. With one hand, he gathered the fabric of the scapular. He twisted it. He knotted the ends together.

It wasn't perfect. It would have to do. He admired the work. The woman's face was now buried in the grass. Her legs were spread. The flesh gleamed in the moon. The woman rolled to her side. She kicked. Gheorghe grabbed her legs. He forced them together. He twisted the woman onto her stomach. He took hold of her hips. He lifted her. He realized his pants were on.

He let go. He unbuttoned his waistband. The woman crawled away like a worm. Gheorghe got his pants off. He jerked down his underwear. He only had patience to get them past his knees. He hopped after the woman. He snagged her by the ankles. He pulled her in. He seized the upper reaches of her thighs. His thick thumbs dug into her crotch. He spread apart her lips.

Gheorghe leaned in. He smiled. He said incredulously, "You're a blond?" The question went unanswered.

As soon as Gheorghe was done, he left the woman alone on the Bagatelle. He walked back to the car. The passenger-side door was open. The engine was running. The lights were on. Nikky was still passed out in the back seat.

Gheorghe climbed inside. He shut the door. He put the car in gear. He drove.

At some point, he turns on the radio. A song plays. He starts humming along.

The song gets louder. I realize I am awake. The song is on my radio. I can't remember leaving it on. The key changes. The climax approaches. I rub my eyes. I recognize the tune. I like it. I find myself humming along.